# Stay with Me

## KELLY ELLIOTT

This book is dedicated to

Karen Wilcox

Thank you so much for all of your input and help with this book.
You are so sweet and thoughtful! This one is for you!

## prologue

### Thano

TAKING IN A DEEP BREATH, I slowly released it and rocked back and forth while I looked at myself in the mirror.

"Bro, you look good, so stop worrying. Besides, everyone is going to be looking at Savannah and not paying any attention to you."

I grinned as I gave my older brother Thaddeus a wink. Savannah and I had been dating since high school, so it was no surprise to anyone when I asked her to marry me our last year of college. "I do have a breathtaking bride, don't I?"

With a slap on my back, he replied, "Yes, you do. And you got our parents to like her. Lucky bastard."

Turning around, I tried to get my breathing under control. My parents came over to this country from Greece as young children, and Savannah was sure they would hate her the first time I brought her home. She was after all . . . not Greek. My family was very big on keeping with tradition, so it was no surprise my grandparents settled into an area of Colorado with a large Greek community. Of course, Savannah won them over with her charm just like she did me. It was keeping my oldest brother Nicholaus away from her that proved to be the challenge.

A light knock on the door had me glancing over as my mother walked in and headed my way.

She smiled sweetly while she brushed imaginary lint from my jacket. "Nervous. Very nervous. She told her mother she needed to talk to you."

I gave her a concerned look. Was Savannah having second thoughts? I had to admit I was feeling more confused today than ever. I prayed we were doing the right thing.

Seeing my look of concern, she smiled big. "But she looks happy. Oh my, the girl is bouncing off the walls she is so happy. She keeps saying her heart is racing and she feels short of breath. Her chest was hurting for a bit."

A sinking feeling moved through my body. "Her chest hurts? Is that normal?"

She gave me a wink. "I'd say so. I was a nervous mess when I was marrying your father. My hands shook like a leaf on a tree in a summer storm. My father thought I was going to shake my flowers off the stems before I even made it down the aisle."

I let out a laugh and kissed her on the cheek. "You always did know how to put me at ease, Mama."

Patting me on the chest, my mother turned to my two brothers and put her hands on her hips as she watched the two of them wrestle with each other. Thaddeus, or as we called him, Thad, was the middle son. Nicholaus had Thad in a headlock. It wasn't uncommon for the two of them to get into wrestling matches. One was always trying to prove to the other how much stronger he was. You'd think they were still in high school with how they acted.

"Stop this, you two! Your brother is needed in the church. All of you get out there and greet the guests and families."

Nicholaus dropped his hold on Thad and gave him a push as he headed to the door. Shaking my head, I followed them and my best friend Gus out the door.

Gus gave me a slight push and said, "This is it. Last chance to bail."

My heart sunk for a quick moment before I came to my senses. "No way in hell. I can't imagine my life without Savannah in it."

Taking in a deep breath, he slowly blew it out and said, "Yeah, if I had hot sex like you two do, I wouldn't want anyone else either."

Giving him a push, I hissed, "Shut the hell up you asshole. If my mother hears you I'm going to kick your ass."

Gus let out a laugh as he walked ahead of me. I'd been living with Gus since college. We met our freshman year and hit it off from the get-go. Savannah spent more time at my place than hers. We often forgot the walls were thin and Gus got his fair share of hearing us making love.

Doing my duty, I made my way to as many of my family members as I could. Savannah's side of the family was much smaller. It was her parents, her grandparents, her older brother Sam, and a few cousins who were attending the wedding. My side of the church was packed.

Walking up to Savannah's grandparents, I reached out for her grandfather's hand and gave it a firm shake. "Mr. Thompson, how are you doing this morning?"

Giving me a head nod, he said, "Fine. Just fine, young man. You ready to marry my grandbaby?"

"Yes, sir. I am, indeed."

The priest walked up to me and spoke closely to my ear. "It's time, Thano."

Nodding, I gave Mr. Thompson a wink and said, "It's time."

"Good luck!" he called out as I smiled. I couldn't shake the feeling that something wasn't right as I walked back to the altar.

*Is this doubt I'm feeling? Am I second-guessing this?* No. I loved Savannah.

Standing at the altar, I watched my parents walk to their seats. Then Savannah's mother was walked down the aisle by Nicholaus. Taking his place next to me, he squeezed my shoulder slightly. "This is it. The beginning to your life of one woman forever."

Grinning bigger, I laughed. *I can't believe I'm marrying Savannah.* My heart pounded in my chest as I drew in a deep breath.

The music changed and I watched as Savannah's best friends all made their way down the aisle one at a time. Each one was dressed in the light-blue dresses it took Savannah forever to pick out. One of Savannah's cousins had a four-year-old little girl, Michelle, who was our flower girl. I couldn't help but laugh when she skipped down the aisle and called out, "Savannah is coming! Savannah is coming!"

Chuckles erupted around the church. With a quick glance to my parents, I felt my heart warm as I looked at how happy they were. It was a far cry from the first time I told them I loved a girl who wasn't Greek.

The music started and everyone stood.

The moment I saw her, my breath stilled.

Beautiful couldn't describe her.

Savannah glanced around at a few people before looking up at me. Our eyes met and we both smiled. My heart hammered in my chest while she made her way to me. There was something missing, though. The spark in her eyes was gone. For a moment, I swore I saw doubt.

Shaking my head slowly to erase my erratic thoughts, I watched as she made her way down the aisle. Savannah sobbed and pressed her lips together as tears began streaming down her face.

Halfway down the aisle, Savannah's smile vanished. She stopped walking and clutched her chest. *Something is wrong.* Looking at her father and then me, she dropped her bouquet and called out, "Thano," before she collapsed to the ground.

I stood there for a brief moment in total shock before I ran over to her. I fell to the floor and pulled her into my arms. "Savannah! Baby, what's wrong?"

Tears ran down Savannah's face while she struggled to speak. "I really do . . . love . . . you."

"Baby, no. No, don't do this to me!" Looking up, I glanced around at everyone as I screamed out, "Somebody help her!"'

My father, who was a doctor, rushed to my side. "She's having a heart attack."

My eyes widened as I fell back and watched my father. Someone yelled out, "Call 9-1-1!"

Savannah's eyes were closed as my father began CPR. My mother wrapped her arms around me as she quietly began praying.

Wiping my tears away, I took Savannah's hand and pleaded with her, "Baby, please don't leave me!"

My pleas went unheard.

*one*

FOUR YEARS LATER

Thano

THE MUSIC PULSED THROUGH MY body as I watched Nicholaus try his best to put the moves on some blonde he had been talking to for the last twenty minutes. It was almost painful to watch him crash and burn.

Letting out a sigh, I glanced around for Gus and Thad. If I knew Gus, he was in the parking lot screwing some girl—and Thad—Lord only knew what he was up to.

I motioned for the bartender. "I'll take another bourbon, neat."

Acknowledging my request, he quickly got my drink and set it in front of me. Sliding him a twenty, I said, "Keep the change."

Tapping the bar, he smiled and said, "Thanks, dude." Turning to the person who sat next to me, he asked, "What will it be, pretty lady?"

The air around me changed as I glanced to my right. A girl with brown wavy hair sat and said, "Jameson on the rocks."

I lifted my drink to my lips and smiled. Taking a sip, I said, "A woman who knows how to drink."

Feeling her eyes on me, I turned to look at her. What happened next was totally unexpected. My breath hitched as the most beautiful green eyes looked into mine. The first time in four years a woman had any sort of effect on me and it had to be in a fucking bar.

"Yeah, well, my daddy taught me two things. How to shoot a gun and how to order a drink."

Lifting my eyebrows, I slowly nodded my head. "Remind me not to piss you off after you have a few of those."

She gave me a polite chuckle and said, "You're safe. Now my so-called best friend, not so much."

*Okay, I'll bite.*

"Why, what did she do?"

The girl took her drink and damn near drank the whole thing in one gulp. Letting out a frustrated sigh, she shook her head and turned her body toward me. "Listen, you're cute . . . really cute . . . but I'm not interested in getting picked up by some overly-gorgeous guy who is out for a one-night stand. So you're wasting your time with me."

Oh, I'm so very intrigued now.

"Which one is it?" I asked as I gave this girl my best smile. The one where both dimples pop out and my green eyes light up. At least, that's what I've been told anyway. I was certainly blessed with my Greek heritage and I knew when to use it.

Dropping her shoulders, she looked at me. Her eyes moved to my dimples, then on to my lips, and finally they settled on my eyes. "Excuse me?" she asked just above a whisper.

"You said I was really cute, and then you said I was overly gorgeous. I'm curious which one I am. Cute? Or gorgeous?"

Her mouth dropped open as she let out a gruff laugh. "Seriously?"

I finished off my drink and set it down. "Yeah. Seriously. And by the way, I'm not trying to pick you up. You're not my type."

Narrowing her eyes at me, she smiled slightly. Slipping off the bar stool, she grabbed her drink and finished it off. Her green eyes pinned me to where I couldn't move even if I wanted to. "Gorgeous."

I gave her a quick nod of my head as I smiled bigger. Tilting her head, she said, "But your eyes are sad."

My smile faded as we stood there staring at each other. Looking away, she quickly said, "Enjoy your evening."

I stood there frozen in place as I watched her make her way through the crowd. Stopping at a couple on the dance floor, who I assumed was the best friend, she said something and then made her way out of the bar.

Turning back toward the bar, I stared at my empty drink. Pulling out my phone, I sent Gus and Nicholaus a text.

*Me: Catching a cab. Don't stay out late, Gus. Cooking class 9am.*

Making my way toward the entrance to the bar, I was stopped three times by women looking either for a dance or to share a drink. Politely turning them each down, I pushed the door open and stepped outside into the cool fall air.

I let out a sigh of relief as I dropped my head back and took in a few deep breaths. Something about the air here in Colorado felt so clean. I moved to Houston, Texas for a year after Savannah had passed away. I needed to be away from anything that reminded me of her. Gus had a friend who needed some help on an oil rig. Needless to say, my parents weren't too happy when I said I was leaving my job as a marketing manager and heading to Texas. I hated every single minute of it and couldn't wait to get back to Colorado Springs. The mountains, the fresh air, the snow-covered slopes. The only thing good about that year was that I was busy working. If I was busy, I didn't think about Savannah.

The day I realized I couldn't keep ignoring the fact that she was gone, was the day I packed up my stuff and headed home. Life moved on everyone kept telling me. The problem was I didn't want to move on without her.

A honking horn pulled me out of my thoughts as I waved down a cab. Jumping in, I said, "Eleven-eleven Summit Road."

"Manitou Springs?" the cab driver asked.

"Yeah," I said as I dropped my head back against the seat. The moment I closed my eyes, green eyes invaded my thoughts. Snapping my eyes open, I shook my head and whispered, "What the fuck?" Sighing, I dragged my hands down my face. For the first time in four years, another woman besides Savannah occupied my thoughts, and I wasn't sure how I should be feeling.

My phone buzzed in my pocket. Taking it out, I saw Gus's name scroll across the screen. Swiping across my phone, I read his text.

> Gus: *Tell me you've got a girl with you. Please tell me you're gonna get fucked tonight. You need to get laid!*

Rolling my eyes, I pushed my phone back into my pocket. I'd been with a few women since Savannah passed away. Most of them had been one-night stands. I had tried to date two of them more than one time. I couldn't get past the fact that they weren't Savannah. No one would ever be Savannah.

No. One.

## two

### Thano

GUS PULLED UP AND PARKED next to me as I leaned against my door. Grinning from ear to ear, I took a sip of my coffee as I pushed off my car and made my way over to him.

The door to his Toyota Tundra flew open as he stumbled out. "Who in the fuck decided we needed to cook at nine in the damn morning?"

Giving him a slap on the back, I said, "You did."

With a dramatic sigh, Gus rubbed his hands down his scruff-covered face. "Fucking hell. I never imagined when I went to college to get my degree in marketing I'd be going to a damn cooking class."

I let out a chuckle. "What better place to get into the heads of women who buy pots and pans than a cooking class. Isn't that what you said?"

"How did we get stuck with this account? I mean seriously. We are manly men. We should be doing the marketing campaign for the new lingerie campaign."

My head dropped back as I let out a roar of laughter. "Oh, yeah right. Like they would put you on that account. We'd get a sexual harassment charge after the first day."

Grabbing my coffee from my hand, Gus pushed me away from him as he said, "Fuck you, Grivas. You good-looking Greek bastard."

Laughing, I shook my head as I followed him into Onion Creek Gardens. It was a small restaurant that was only open Thursday through Sunday; on the days the restaurant wasn't open, one of the owners held cooking classes. "Why do you always bring up the fact that I'm Greek?"

Gus stopped and looked at me. "Have you looked in the mirror lately, asshole? The dark hair, the dark skin. Women flock to you. It makes me sick."

Grinning at the young woman standing in the hostess section, I gave her a wink. "Don't listen to him; he's hungover and feeling a tad bitter this morning because this was his idea."

Letting out a giggle, the young girl waved as if she wasn't paying any attention to us.

It didn't take Gus long to start flirting with her. "What time do you get off, sweetheart?"

Chewing on her lower lip, the girl smiled and said, "Oh, um, not until two this afternoon."

Gus reached out and grabbed a piece of paper and scrolled his cell number down on it. "Call me. Maybe we can get dinner."

Her eyes quickly moved over to me and then back to Gus. I knew it wouldn't take her long to answer. Gus was one of those guys who just had to smile and girls were falling over him. He was as tall as me at five-feet-eleven. We both worked out almost every day and had the same build. The only difference was he was blond with blue eyes and I had dark-brown hair and green eyes. My Greek heritage accounted for my darker skin tone.

Taking the paper from Gus, she winked and stuck it in her pocket. "Sounds like a solid plan."

I grabbed Gus and pulled him toward the interior of the restaurant. We were all to meet in the small dining room and then go to the kitchen as one unit. At least that's what the brochure said would happen. "Jesus, don't you ever get tired of this game, Gus?"

"What game?" he asked with a shrug.

A blonde walked by and I thought Gus was going to break his neck as he watched her. "This game of hooking up with random women and having sex with them."

"Bite your tongue. There will never be a day I get tired of this. Are you kidding me? Right now I'm in my prime."

Snarling my lip, I slowly shook my head. "In your prime, huh?"

"Yep. I mean look at me. What woman wouldn't want me between their legs?"

Two women turned and looked at us. One smiled and the other one frowned. This was going to be a hard crowd to crack, especially with Gus already acting like a dick.

Gus took a drink of my coffee and asked, "What are we cooking?"

"Breakfast and a smoothie or something," I said as I looked around the room full of women. Of all the cooking classes, this one seemed like the easiest one. How hard could it be to fry up some eggs and blend some fruit together?

A few more women walked in, each one zeroing in on us. I was pretty sure the redhead moaned when she looked at us.

"Yeah. In my prime. Endless pussy," Gus said as he looked around. "Jesus, I've died and gone to fucking heaven. And we get breakfast out of it. Score."

The door to the kitchen area opened and a woman about my age, twenty-seven or so, walked out with a huge smile on her face.

"Good morning, cookers!"

"Good morning, Claire!" everyone said in unison.

Gus and I smiled and looked around the room before my eyes landed on the instructor. Tilting her head, she asked, "Were you boys looking for the gym next door?"

*Holy shit. Did she really just stereotype us?* With a grin, I responded to her question. "No. We're here to improve our cooking skills. Learn how to do more for the special women in our lives." She didn't have to know my mother had me in the kitchen cooking from the time I learned to talk.

Gus snapped his head and glared at me.

Someone standing behind me whispered, "My ovaries just exploded."

Gus cleared his throat. "Excuse me, Thano, but speak for yourself. I'm single, ladies, and yes I am a man. That doesn't mean I'm only a gym rat. I'm looking to enhance my cooking skills so I can cook a meal for a beautiful woman that will have her begging for more."

Okay. He one-upped me on that one.

Bastard.

The instructor let a small chuckle slip from her lips. "Okay, ladies . . . and gentlemen . . . follow me into the kitchen."

As she walked, she gave us a brief intro into the class and started rattling off everything we were going to make.

"We're going to start with our smoothie. I like to call it the woman's . . . or man's . . . happy skeleton blast! We've got spinach and flax seeds with a bit of molasses and other goodies."

Gus dropped his mouth open. "I'm not drinking that shit."

Hitting him on the chest, we walked up to a cooking station and looked at everything set out.

"What is this stuff?" Gus asked in a whispered voice.

With a shrug, I replied, "I have no idea."

"If you boys need any help, I'm more than happy to assist."

Glancing up, there was a woman who looked to be a few years older than me. Her tits were practically spilling out of her shirt. She stood there waiting for our response.

"Julian, please head on over to your station. Kilyn will be here soon to help out."

Claire looked at me and winked. "Kilyn is my assistant. She's notoriously late. She can help you boys out."

With a nod, I smiled.

Clapping her hands to get everyone's attention, Claire kept talking. "After we make the smoothie, it's on to the eggs benedict."

"The what?" Gus mumbled.

Oh. Shit. I think I signed up for the wrong cooking class.

"We'll start with the hollandaise sauce."

"The what?" Gus asked with a panicked look. "Holiday sauce? Which holiday is coming up? Thanksgiving, right?"

I looked down at the ingredients Claire set at our station on a blue tray.

Eggs, lemon juice, butter, salt, and pepper. That seemed easy enough.

Leaning over, I said, "Dude, don't worry. We've got this shit. I cook with my mother all the time."

He moaned and scrubbed his hands down his face. "I'm hungover, I'm surrounded by hot women, and now we're baking desserts for the holidays! It's too much. I'm on overload."

Claire continued to talk. "After we make the hollandaise sauce, we'll make the eggs benedict. Then we'll finish it off with a creamy strawberry crepe."

Gus and I snapped our heads and looked at each other. "French shit? What the fuck did you get us into, dude? I'm telling your mother you brought us to a French cooking class!"

"Shh!" I said as I pushed his shoulder.

"Don't worry, boys, you'll have help as soon as Kilyn gets here. She is our crepe specialist. Makes them all the time."

I forced a smile. *Great. Just what I need.* Some old French woman yelling at me while trying to tell me how to make fucking crepes.

"Okay, let's heat up those pans and get our butter melting."

Gus placed the wide pan on the small portable stove as I took the butter and dropped it into the pan.

"If you feel like getting fancy, clarify the butter by skimming some of the milk solids off. It will make the sauce thicker, but less rich."

Claire looked at what I was sure was a *holy fuck what did she just say* look on my face.

She was about to say something when the door to the kitchen flew open and someone came running in.

"Shit! Sorry! I thought sneaking in that yoga class might be a mistake and it was!"

I kept my eyes focused on the butter as I tried to figure out what the hell I had to do to skim the milk.

"Dude, I found the woman I'm going to marry," Gus whispered to me as I looked at the girl next to me to see what she was doing with her butter. I gave her a grin as she smiled back.

"First time?" she asked.

Taking in a deep breath through my nose, I nodded and said, "Yep.

It said breakfast. I thought fried eggs or something."

She gave me a huge smile and replied, "You won't find Claire or Kilyn cooking anything easy like plain eggs."

Gus hit me on the arm. "Dude, I'm serious. I'm in love."

Looking back at him like he was nuts, I shook my head. "What in the hell are you talking about?"

Gus pointed with his mouth to the floor. "Dude, my future wife is standing next to our French chef."

Looking over to Claire, I watched as a girl was bent over pulling her hair into a ponytail. When she stood back up, our eyes met. My mouth dropped open at the same time as hers.

"Holy shit," I whispered as Claire called out to me.

"Dark-haired dreamy man in the back, stop staring at Kilyn or your butter will burn."

*Kilyn.*

Her green eyes sparkled as she shook her head and made a tsking motion with her finger and winked. Walking up to us, she grinned and my breath was taken away. *What in the hell? That hasn't happened in one hell of a long time.*

"Are you following me?"

Pulling my head back, I gave her a fake as hell stunned look. "That would be hard to do considering I was here first."

She flashed me a drop-me-to-my-knees smile.

"We're here for research," I said.

She lifted her brows and turned to Gus. "Research, huh?"

Gus slowly nodded his head. "Marketing. Pots and pans. Women."

Turning to look at Gus, I mumbled, "Women?"

Kilyn tried to hide her chuckle, but she failed.

"I see. Well, it looks like you need some help with that sauce."

"Yes. God, yes. What holiday are we making this for?" Gus asked.

Rolling my eyes, I looked away. Kilyn laughed and I was stunned by how it affected me. It rolled over my body like a warm blanket. I found myself wanting to hear her laugh again.

"Hollandaise sauce—not holiday," she said with a grin.

"Oh. Well, hell, I feel stupid."

"Nonsense. Let's grab a double boiler and get this moving along."

For the next two hours, Kilyn showed us how to make a kick-ass sauce, eggs benedict, which I instantly loved, and finished it all off with showing me how to make the perfect light and fluffy crepe. Gus had long given up and moved over to the table next to us and sat on his ass and flirted non-stop with the two women. Every now and then, I would hear him ask about why they liked a certain pot or pan. *At least the bastard was working.*

I took the crepe out of the pan and set it on a serving plate. Kilyn jumped and clapped her hands. "That's perfect! Now take a quarter cup of the strawberries and one third cup of cream cheese and fill the crepes. You'll roll it up and top with a small dollop of the cream cheese filling and a few sliced berries." I did everything as she said it, dropping a few fresh strawberries on the top of our beautiful creation to finish it off.

"And voilà! Your strawberry and cream cheese crepe."

Cutting into the crepe, I brought it to my mouth while Kilyn watched intently. Her eyes turned dark as they roamed across my body. I was almost positive I saw something in them that resembled lust. When she focused back on my lips, she licked her own.

"Holy shit. This is amazing!"

Kilyn chuckled and began cleaning up. "I'm glad you liked it. I hope you learned something about cooking this morning."

"I learned having a beautiful woman by my side to cook with is a benefit."

She smiled bigger. "Well, having a cute guy next to me isn't so bad either."

"Gorgeous. Last night you said I was gorgeous."

Scrunching her nose up in the most adorable way, I couldn't help but take in every single thing about her. Her brown hair was pulled up into a ponytail with a few curls hanging down. She didn't have a stitch of makeup on and sure as hell didn't need any. Her green eyes looked tired, but her skin seemed to glow.

"Oh, that's right. How could I forget?" she replied sarcastically.

With a shrug, I helped her carry the dishes over to the restaurant's massive sink where two young guys were working. "How did you like the class? Claire is my best friend and teaches it."

"I really enjoyed it."

Kilyn motioned with her head over to Gus. "It looks like your friend did as well."

Sighing, I apologized for him. "I'm really sorry about him. If he thinks he even has a chance, he'll pounce."

Waving my comment off with her hand, she headed back to our station. It was about then Gus turned and jumped up.

He pushed me out of the way as he stuck his hand out to shake Kilyn's hand. "I'm not really sure how you know my good friend Thano here, but I'm Gus. We neglected to introduce ourselves before we got lost in the world of cooking."

*Oh brother.*

Kilyn shook Gus's hand and said, "Pleasure." She motioned over to me and said, "We met last night at a bar."

Gus snapped his eyes over to mine and then back to Kilyn.

Tilting her head and giving me the sexiest look I'd ever seen, she practically purred, "Thano? What an unusual name."

I couldn't believe we had stood next to each other for two hours and never introduced ourselves.

Gus waved me off. "Yeah, yeah, it's Greek. So, what do you say I take you to breakfast? We can ditch Thano and get to know each other better."

Kilyn pulled her eyes from mine as she took Gus in. "Um . . . we just ate breakfast."

Gus pinched his eyebrows together. "Well, how about coffee?"

Was this asshole really moving in on my turf?

*My turf? What in the hell makes me think Kilyn is my turf?*

Kilyn gave a polite smile and replied, "Thanks, but I have a meeting in a few minutes. It was great seeing you again, Thano. Have a great day, guys."

And just like that, she was walking away from me again. Stopping to talk to Claire, Kilyn kissed her on the cheek and rushed out the door.

"What I wouldn't do to get that girl's number. Holy shit. She was hot."

My body felt as if a heatwave rushed through it as I thought of Gus and Kilyn together. "Yeah. She was cute," I said as I took off quickly toward the door Kilyn walked out of.

Gus came up next to me as we made our way through the restaurant and outside. Dragging in a deep breath, I pushed aside those hauntingly beautiful green eyes.

"I'm going home to change and then going for a run."

Running was the only thing that cleared my head, and I needed my head cleared. Fast.

three

Kilyn

"PENNY FOR YOUR THOUGHTS."

I pulled my eyes away from the Rocky Mountains and turned toward Claire. I hadn't been able to stop thinking about Thano for the last week. The way he looked at me and caused my heartbeat to quicken. His smile seemed to invade my thoughts every time I closed my eyes. I wasn't used to a man making me feel like this. "Trying to get into the zone with the Peterson design."

With a regarding look, she folded her arms across her chest and gave me the same look my mother used to when I had told a lie.

"The Peterson house? Seriously, that was the best you could do?"

Dropping my feet to the floor, I walked over to my desk and flopped down. "Yep."

"You were taken with him."

"With who?" I asked, knowing damn well she meant Thano.

*Thano. What an interesting name.*

Pulling up my computer, I typed in *Meaning of the Greek name Thano.*

"The hotty from cooking class. What was his name again?"

"Thano," I replied a little too quickly.

Peeking up at her, she shook her head. I swear it was as if Claire had an inside line to my thoughts. We were practically sisters, so I shouldn't be surprised she would be on to me. "You knew damn well who I was talking about. How in the hell do you remember a name like Thano if he didn't make some sort of impression on you?"

"Pesh. Please, it's an unusual name. How could I forget it? Besides, I wasn't taken with him."

She leaned back in the chair and stared at me. Her brown hair was pulled up into a tight bun and her makeup done perfectly. The tight white blouse she was wearing was open enough to give a small taste at what could be underneath. The whole outfit was finished off with a pencil skirt and black pumps. Let's not forget all the jewelry she was draped in. Claire always made sure she was put together. She'd been like that since seventh grade when George McDoogle told her she dressed like a boy. That's when we both discovered what the power of a dress and makeup could do to a boy.

"Why are you staring at me like that?"

Tilting her head, she gave me a slight smile. "Kilyn, when are you going to open your heart to the idea of someone?"

With a shrug of my shoulders, I replied, "When that someone comes along. I'm in no rush to settle down. I'm having too much fun."

Looking back at my computer, I quickly scanned the search results.

The name Athanasios was at the top. Greek meaning for immortal.

*Huh. If only a person could be immortal.*

"Kilyn, I know a lot of terrible shit happened to you, but not all guys are scumbags like he was."

Swallowing hard, I closed my eyes. I needed to get refocused and get Thano out of my mind. "I don't want to talk about it, Claire. I think I'm going to head home. Go for a run and clear my head. I'll have some sketches of the kitchen for you by tonight."

Running was something I had started up in high school as a way to escape reality for a bit. Something about it felt as if it freed my soul.

With a sigh, she stood. "Don't rush. I won't be back on my computer until tomorrow afternoon. It's date night with Blake."

Forcing a smile, I replied, "Have fun tonight and behave."

She laughed and grabbed her phone and began typing. I imagined she was sending her husband another dirty text. I swear, Claire had more action sexting Blake than I've had in my entire adult life.

"I don't know the meaning of that word."

Laughing, I gathered up a few things and headed out the door to my car. My best friend Claire was an overachiever. She always had been. Not only was she business partners with me in my interior design company, but she co-owned Onion Creek Gardens.

I was good to just get by in college. My life was nothing like Claire's. I loved her like she was my sister, but we were opposites in every way. She was daring, I was cautious. She took chances. I researched the shit out of things. But there was one thing we had in common. We loved life and didn't take a day for granted.

Pulling my jacket around me tighter, I smiled at the young couple walking toward me holding hands.

I loved love. I was just not lucky in it.

Ever since my parents passed away, I wasn't lucky in anything.

My phone buzzed in my pocket. Reaching in, I pulled it out and answered it without looking.

Huge mistake.

"Hello?"

"Kilyn. Baby, how are you?"

Ugh. It was Jack. We met at a cooking class and I agreed to go out with him one time. Worst two hours of my life.

"I'm doing well, Jack. How are you?"

"I'd be better if you were here next to me."

With an internal groan, I opened the door to my car and slid in. "Jack, we talked about this. I'm not interested in you like that."

He laughed. "I know! I know! Listen, I'm in the mood to get my shake on. Please say you'll go with me. I've had a hell of a shit week."

Letting out a frustrated sigh, I dropped my head back. "I'm sorry. I have to pass. I've got to get some designs done up. Maybe next weekend or something?"

"Yeah. Sounds good."

"Bye, Jack, be careful and have fun."

The sooner I got home and changed, the better. The drive to my new condo in Manitou Springs wasn't far from my office. I'd change into my running stuff and clear my head with a good long run.

"KILYN?"

The sound of his voice made my heart stop, and I swear I was involuntarily holding my breath.

Glancing over my shoulder, there he stood.

Good. Lord. Help. Me.

Thano smiled that big smile of his, showcasing the two dimples and his straight white teeth. My eyes traveled down his body and I swear the ground shook.

Breathe, Kilyn. Breathe.

"Um . . . ah . . ."

I couldn't utter a word. Not a damn word. I'd never had a man make me feel like this and it scared the piss out of me. Maybe I was so affected by him because of how insanely good looking he was.

He held up his hands in defense and said, "I swear, I'm not following you. I was out for a run and I looked over here and saw you. I can't believe we've run into each other twice since that night in the bar."

*Talk, Kilyn. You idiot! Talk!*

"I um . . . I just moved to Manitou Springs not too long ago. Do you live around here? Close by? I mean, you don't have to tell me where you live. I live a few miles that way."

Damn it. I sounded like a teenager. And the worse part was I actually pointed down the street as I was talking.

*Where is the rock for me to crawl under?* Pulling my lip in, I chewed the hell out of it. I couldn't help but notice his eyes grow darker while he zeroed in on my lips.

The throbbing between my legs was getting to the point where I was going to have to do something about it and soon.

Holy hell. Has it really been that long since I'd had sex? Or was it just him?

"I live in town, but I'm also building a log cabin up in the mountains.

Hopefully to live there full time someday."

Please take me there and ravage me!

*No. Wait. Jesus, Kilyn, pull yourself together, woman!*

"I like cabins. And love the mountains."

That was all I could come up with. I was slowly dying inside. I'd never been at a loss for words no matter who I was talking to.

His smile grew bigger as he replied, "Me too. Another thing we have in common."

My eyes shot up while I watched him push his fingers through his sweat-soaked dark hair. His comment snapped me out of my current daze. "Another thing?"

"Yeah," he said with a wink. "We both like to run and we both love the mountains."

Why did my knees feel weak? Did I run too hard? Maybe I was tired.

With an awkward chuckle, I nodded. "I'd kill for a weekend in the mountains. Anything to get away. You're lucky."

He lifted his eyebrow and something moved across his face.

*Change the subject, Kilyn. Fast.*

"Hey, so is Thano short for something?"

"It is," he said with another drop-my-panties smile. "My full name is Athanasios."

*Dear. God. Why does that make my panties soaking wet?* It's the way he said it. Those green eyes of his confused me. They held a sad secret, but every now and then he would look at me like he wanted to rip my clothes off.

I would so be down with him ripping my clothes off. My eyes moved to his arm and the tattoos on it. Licking my lips, I forced the moan to stay in.

"That's . . . a really cool name."

He tossed his head back and laughed. "Gotta love my Greek parents."

I needed to know his full name. Okay, that's not true. I didn't need to know, I just wanted to hear him say his name again.

"So what's your full name? Do the Greeks use like a thousand different names for members of the family? You know, like ten middle names?"

When he laughed again, I couldn't help but notice how a crazy feeling zipped through my body. My eyes lingered a little too long on the scruff that covered his perfectly beautiful face. "No. It's Athanasios Adrax Drivas."

And there it was.

I was positive Thano could get any girl he wanted merely by saying his name. Another reason to stay away from him. With those looks and that name . . . let's not forget the rocking body. Yep. He had player written all over him.

Thano opened his mouth to talk and his phone rang. With a smile, I lifted my hand and said, "Well, it was great seeing you again. Maybe I'll see ya around."

He looked conflicted. "Wait! What's your last name since you know mine?"

I couldn't help but notice how my chest fluttered. "O'Kelly is my last name."

The smile that spread across his face made me smile.

"Irish."

"Yep." Glancing to his phone, I pointed. "You better answer that."

He nodded and said, "Yep. See ya, Kilyn."

I lifted my hand and said, "See ya."

Turning, I took off running. I'd never run so fast in my life. It was as if I was running from the way he looked at me.

Or worse yet, from the way he made me feel.

## four

### Thano

WALKING THROUGH THE CABIN, I tried like hell to forget about my conversation with Kilyn. Blowing out a deep breath, I shook my head to clear my thoughts.

"How's it looking?" Mike asked. He was the contractor handling the building. He was also a friend of mine since high school.

With a smile, I replied, "It looks great. What's left to do?"

"If you're happy with everything, we're done. We had a few paint touch-ups to do that the guys took care of earlier this morning. The inspector came in and all is looking good. You my friend, have your cabin in the woods."

My chest tightened. Savannah and I talked about building a place in the mountains. She would have never gone for how simple this cabin was though. She grew up in a very wealthy family. A three-bedroom cabin would never have made her happy. But being up here would have.

She should be here.

"Hey. You okay, Thano? You look pale."

Clearing my throat, I nodded and hit him on the side of the arm. "Yeah. I'm great. It all looks great, Mike."

"Did you ever tell your parents?"

With a halfhearted chuckle, I looked around again. "Hell no. My mother would have been all over you. Picking paint colors and adding this or that. In a way, I did it for you, Mike."

He narrowed his eyes and stared at me with a disbelieving look. "For me? How's that?"

"If she had known I was building this place, she would have been calling you on the phone every day. You and I both know it. My mother gives new meaning to the word control freak."

He nodded. "That's true. She would have been, but I also bet I'd have gained forty pounds with her cooking."

"See. Me not telling them was a good thing."

"Uh-huh. You keep telling yourself that, Thano."

THE MOMENT I OPENED THE door to my parents' house, my mother called out my name, "Athanasios! It's about time!"

With a slight smile, I made my way through the house and into the kitchen. My mother was jabbering away in Greek as she moved about. Her black hair was pulled up into a bun and she wore just a touch of makeup. My mother was beautiful. Beyond beautiful. She was only fifty-five-years-old and didn't look a day over thirty.

"Mmm, smells good, Mama."

"Of course it does. No one cooks moussaka like I do."

With a chuckle, I agreed. "No one does, Mama."

The smell of the ground lamb and garlic cooking made my mouth water. Damn, I loved my mother's cooking.

"How has your week been?" she asked as she laid the eggplant in the baking dish. It was a very rare occasion for her to be alone in the kitchen.

With a shrug, I replied, "It's been uneventful."

She turned to look at me and raised her eyebrow. "Is that so?"

I knew that look. It was the look that told me I better rethink my answer.

"Um . . . yep. Why do you ask?"

She turned back to what she was doing and pursed her lips.

"Rosemary, Aunt Marie's friend, saw you talking to a girl on the street near your apartment."

"Rosemary? Why was she in Manitou Springs?"

"Ah, so you do not deny you were with a girl?"

I popped an olive into my mouth and sat at the island while I watched her. "I wasn't with any girl, Mama. I was talking to a girl."

She huffed. "What's the difference?"

"There's a huge difference."

"Is she a friend?"

I thought for a moment. Was Kilyn a friend? We hadn't exchanged phone numbers and I just found out what her last name was.

"No. Gus and I met her at a cooking class and she—"

Taking a step back, my mother clutched her chest. "A cooking class! What is this? You take a cooking class from this girl? What can this girl cook better than your Mitera?"

Oh hell.

"No, Mama. I don't know how she cooks to be honest with you."

Her eyes widened in shock. "You date a girl and you don't know how she cooks? Does she cook a good pastitsio? What about a spanako-pita or baklava?"

I closed my eyes and prayed I'd get through this meal. "Mama, I'm not dating anyone and I highly doubt Kilyn knows how to cook any of that."

Her face turned white and, right on cue, my father and Thaddeus walked in.

"Katerina, are you okay?" my father asked my mother, rushing to her side.

She held up her hand and gave me a look that should have turned me into dust.

"And why can she not cook those meals, Athanasios?"

Thaddeus tossed an olive up and caught it in his mouth as he leaned back and looked at me. Gus had already filled him and Nicholaus in on the hot girl in cooking class I met at the bar the night before.

"Yeah, Thano, why?"

I shot him a dirty look before turning back to my mother. "She's

Irish, Mama. I seriously doubt she knows how to make a baklava."

Stepping back, my mother cursed in Greek while my father shook his head. "Not again," he mumbled. "Katerina, the world is not filled with Greek women."

Closing her eyes, my mother cried out, "Why do you try to break my heart, Athanasios?"

I stood and rolled my eyes. "I'm not breaking your heart, Mama, because I'm not dating Kilyn. I barely know her. What Rosemary saw was me out running and I happened to see Kilyn running. I was being polite in saying hi. She helped Gus and me out in class."

She let out the breath she had been holding in. "This does not explain your betrayal of going to a cooking class!"

Thaddeus busted out laughing but quickly stopped when my father gave him a look.

"Katerina, let the boy explain before you go off jumping to conclusions."

"Thank you, Dad." Turning back to my mother, I said, "We are about to market pots and pans. We were doing research. Seeing what women like to use when they are in the kitchen."

Anger moved across my mother's face and I involuntarily took a step back. As did Thaddeus, hoping to escape the wrath of our Greek mother. Because when she got pissed. She. Got. Pissed.

"Am I not a woman?" Spinning around to look at my father, she shrugged. "Dimitris? Did you not marry a woman who knows pots and pans?"

I could tell my father was holding back a smile. "I did. I'm sure Thano was going to seek out your knowledge soon, my love."

He walked up and wrapped his arms around her waist and pulled her to him. Placing his lips on hers, he kissed her passionately. I'd long ago gotten used to my parents' displays of affection. My father never could seem to keep his hands off of my mother. He'd give her the world if he thought he could, but he tried hard to make everyone believe he wore the pants in the family, which was not the case. He was true to his Greek roots—but our mother—she was hardcore old Greek.

Breaking their kiss, he winked and said, "Now, leave the boy be and let him do his job the way he wants."

I swear my mother melted when in my father's arms. He knew it too and worked it well.

"Fine. I'll let it go." Turning and pointing to me, she continued. "This time!"

DINNER PROVED TO BE LIKE every other time I came home to eat. My brothers argued like cats and dogs. My mother informed me of the perfect girl for me. One of her Greek friend's daughters. My father talked about going camping, even though we all knew he'd never take the time off from his practice to actually go camping. Aunt Maria, Uncle Nick, and my two cousins also showed up for dinner.

Getting up, I walked out onto the deck and stared out to the mountains. Closing my eyes, Kilyn popped in my head. I quickly opened them and ran my hand across the back of my neck.

What was happening to me? Why couldn't I get her out of my head? I was torn between wanting to find out more about her and not wanting to forget Savannah.

Glancing over my shoulder, I watched my father take a seat. My father was a handsome man. For as long as I could remember, women would flirt with him endlessly. He never paid them any attention though. He only saw my mother and that was something I truly admired about him.

He looked straight ahead and nodded, as if saying something to himself. "I believe you are struggling with something, Athanasios."

I never knew how he did it, but my father always knew when something was bothering one of his sons. He saw it in me after Savannah died, and when he told me to find myself again, he didn't mean run off to Texas. I knew he was upset I left my job and went to work on the oil rig. But he never told me so. I saw it in his eyes though.

"Nah, I'm just tired. Work's been busy."

He slowly nodded. "You feel as if you are betraying her. Is that it?"

Pinching my eyebrows together, I asked, "Who?"

His eyes flicked up to meet mine.

"You know who . . . don't skirt around it. You're interested in this girl. Maybe this is the first girl who has sparked something inside you, huh? That makes you feel guilty."

I let out a laugh. "Kilyn? Dad, please. I don't even know the girl, and just because Mama's friend saw me talking to her means nothing. I ran into her and said hello."

"Have you been with a woman since Savannah? Sexually?"

My mouth fell open. My father was not asking me this. Squeezing my eyes shut, I cleared my throat and looked away. I knew if I avoided his question or tried to change the subject, he was not going to give up. "Yes, I have been with other women since Savannah. None of them meant anything. None of them ever will. I loved Savannah and no one will ever make me feel the way she did."

He gave me a regarded look and stood up as he looked out over the mountains.

"Then ask yourself something, son. Why do you stand out here with such a conflicted look on your face if your heart is not arguing with your mind?"

Opening my mouth to say something, I snapped it shut.

"Life moves on, Athanasios."

"I wish it could for me."

With a sad look on his face, he looked into my eyes. "It could . . . if you let her go."

My eyes stung with the threat of tears. "I can't. I want one more day to tell her I love her. To show her no one could ever love me like she could." My voice cracked and I sucked in a breath. "I want to hold her in my arms one more time."

# five

## Kilyn

"YOU SAW HIM AGAIN AND you're telling me that's not a sign?" Claire asked as she followed me into the elevators.

Sighing, I closed my eyes. "I'm not interested, Claire."

Grabbing my arm, she turned me to face her. Her eyes looked so sad and I knew what was about to come. "Kilyn, when are you going to let go of the past and move on?"

My lip trembled as the memories rushed through my mind. Pushing them out, I stood taller. "I've moved on, Claire. Just because I don't like to talk about it doesn't mean I haven't moved on."

She shook her head. "Then why won't you open your heart? Why?"

With a forced smile, I said, "I have a black heart."

My phone buzzed, saving me from any more of Claire's questions. Reaching into my purse and pulling out my phone, I smiled when I saw his name.

"Cody," I said as I lifted my eyebrow. Claire made a gagging sound and looked away. Cody had been the only constant in my world, or as Claire would say, he was my fuck buddy.

"Hey sweet thing. You down for some dancing?"

"Dancing? Tonight?"

"Hell yes! You in?"

With a smirk, I replied, "Count me in. How about I meet you there?"

"Smartest thing you've said all day," Claire mumbled.

I reached over and hit her on the shoulder.

"Sounds good. And Kilyn, don't wear panties."

My smile grew bigger. This was what I needed, I was sure of it.

"Oh, I'm sure I can arrange that. See ya tonight."

Hitting End, I dropped my phone back into my overly-expensive periwinkle Dooney and Bourke purse. The only reason I bought it was because I loved the color.

"Please tell me you're not going to have sex with him."

The doors to the elevator finally opened on the twenty-first floor. Glancing over my shoulder at Claire, I winked and said, "That's exactly what I intend on doing."

"Oh gawd! What do you see in him?"

"Nothing. That's what makes it work, Claire. He wants nothing from me but a fun night out. Same goes for me."

Walking up to the receptionist's desk, I flashed a bright smile and said, "Kilyn O'Kelly and Claire Paige here for our one o'clock appointment."

The young blonde nodded and replied, "I'll let Mr. Conner know you're here."

"Thank you!"

I knew I was being a tad over the top, but for some reason knowing I was going to relieve this insane need for an orgasm tonight had me flying high.

As the girl walked away, Claire leaned over and whispered, "Are you that excited to see Cody?"

Not bothering to look at her, I stared straight ahead at Mr. Conner walking toward us. "No. I'm that excited to get laid."

"Ugh. I just threw up in my mouth, bitch."

Extending my hand, I flashed a smile at the head of Conner Law Firm. He was redoing their lodge in Chipita Park as a surprise for his wife.

"Tell me you have something to knock my socks off."

"Oh, I think you'll be very pleased," I replied.

THE SECOND WE GOT INTO my car, Claire let out a squeal of excitement. "We got the job! I can't believe we got the job!"

With a smile on my face, I pulled out and headed back to the office. "This is huge for us. If we can move more into home interior, we can actually take on additional jobs!"

"I feel like celebrating!" Claire giggled.

"Why don't you and Blake come out with me and Cody tonight?"

Claire moaned. "Ugh . . . Cody."

Shaking my head, I replied, "Why do you hate him so much?"

I could feel her eyes on me. "Seriously, you don't know why?"

With a shrug, I quickly glanced at her. "Nope. No clue."

"Kilyn, he uses you for sex."

Letting out a roar of laughter, I tried to ignore the tightness in my chest. "And you don't think I do the same? Claire, that's what I like about Cody. He's upfront and honest. And he's not bad in bed."

"So you'll have meaningless sex with him?"

Coming to a stop at a light, I turned to her. My smile was gone and the feeling in my chest was heavier. "I've had sex with two guys in my twenty-eight-years, Claire. Two. And one of those . . . one was—"

My voice cracked and I turned away and forced myself to talk. "I'm not a slut, Claire. I just want to have fun."

Claire took my hand in hers. "I know you're not a slut. I didn't mean anything by it. I only want you to be happy, Kilyn. I'm sorry."

I reached up and quickly wiped a tear away while trying not to get pissed at Claire. I vowed I would never let Peter make me cry ever again. Closing my eyes, I was haunted by the sound of his breathing.

Quickly snapping out of it from the honk behind me, I hit the gas and didn't utter another word to Claire. I didn't have to. She knew me well enough to know I needed silence.

Twenty minutes later, I walked into my office and shut the door. Dropping into my chair, I pulled in a few deep breaths and tried to clear my head. The light knock at the door had me moaning internally.

"I'm fine, Claire. I need a few minutes."

She didn't say a word, but I knew she was still standing there. She'd probably stay there until I got up and opened the door. I never kept my office door shut. Not even during meetings. It was just the three of us. Claire, Kasey, the office manager, and me. Kasey kept this place running by doing everything from paying bills to running and grabbing coffee on late nights.

My phone buzzed in my purse. Pulling it out, I saw I had a message from Cody.

*Cody: Can't make it tonight. Something came up. Sorry.*

With a sigh, I dropped my head back against my chair. I knew what that meant. Someone better came along to occupy his time. Claire was right. I didn't need that asshole. I had a perfectly good vibrator waiting at home for me.

Pushing my chair back, I grabbed some files and my purse. I needed to get out of here and get some fresh air.

Before I had a chance to even gather everything up, there was another knock on my door.

"Claire, I'm fine!" I called out.

The door opened and Kasey walked in. "Um . . . Kilyn, it's not Claire. There is someone here to see you about some decorating."

I rolled my eyes and looked at her. "Did they have an appointment?"

She pulled the corner of her lip in between her teeth. "No. But I think you might know him. When he saw your name he started laughing pretty hard. Like, it took him a good minute or so to get himself together."

Narrowing my eyes at her, I contemplated on what to do. On one hand, I couldn't care less who was out there and what job they wanted us to do. On the other hand, I was intrigued.

"He doesn't want to make an appointment?"

She shook her head and stepped into my office. Quietly shutting the door, she smiled. "I could ask, but he is drop-dead freaking gorgeous. I mean, I'm pretty sure he melted my heart the second he looked at me and smiled. I've never in my life seen someone so good looking."

She leaned in closer and whispered, "And he has tattoos. Lord. Help. Me."

Giggling, I shook my head. "What was his name?"

"Oh, I think he told me, but I was too distracted by his body."

My hands came up to my hips. "Kasey! Good Lord, you act like you've never seen a man before."

She smiled. "I've never seen one I wanted to crawl on top of and—"

Curling my lip, I held up my hands and said, "Stop! I'll see him. Where is Claire?"

Her smile faded. "She said she was going home. She left after she knocked on your office door and you told her you were fine."

My heart pained for a moment. I knew it was just as hard for her as it was for me. After all, Peter was her brother.

Shaking my head, I said, "I'll call her after I meet with this potential client."

Kasey wiggled her eyebrows. "Want me to have him come in?"

Glancing down at my desk, I began arranging the files I was taking home. "Sure. Have him come in."

Kasey spun on her heels and headed out of my office while I placed a few files in a bag.

Something in the air changed. Almost as if electricity was being charged through the air. Goose bumps spread across my skin as I glanced up.

My heart dropped and I fought against the lump in my throat.

How did he find me?

*six*

## Thano

THE MOMENT I WALKED THROUGH her office door I felt it. The same pull in my chest that I had every time I saw her. Those hauntingly beautiful green eyes caught mine. Her mouth parted slightly, but she didn't say a word.

With a smile, I walked up to her and let out a chuckle. "A cook and an interior designer. I'm impressed."

Kilyn took a few steps back until she bumped into her chair. It took her all of five seconds to square her shoulders off and give me that beautiful smile of hers.

"I'm beginning to think you're stalking me, Mr. Drivas."

My eyes couldn't help but to roam quickly over her body before settling back to her eyes. I lifted my hands in defense. "I swear, I was shocked when I saw your name."

She folded her arms over her chest and lifted her brow as if questioning me. "Uh-huh. So you're telling me it's strictly a coincidence you ran into me running and now you're standing in my office. What in the world could you possibly need an interior designer for?"

I couldn't blame her. I'd be a little hesitant if I were her. Flashing her a smile, I watched as something moved across her face. She pressed her lips together before she caught her lower lip between her teeth.

Damn if that wasn't the cutest thing I'd ever seen.

"The cabin."

Her eyes lit up while her mouth parted slightly.

"The one you're building?" she said with a bit of excitement in her voice.

I wasn't sure if I liked how Kilyn made me feel. She brought a piece of me back to life I wasn't sure I was ready to face. No one had made me feel a damn thing since Savannah. But this girl lit up something inside of me I was having a hard time ignoring.

"It's finished. Now I need to make it look like someone actually lives there."

Her eyes searched my face quickly. "How big is it?"

"Twelve hundred square feet. Two bedrooms, two and a half bathrooms, a kitchen, dining area, and a living room. There is also a loft above the garage which is about six hundred more square feet with another bathroom."

When she licked her lips, my dick jumped in my pants. I'd never felt so damn confused in my life. Was I having feelings for her because we kept running into each other, or was there something about her that drew me to her?

"I normally do large homes and commercial properties. I haven't done a smaller project in a long time. It could be fun."

"Would it be terribly rude if I asked to see some of your work?"

She smiled slowly and tilted her head. "I'd be worried if you hadn't." Motioning for me to take a seat, I moved swiftly and sat.

Scanning her desk, I tried to hide my grimace. It was a mess. Files were everywhere. Pieces of paper scattered all over the place with one or two things written on them. I was beginning to regret walking into her office. If her work was as sloppy as her desk, how in the hell would I get myself out of this?

I pushed my hand through my hair and cursed under my breath. Shit.

Kilyn reached into her bag and pulled out a file that said, 'Conner, Chipita Park Project'.

She opened the file and handed me a few pieces of paper. "If you'd like to see the 3-D designs, I can get my laptop back out. I just presented this to Mr. Conner this afternoon. As you can see, this project is much bigger than yours. The total square footage we will be designing is six thousand square feet and that includes the outdoor pool area as well as a small guesthouse by the pool. Mr. Conner's taste is somewhat . . . different. He hunts a lot in Africa and is going more for that look. Now, I don't know what your style is, but I'm confident I'd be able to deliver exactly what you were looking for."

Glancing up at her, I couldn't help but feel a sense of pride. I had no clue why. I hardly knew this girl, but to see how she handled herself as if standing in front of a room full of board members hell-bent on selling them her product. Confident and so in control. It was a turn on.

I took in a deep breath through my nose and filled my senses with her smell.

Damn. Now I couldn't concentrate because I had to know what kind of perfume she was wearing. What I wouldn't give to have her leave that smell on my bed sheets each morning.

*Shit. What in the fuck am I doing?*

"Thano? Did you hear me?"

Her sweet voice pulled me out of my wayward thoughts. "Sorry, I um . . . I got distracted by your perfume."

A small smile tugged at the corner of her mouth as she pulled her head back in surprise. "My perfume?"

For the love of God. Why would I say that? Now I do sound like a stalker.

"Yeah, it brought back memories of my great-grandmother."

My body shuddered. Holy shit. I was just thinking of having sex with her and I brought my great-grandmother into the picture.

With a wink, she replied, "Oh. Well, I'm not sure if that is a compliment or if you were comparing me to an old lady smell."

With an awkward laugh, I shook my head. "No, you smell amazing."

She grinned and replied, "It's Chanel Number 5."

I needed to make a note of that.

Clearing my throat, I motioned with my head toward the plans.

"What were you saying?"

Her eyes dropped to my lips and I'd have given anything to ask her what she was thinking.

"Um . . . I was . . ."

She stood up and barely shook her head as if trying to remember her own thoughts. "I asked what style were you thinking?"

*You on top first, making yourself come, then it would be my turn, taking you from behind fast and hard.*

Son-of-a-bitch.

*Stop this, Thano.*

"How would you decorate it if it were yours?"

Her mouth fell open in surprise. I could see her chest begin to rise and fall faster, and I wanted to punch myself in the face.

Why in the hell did I ask her that? I really wanted to know. If that cabin were hers, how would she decorate it?

"I've never had anyone ask me how I would decorate a room be-fore." She lifted her eyes in thought before looking back at me. "Is it surrounded by trees?"

With a laugh, I nodded. "There is a wraparound porch with views of the mountains and a stream that is a few hundred feet from the back of the house."

She slowly sank into her chair. "That sounds like heaven. Pure heaven."

I grinned. "It is."

"Okay, well, if it were mine I think I would go for more of a rus-tic cabin feel. Of course, I'd have more feminine touches throughout, but nothing dramatic. I would think you'd want to do that as well, for you know, when you bring your girlfriend or someone up there, they wouldn't feel like they were in a guy's bachelor pad getaway cabin. Does your girlfriend not want to have any input in the decorating?"

"I don't have a girlfriend."

There was no doubt in my mind her eyes sparkled when I said I didn't have a girlfriend.

"Do you never plan to have one?"

My heart dropped as Savannah popped into my head.

"Why would you ask me that?" I snapped.

Kilyn pinched her eyebrows together and readjusted herself in her seat. "I wasn't meaning anything bad by it. I was simply stating that at some point I'm sure you'll bring a girl up there for some sort of romantic weekend. Maybe for a few days or maybe longer. Maybe someday you'll ask someone to marry you there. I don't know. I'm simply stating—"

"I get what you're saying," I said as I cut her off. "I have no plans for any of that right now. A girlfriend is the last thing on my mind."

Clearing her throat, she stood and began gathering the plans and putting them back into a folder. "Right. Well, anyway, it's your house so you really need to decide how you want it to be decorated—not me."

She pulled out another file and opened it, dropping it in front of me, this time not bothering to take out the designs.

"This is a dentist office I designed. The work has been completed on it if you'd like to call and ask them for a tour."

Damn it. Clearly, I pissed her off with how I acted. She was no longer energized by talking about her work. Her voice was cold and distant, almost as if she didn't care if I hired her now or not.

"Kilyn, I'm sorry I snapped like that."

Her eyes looked briefly into mine. She looked as if she wanted to ask me something, but she looked away. "I really do need to be going, and since you didn't have an appointment, I can gather up a few other designs and send them your way if you'd like. I'll need your email address."

Fuck! I needed to figure out how to turn this around.

Standing, I nodded as I pulled out my wallet and took out my business card. "I'm sorry. I didn't realize you had somewhere to go."

She didn't even bother to look at me as she took the card. "No worries. I was supposed to go dancing with a friend, but he canceled on me."

The zip of jealousy that raced through my body shocked the hell out of me. I quickly decided this was my opportunity to get to know Kilyn a little better.

"What kind of dancing?"

She stopped what she was doing and looked at me. "Country western."

Scrunching up my nose, I groaned.

Her hands immediately went to her hips and I saw a playfulness in her when she tried to hide her smile. "You don't like country music?"

"No. Not at all."

Tilting her head, she went back to accessing me. "Have you ever listened to it, Thano?"

"Only pussies listen to country music."

Her mouth gaped open. "So you're saying I'm a pussy?"

My heart slammed in my chest. *Fucking hell, how do I keep doing this?*

"No! Wait, I didn't mean women. I meant men who listen to country music are pussies."

Slowly shaking her head, she placed her hand over her heart as if I had mortally wounded her. "I'll have you know, some of the only men I'd ever bend over this table for and let them ravage my body are country music artists. Oh my God! Dierks Bentley. Hell. Yes. Keith Urban? Yes please! Oh, and let's not forget about Sam Hunt. I'd let him do things that would make even you blush."

I cleared my throat. Is it getting hot in here?

She closed her eyes and smiled. "Oh! Then you have Dan and Shay." Looking straight at me, she kept going. "Hell, I'd even get into a threesome for those two. Sandwiched between the two of them . . . hell to the yes."

Swallowing hard, I cracked my neck and rubbed the back of it. "Um . . . Kilyn, can we change the subject? It's been a long . . . dry spell if you would."

Her eyes darkened before she turned away and looked out the window. "Sorry. I'm passionate about my country music."

"I see that," I barely mumbled.

Grabbing her bag, she reached for her purse.

Fuck. What was it going to take to get back on her good side?

Before my mouth had time to catch up to my brain, I blurted out, "Why don't you come up to the cabin this weekend? You can take a look around and decide if it's something you want to take on."

She had been rounding her desk when she stopped directly in front of me.

The smell of her perfume wrapped around my body as she continued to stare at me. I took that as a chance to quickly glance around the rest of her office. There was a small sitting area off to the side with fresh flowers and a few magazines neatly spread out over the coffee table. There was a bookcase behind that with books color-coded by their covers. At least the rest of her office was neat and organized, unlike her desk.

"You want me to come up to your cabin with you?"

"Just to check it out. I'm not asking you up there for the weekend or anything. I mean, the only thing up there is a chair and a bed," I said with a laugh.

Kilyn narrowed one eye as she continued to give me the evil eye.

"Oh, cause the fact you only have a bed up there makes me feel so much better."

I closed my eyes and sighed before looking at the floor. The last thing I wanted her to think was I only wanted in her pants. "I went up there a lot when they were building it. It's my escape. All I needed was a place to sit and sleep."

Her facial expression softened and a slow crooked smile moved across her face. "I'll go and look at your cabin, if you go dancing with me tonight. Country western dancing."

I let out a roar of laughter before I noticed she was giving me a dead serious look. "Wait. You're serious? In order for you to come look at the cabin, I have to go dancing with you?"

"Country western dancing."

I swear, if I didn't want to be around her so much, I'd turn and walk away. Interior designers were a dime a dozen.

"Fine."

With a smile almost too big for her face, she asked, "Really?"

Rolling my eyes, I tried to figure out how to keep this from my brothers. No matter what I did to hide it, I was sure they would find out about it.

"Yes. But if you think I'm doing any of that line dancing, you are crazy."

Her teeth sunk into her lip, making my thoughts wander to where they shouldn't.

"You say that now, Mr. Drivas. I have your number," she said as she held up my card. "I'll call and let you know where to meet me."

"Meet you? You don't want me to pick you up?"

With a wink she replied, "Nope. I'll meet you."

She headed for her office door. Lifting her hand, she waved good-bye to the receptionist.

"Don't forget, Kasey. It's a long weekend for me. I'll be back in Monday."

Kasey smiled at Kilyn and then looked at me. She slowly licked her lips and pushed her chest out a little more.

I tried like hell not to look directly at her chest as I passed by. "Good afternoon, sir."

"Good afternoon," I replied and quickly followed Kilyn.

We rode down in the elevator in silence. The whole time I was trying to think of how to get myself out of this damn situation I had gotten into. The last thing I really wanted to do was go dancing. I hated dancing.

The doors opened and Kilyn stepped out. I opened my mouth to talk when she stopped and I ran right into the back of her. Spinning around, she flashed me an evil smile.

"Not yet there, Mr. Drivas. Save it for tonight."

"Yeah, about that, Kilyn, I . . . I um . . ."

Narrowing my eyes, I took in the look on her face. She actually seemed excited about the idea of me going dancing with her. All I wanted to do was be around her. Maybe I needed to get it out of my system; if that meant spending an evening listening to pansy-ass music, then so be it.

"What should I wear?"

Her eyes lit up like it was Christmas morning. Something in me wanted to make her look that happy every single day.

Pushing that thought as far away as possible, I waited for her response.

"Jeans, a T-shirt, and a pair of boots. Cowboy boots."

With a sly look, I asked, "What if I don't own any cowboy boots?"

Taking a few steps back, she winked and said, "You better go buy some then. Talk to you soon . . . Thano."

My heart stopped as my name trickled off her soft plump lips. My breath hitched and I was frozen in my steps. I watched as she walked away while I tried to figure out what in the hell was happening to me.

By the time I got to my car, I was fighting for air. Dropping my head back against my headrest, I closed my eyes and whispered, "I can't forget her. I won't forget her."

## seven

### Kilyn

"WHAT DO YOU MEAN CODY won't be there?" Claire asked.

Leaning forward, I carefully applied my mascara. I wasn't sure why I felt the need to take a shower, shave, wash and dry my hair, and reapply all of my makeup. I wouldn't have done any of that if I had been meeting Cody.

"He bugged out on me."

"But we're all still going dancing? I thought maybe you were mad at me and didn't want me to come."

With a long sigh, I replied, "Nonsense. Is Blake coming?"

"Yes. He has tomorrow off, and since you're taking a long weekend, I thought I would as well. We talked about going up to the mountains, but they are saying a storm might blow in."

"Please, they keep saying that and nothing happens. You should go. Enjoy your weekend."

The silence on the other end of the line told me I needed to make things better. If I didn't, Claire would beat herself up all night and not enjoy her time with her husband.

"Claire, it's okay. I'm okay. I promise."

A sniffle came over the phone. "I hate that it is even there between us."

"It's not. It has nothing to do with you. Nothing."

"It has everything to do with me, Kilyn. Everything."

Dropping my hand, I stared at my reflection in the mirror. Where once was a girl so broken, now stood a confident woman. I talked about what had happened to me plenty of times. But talking about it with Claire. I couldn't. I wouldn't.

It was time for a subject change.

"Thano is going tonight."

Claire gasped. "What? How? Why? Where did you see him?"

Attempting to hold back my giggles, I gave her the answers she was seeking.

"Thano is meeting us at the club. He stopped by the office today looking for an interior designer for a new cabin he built up in the mountains. He had no idea it was our firm."

"Oh. My. God. It's like the gods are throwing you two together."

With a roll of my eyes, I went back to applying my mascara. "Please."

"Okay, so how did it end up that he is coming dancing with us?"

"He said country music was for pussies. I was not about to let that go. I told him the only way I'd go and look at his cabin to see if we wanted to take on the job was if he came dancing tonight."

Claire started coughing. "Hold on. Choking here."

Blowing out a frustrated puff of air, I waited for her to get it all out of her system. I knew Claire better than anyone. We grew up together. She was like my sister and I knew what was about to come.

"You like him!"

And there it is.

"No, I do not. I needed someone to dance with tonight since Cody backed out on me."

With a loud laugh, Claire replied, "Oh, because the hundreds of single guys at the club aren't good enough?"

"No. Because the moment he said that, I had to prove him wrong. I'll get him loving country music by the time we finish his cabin if it kills me."

"So you've already decided you're taking on the cabin? What about the Conner project?"

Dropping my mascara back into my makeup bag, I dug around for my blush.

"Don't worry, Claire. You're always worrying. Are we all driving together or what?"

She sighed, and I knew this conversation was far from over. "We'll pick you up at seven."

"Perfect!" I said. "See ya then!"

THE NICE COWBOY SPUN ME around and dipped me at the end of the song, causing me to let out a laugh.

Pulling me back up, he searched my face. "Tell me you're here alone."

With a pout, I said, "Sorry, cowboy. Waiting for my date to show up."

"Lucky him."

I smiled and headed toward the bar. Even though I was dressed in a lightweight baby-blue shirt and shorts, I was still sweating my ass off. My mother had hated when I wore my cowboy boots with shorts, but that was when I was fourteen. I was older and I knew it made my ass look good.

Trying to catch my breath, I motioned to the bartender for another Bud Light.

"Better slow it down there, ladybug, if you're too drunk you can't teach me to dance."

Goose bumps ran down my neck and over my body as his hot breath touched my skin.

"How long have you been here?" I asked, taking the bottle of beer and pressing it to my lips. When I turned around, I damn near choked at the sight in front of me.

"Holy hell," I whispered as my eyes looked at the Greek god standing in front of me. His dark hair and skin were made darker by the ul-tra-tight white T-shirt he had on. Moving my eyes down, I took in the jeans that certainly were not new. When I finally reached his boots, I smiled wide.

My heart skipped a beat and I fought like hell to ignore it. "You bought boots."

His hand wrapped around my waist and he pulled me closer to him. My breath caught and I was positive he could hear my heart pounding against my chest.

Jesus. Was he always this touchy? I certainly hoped like hell he was.

"I did, and let me tell you something, they were expensive as hell." He smiled and those damn dimples popped right on out. The urge to push my hand down my panties was real. So real, I let a small moan slip from my lips.

Thano leaned in closer, placing his lips next my ear. "But don't worry, the saleslady assured me they would work when I told her I was trying to impress a country girl. I told her if they didn't, I was bringing them back."

Trying not to, I busted out laughing. Placing my hands on his massive chest, I ignored the pull in my lower stomach. With a good push, he took a few steps back. Not even bothered by the fact that I had used all my might to push him away and he only took two steps back.

*I need to get to the gym.*

"You wouldn't think of returning them!" I gasped.

"I would! I totally would. So you better make it worth my while."

The burning in my chest was something I wasn't familiar with. I'd never had a guy make me feel the way Thano did. I was positive it was because of this whole running into each other bullshit we had going on. Maybe someone was trying to tell me something. If they were, I was going to keep ignoring them. A guy like Thano surely had to have a revolving door when it came to his bedroom and the girls he invited in. That had to be the reason he didn't have a girlfriend.

When Dirks Bentley's "Drunk on a Plane" started, I grabbed Thano and pulled him out onto the dance floor.

"Okay, now all these people are doing the two-step. It's really simple once you get it down. When you get a little comfortable with the steps then you can try giving me a spin or two!"

He smiled, but it was almost an evil smile. Like he knew something I didn't. "Thélis na horépsis mazí mu, Kilyn?" he called out.

I froze and couldn't move an inch. Never mind the fact that I had barely gotten over how damn good he looked, now he pushed me right in front of the MAC truck and tried to finish me off by saying something in what I could only assume was Greek.

*Jesus, Kilyn, pull yourself together.*

Swallowing hard, I licked my lips and tried to speak past the lump in my throat. "What did you say?"

"Would you dance with me, Kilyn?"

Dear God. Talk to me like that again and I'll let you do whatever you want to me.

"Um . . . yes. I mean okay."

When he took me into his arms, my breath caught and I was pretty sure he knew he was having an effect on me.

"Show me how to two-step."

Can't. Think. Body. On. Fire.

"Give me a second. Your whole speaking to me in Greek threw me and I'm trying to get myself back together."

His head dropped back and he let out a roar of laughter.

After adjusting his hands into the right position, I showed him how to take the correct steps. He was catching on pretty good and I was honestly impressed with how fast he was learning. There might be hope for him after all.

We stopped after two songs and got a drink. "You're learning pretty fast."

Thano flashed me a sexy-ass grin and said, "I'm a fast learner."

I bet.

When LOCASH's song "I Love This Life" started, I jumped up.

"I love this song!"

Thano finished off his beer and took my hand. "Then let's go dance."

A part of me was bummed out because I loved cutting up the floor with this song and was kind of hoping to hook up with another dancer. Thano pulled me into his arms and we took off.

He guided me around that dance floor like he'd been two-stepping all his life. Then he spun me and pulled me back to him without missing a beat. I'd never danced with anyone who knew how to lead like this guy was.

Giving him a look only a mother could give, I yelled, "You already knew how to two-step, didn't you?"

He winked and spun me again. Laughing, I let it go and enjoyed being in his arms and listening to my song as we danced our asses off. We were a force to be reckoned with as Thano spun me around, dipped me, and even did some fancy move where he whipped me around his body.

I'd never had so much fun.

A slow song came on and I quickly headed to our table where Claire and Blake were. Any closer contact with Thano and I was positive I'd be begging him to make me scream out his name.

Trying like hell to catch my breath, I dropped in my seat while Thano reached across the table and shook Blake's hand.

"Sorry!" I shouted. "You remember Claire, right? This is her husband, Blake."

Thano smiled and gave Claire a friendly nod. "The cooking queen."

Claire laughed. "That's me! And part time interior decorator as well."

Thano looked between us. "You work together?"

I nodded. "Yeah. Claire mainly handles everything after the designs have been approved. The contractors and such. She also designs most of the kitchens, since that is her thing."

Thano stared at me with a goofy smile. "What?" I asked.

"It's just, someone your age to have your own company and already be so well-known in what you do . . . it's impressive. Very impressive."

I could feel my face turn hot. Looking away, I couldn't help but notice the shit-eating grin on Claire's face. "She started her company when she was still in college. Kilyn somehow talked one of her professors into letting her design her new house. It was supposed to just be the paint color but when Kilyn started making suggestions, the professor hired her on the spot."

Needing to change the subject, I turned to Thano. "Let's forget about that. Do you want to explain to me why you lied?"

He jerked his head back in surprise. "What do you mean? I haven't lied to you about anything."

I shook my finger at him. "Oh, oh please. You clearly knew how to two-step, Mr. Drivas. You probably do it better than me!"

Leaning closer to me, I felt myself pull back. "I never said I couldn't two-step, Ms. O'Kelly. I said I didn't like country music."

My head was spinning. "You said you didn't listen to it! If you don't listen to it, how in the world can you dance to it? Plus, you asked me to teach you."

He lifted his beer and took a drink. I watched as the muscles in his throat worked while he swallowed. *Why in the hell is that turning me on?*

Placing the bottle on the table, he looked directly into my eyes. "My mother started all her sons in dance class at age six. I can probably dance to any type of music you asked me to. My favorite is ballroom dancing."

Claire leaned forward and shouted, "If I wasn't married, I'd crawl over the table and have sex with you right now."

My head snapped over as I yelled, "Claire!"

Blake laughed and chimed in. "That's my cue to get my wife out onto the dance floor and take her for a spin. Clearly, I've been neglecting her."

I watched as Blake and Claire took off toward the dance floor. When I turned back to Thano, he was staring at me with black eyes. My entire body trembled from his intense stare.

Luke Bryan's "Strip It Down" started and Thano took my hand and pulled me up.

"Let's dance, ladybug."

That was twice he called me that, and I had to admit I kind of liked it. It was cute, but still made me feel . . . sexy. But why ladybug?

Pulling my body up against his, I buried my face and tried to pretend I was dancing with someone who didn't drive my body crazy and make my stomach feel like I was on an endless roller coaster.

His thumb rubbed against the skin on my hand, leaving a trail of fire in its path. Every time he moved his hand across my back, my breath caught and my stomach dropped.

*For crying out loud. I'm not in high school. What in the hell is up with these feelings?*

I prayed for the song to end and a fast one to start. When Garth Brooks "Friends in Low Places" started, we danced hard and by the time it was over, I was gasping for breath. Clearly I was out of shape and Thano was so much better at two-stepping than Cody ever would be.

I wondered if he would be better in bed, also.

*Stop this, Kilyn.*

"You want to stop for the night?"

My heart dropped as I looked at Thano and asked, "What makes you think I want to stop?"

He looked confused. "You said to stop. I assumed you meant you were ready to stop for the night."

"Are you ready to stop?"

His eyes turned dark again. "Baby, I could go all night long."

Feeling my heartbeat increase, I whispered, "I bet you could."

## eight

### Thano

ANYTIME I WAS WITH KILYN, the walls I'd built around my heart felt as if they were shaken. A small crack was made each time she smiled at me or laughed that beautiful laugh of hers. Tonight was no different. *I hadn't felt this happy in a very long time.*

"Stop this, Kilyn," she whispered.

Feeling a tightening in my chest at her words, I didn't want the night to end. "You want to stop for the night?"

She looked at me with an incredulous stare. "What makes you think I want to stop?"

Okay, did I hear her right? "You said to stop. I assumed you meant you were ready to stop for the night."

"Are you ready to stop?"

Warmth radiated throughout my body at the idea of holding her close to me again. Maybe it was time for a bit of meaningless flirting. At least I would tell myself it was meaningless. "Baby, I could go all night long."

Her eyes glowed and she unknowingly licked her lips slowly before whispering, "I bet you could."

My breath stalled as I looked into her eyes. There was something about Kilyn that brought a piece of my heart to life. I wanted desperately to let my guard down, but did I dare open myself up to that kind of heartache again? Was it a risk I was willing to take?

Another song played and I couldn't help but notice how Kilyn's eyes lit up. It was clear music was important to her. Taking her hand, I kissed the back of it. Her mouth parted slightly before I led her out to the dance floor. Pulling her closer to me, she buried her head into my chest as we started dancing.

Something was holding Kilyn back as much as it was holding me back. A part of me wanted to know what it was.

Placing my finger under her chin, I lifted her eyes to mine and softly said, "Se skeftomai sinehia."

Her eyes lit up and she smiled. "What did you say?"

I wasn't sure why I kept talking to her in Greek. I never did that with Savannah. Not once did I ever utter a word to her in Greek.

Swallowing the lump in the back of my throat, I said, "I'm constantly thinking about you."

Kilyn came to a stop as she stared into my eyes. Placing my hand on the side of her face, I looked deep into those beautiful green eyes while I ran my thumb over her soft lips. "I'm fighting the urge to kiss you."

She sucked in a breath of air and dropped her eyes to my lips. "Ti Káneis gia ména?"

Swallowing hard, she asked, "What did you say?"

My stomach was in knots as I answered, "What are you doing to me, ladybug?"

Her eyes closed as she whispered my name, "Thano."

I needed to see what she tasted like more than I needed air to breathe. Pressing my lips to hers, she gripped onto my shirt tightly while letting out a soft moan into my mouth.

Slipping my hand behind her neck, I grabbed a handful of her hair and pulled, causing her to open more to me, deepening our kiss.

She tasted sweeter than honey and I forced myself to pull my lips away. If I kept kissing her, I'd want more. Need more.

When I opened my eyes, hers were still closed. Releasing her hair, I ran the back of my hand down the soft skin of her face. My God she was beautiful.

Opening her eyes, Kilyn smiled and took a step back. She drew her lip in between her teeth. "We should probably call it a night."

My heartbeat was pounding against my chest so hard I was sure Kilyn could hear it.

With a slight smile, I replied, "We probably should. Do you want me to give you a ride home?"

I regretted asking to take her home the moment it slipped from my lips. The attraction I felt for Kilyn was almost too strong to deny. Yet, I wasn't sure if I was ready to move on.

No. I'd never be able to move on, but I also didn't want to lead her on. Use her like I'd used the other women to try and forget for a bit.

"Are you sure? Claire and Blake live in the opposite direction of me and it would help them out if you could drop me off."

It wasn't lost on me how she stressed me dropping her off. Maybe Kilyn wasn't any more ready to take the next step than I was.

Giving her a soft smile, I replied, "Sounds good."

After telling Claire and Blake I was taking her home, Kilyn grabbed her small purse and coat. We walked in silence out to my car. Walking up to the passenger side, I unlocked it and opened the door for her.

With a huge grin, she shook her head and whistled. "A BMW M2 Coupé. Very nice."

"Very stupid," I replied with a chuckle. "My parents told me to go sensible and I didn't listen. I pay more for the car than my rent, I swear."

Kilyn laughed, leaving my body feeling strange in its wake.

"Well, I'd take yours over mine any day."

She slipped in and I couldn't help but notice how damn good she looked in my car. Shutting the door, I raced around the front and quickly jumped in. Putting it in drive, I took off toward Manitou Springs.

"What kind of car do you have?" I asked.

"Honda Accord two door."

Glancing over to her, I asked, "You don't like it?"

"I do. I let Claire talk me into it when I wanted something else. It still pisses me off I let her do that to me."

She turned and looked out the window, wringing her hands over and over.

"Why do I get the feeling Claire talks you into, or should I say out of, things often?"

With a gruff laugh, she replied, "Oh, yeah. She's good at talking me out of stuff, even if I don't need her to." Her smile faded some as she continued. "She's done a ton more stuff than I have. I envy her in a way."

"How so?" I truly wanted to learn more about Kilyn. She had a bit of a mysterious air about her.

Stopping at a light, I looked over at her. She was staring straight ahead. "She's been horseback riding. I haven't, even though I'd love to. Oh, yeah, and she's been on a Ferris wheel. That's something I've never had a chance to do."

"Really? You've never been on a Ferris wheel?"

"Nope," she said with a chuckle. "I've never even been to a carnival, which really makes me sad."

I clutched my chest and sucked in a breath of air. "How? That's like a staple of every childhood."

Her smile faded before she looked away. "Well, I didn't have a normal childhood."

The pain in her voice bothered me and I couldn't explain why. "Do your parents live around here?"

Turning her head, she slowly blew out a deep breath. "No. They don't."

I wasn't sure if I should push her for more of an answer or not. I quickly decided I should.

"Do you not talk to them anymore?"

Her chin trembled before she plastered on a fake-ass grin. "My parents died in an accident when I was fourteen."

My heart dropped. "Shit. I'm so sorry, Kilyn. I wouldn't have pushed if I had known."

With a shrug, she gave me a wink. "How would you have known?" She looked straight ahead and pointed to a building. "That's me. You can pull up and I'll jump out."

I was pissed at myself for feeling the way I was. A part of me was disappointed she wasn't asking me up, but the other part of me was breathing a sigh of relief.

"Will you be okay walking up on your own?"

She narrowed her eyes and gave me a look I couldn't read. "I mean, I can walk you up if you want?"

With a breathtaking smile, she opened the door and got out. "Nah, Dave the doorman will make sure I get in okay."

The relief I felt knowing she would be okay surprised me. "Hey!" I shouted before she shut the door. "Are you off tomorrow?"

Leaning in, she flashed me a sultry look. "Why? You want to go salsa dancing? I bet you can do that as well."

My cheeks almost burned, I was smiling so big. "I can, but that's not what I was going to ask. There's a storm blowing in later this weekend, but I thought maybe we could head up to the cabin earlier in the day so you can take a look at it."

"That's right, me going up to your bachelor pad in the mountains was part of the deal wasn't it?"

"Yes, it was. So what do you say?"

Pulling her lip between her teeth, she studied me for a few moments.

"I think tomorrow will work. What time?"

There was no way I could ignore the mixed emotions I was having. No doubt I was excited to spend more time with Kilyn, but I was also feeling tremendous guilt at the same time.

"Ten too early for you?"

Taking a step back, she scrunched her nose up in an adorable way. "Puh-lease. I'll already be back from the gym and ready to go."

Putting my car in drive, I nodded. "Ten it is then."

I couldn't really see those beautiful green eyes of hers, but I imagined they were sparkling like they always did when she was happy or excited. "Night, Thano."

"Good night, Kilyn."

She shut the car door and walked into her building, not once turning to look back at me.

I drove off trying to decide if I was bothered by that or not.

*nine*

## Kilyn

BY THE TIME I WALKED out of my kickboxing class, I was covered in sweat. All I wanted to do was get home, shower, and get ready for this trip up into the mountains with Thano.

Pressing my lips together, I tried like hell to keep the stupid bubbly feelings of excitement down. This was new for me. This whole fluttering in my chest and my stomach dipping like I was driving fast down a road and hit a dip. Of course, I'd never met a guy like Thano either. The way he looked at me, talked to me, held me in his arms like I was something very special to him.

My fingers moved to my lips; I swore they still tingled from his kiss last night. After I had gone up to my apartment, I lay awake in bed and cursed myself for not inviting him up. I didn't want this to be just another fuck buddy type of thing. If I was going to let my walls down, I wanted it to be different.

I shook my head and closed my eyes. Who was I kidding? I'd never fully let my walls down, but maybe, just maybe with Thano I could try.

"Jesus, that is the look of a girl in love."

Snapping my head up, I stared at the girl standing in front of me. What was her name again? She didn't have her nametag on and when I went to look, it appeared I was checking out her fake-ass boobs.

"No, it is not a look of someone in love," I snapped back.

Wiggling her eyebrows, she replied, "You got lucky last night then?"

I let out a fake laugh. "I wish."

Another girl ran up and practically attacked the nameless big-breasted receptionist. "Oh my God, Ann! There he is! The guy who left you that morning!"

"Where?" Ann looked as she lifted up on her toes. Her eyes widened as she gasped, "What is he doing here? Don't tell me he is a member here now."

Now I was intrigued. "What is who doing here?" I asked. If she was going to pry into my sex life, I was prying into hers.

"This dick I met awhile back. I guess to him I was nothing more than another woman to spend the night with." Her eyes turned dark as if remembering that night. "Asshole has no idea what he missed out on."

I couldn't help but laugh. What did she expect to get from a guy who only hooked up with her for sex? "Actually, I only came up to get next week's schedule. Do you have it?"

Ann kept her eyes focused on who I assumed was the dick who poked and ran. She reached for a schedule and handed it to me. "He's coming this way."

"Stay strong, Ann," the other girl said.

Turning to leave, I ran smack into a familiar chest.

"Now I'm beginning to wonder if you're not the one stalking me, ladybug."

My eyes widened while I stood there frozen in place.

Thano.

My mouth went dry as I took him in. His white T-shirt was soaked with sweat and I could totally see every single line of his muscles beneath it.

Yummy.

This was insane. How many times were we going to run into each other? What was life trying to tell me?

"You work out here?"

He smiled that brilliant smile that melted my panties right off. How in the hell was I going to be able to survive this little trip with him when all I dreamt about was him on top of me. Or me on top of him. Oh, from behind I bet would be nice.

I shook my head to clear my wayward thoughts.

"Today is the first day I've tried out this new gym. Gus told me about it."

He looked over my shoulder and frowned when he saw Ann.

My chest felt like a heavy weight was on it as I quickly figured out whom Ann was talking about. Shutting my eyes, I cursed.

Damn it. I knew he was too good to be true. He was a player. Hooking up with women at clubs and then having sex. I should have known.

"You probably don't remember who I am, do you?" Ann said with sarcasm dripping off every single word.

Thano gave her a smile, not the kind he gave me though. "I do. Your name is Ann."

"Wow, I'm impressed you took the time to remember."

Clearing his throat, Thano looked back at me and pinched his brows together. "I need to take care of something really quickly here. I'll still pick you up at ten, right?"

My eyes widened and my mouth dropped open. He was excusing me to talk to his little fuck buddy and making plans to pick me up.

Oh. Hell. No.

"Seriously? Why are all guys such dicks? Maybe you need to find someone else to decorate your fuck pad."

Pushing past him, I headed toward the exit.

"Kilyn!" Thano called out as I picked up my pace. I would have run if I thought it wouldn't make me look like an insane person.

If he thought I was going to be his next one-night stand, he had another think coming. And to think I let his stupid charming smile and sexy Greek words sneak in on me.

I was almost to my car when I breathed a sigh of relief. He hadn't come after me.

Unlocking my car door, I opened it only to have it slammed shut again.

"Wait. Kilyn."

Looking up at Thano, I placed my hands on my hips and shot him the dirtiest look I could muster up.

"Let me go, Thano."

Shaking his head, he said, "No. Not until you let me explain something."

"There's nothing to explain. Ann managed to tell me about the dick who screwed her and left when he got what he wanted."

His eyes narrowed and a look of anger washed over his face. "Is that so? Well, then maybe you should at least give me the same chance to tell my side of the story."

I laughed. "Your side? You fucked her and left her the next morning. What else is there to say? I'm not that type of girl, so you're wasting your goddamn time."

Going to open my door, he blocked me. "Nice mouth, Kilyn. And I have plenty to say and you're going to listen to me."

My entire body began to shake. "I don't do well with being told what to do, Thano."

He pushed his hand through his still sweat-soaked hair. I hated that it made my insides pull with desire. And what I hated even more was how the authority in his voice turned me on. I vowed I'd never let another man have any sort of control over me, but something about when Thano did it was different.

"Kilyn, please let me tell you something, and if you're still pissed at me, I'll let you go and I'll find someone else to decorate the cabin, I swear. But please give me a chance. I don't want you to leave angry."

The sadness in his eyes caused me to take a step away from my car. Crossing my arms over my chest, I let out a huff. "Fine. You have two minutes and then I'm out of here."

He shook his head as if trying to figure out how to talk himself out of this.

"I lost someone very close to me, and for a long time I was fucked up. I hooked up with a few girls and had sex with them and it was all in fun. I always told them I wasn't looking for anything but one night. It was the only way I could erase the pain for a bit. That and alcohol. I only did that with a few girls because the guilt drove me insane for weeks afterwards."

My heart felt as if it were breaking, and I wasn't sure if it was because I knew Thano loved someone so much it would break him, or if it was from knowing he had meaningless one-night stands with other women. Deep down I knew it was a little of both.

"I met Ann months ago at a club I went to with my brothers and Gus. Ann and a few of her friends ended up joining us at our table, and my brothers made sure I got pretty fucked up and kept pushing her on me. We danced a few times and I'm sure I said something that led her on. Ann offered to take me home. I was so fucked up I couldn't even tell her my address. I had no intentions of sleeping with her; I promised myself I wasn't going to get drunk and have sex with someone again. She ended up taking me back to her place and she said we slept together. I barely remembered it and I'm pretty sure I was so trashed I wouldn't have been able to even have sex."

Rolling my eyes, I said, "Ugh. I don't care to hear your details."

"I'm just saying, I don't even think I actually had sex with the girl. I woke up the next morning still in my boxer briefs. She made an advancement toward me and I tried to explain to her I wasn't interested and I apologized for any misconduct on my part. Needless to say, she was pissed I was turning her down. Really pissed. She ended up throwing me and my clothes out onto the street where I had to call Gus to come pick me up."

I thought back to what Ann had said about Thano having no idea on what he missed out on. Come to think of it, she never actually said they had sex. I felt a little silly for the way I acted. It wasn't like Thano was taking me out on a date for Christ's sake. I was going to be working for him.

Tilting my head, I stared at him. "Why are you telling me all of this? What do you care what I think?"

He swallowed hard and shrugged. "I don't know. The idea of you thinking I would sleep around bothered me. I like . . . I mean . . . I want . . . I um . . . shit." He sighed as he closed his eyes and shook his head.

My heart was racing. What does he like? What does he want? Dear God, what's under his shirt?

"Kilyn, you make me feel something I haven't felt in a long time. It both excites and scares me. We keep running into each other and Gus would say it was a sign and, fuck I don't know, maybe it is. All I really know is I want to get to know you better."

My brow lifted. "Get to know me better how?"

His eyes turned dark while he quickly swept them over me. My body responded with a shudder. When he took a step closer to me, my heart was pounding so loudly I couldn't hear my own thoughts.

His hand slipped around the back of my neck, pulling me closer.

Oh. Dear. God.

My knees shook as I reached up and grabbed onto his arms to keep myself from falling. Thano softly ran his lips along my neck and a small moan slipped from my mouth.

I could feel his hot breath on my skin as he talked in a low voice. "I want to know what I do that makes the pulse in your neck beat like this."

My breath caught when he pressed his lips to my neck and whispered, "Eísai tósi ómorfos."

The foreign words swam around in my mind so beautifully. With my breathing labored, I panted out, "I have no idea . . . what you . . . just said. But you can get to know me in any way you'd like."

It might have made me sound like a cheap whore, but in that moment I didn't care. All I cared about was this man was able to bring back feelings I had buried long ago.

And I liked it.

I liked it a lot.

## ten

### Thano

THE WAY KILYN WAS BREATHING had my dick throbbing. I fought the urge to push her into her car and fuck her right here in the parking lot.

Jesus, Thano. Get a grip.

It didn't help matters any when she practically gave me the invitation to do just that.

Kissing along her jaw, I forced myself to pull back.

"I'll pick you up at ten?"

She nodded, her eyes closed and her lips parted slightly. "O—okay. Ten. Yep. Work. Right."

When I stepped back, her body was swaying and I couldn't help but smile. I loved how she reacted to me. No woman had ever responded to me like Kilyn did. Not even Savannah, but that had to be because we were so young when we started dating.

I stopped and looked at her. She still had her eyes closed.

"Kilyn?"

Snapping them open, she jumped. "Right. I'll be ready and have my measuring tape and notepad to assess everything."

When her eyes widened in horror, I laughed.

Lifting her hands, she started babbling and damn it if it didn't make me that much more attracted to her.

"No, wait. I don't mean I'm going to be assessing your size or how well you do. Not that I think we're going to do anything because I totally don't think that, but I have to admit I'm pretty well turned on right now, you know." She motioned with her hands up and down. "Look at you. You're hot and sweaty, and I can see through your shirt, and you kissed my neck and whispered something to me in Greek and . . . and," she looked around, "man, did a warm front come through or something? It's so hot."

I forced the laugh back down as I reached for her hand and gently kissed the back of it. "See you at ten, ladybug."

Her smile made my heart skip a beat. "See ya at ten," she softly replied.

Turning on my heels, I walked over to my car, trying like hell to figure out what in the hell I was doing. I wasn't ready for a relationship, but I was so drawn to Kilyn, I had to have her.

All of her.

"WHAT DO YOU MEAN YOU'RE not coming over for dinner tonight?"

Slipping the T-shirt over my head, I put the phone back up to my ear. "Thad and Nicholaus will be there, Mama. You won't even know I'm gone."

"Why do you assume such things? I will know. Your cousins are in town. I'm making a huge dinner."

Running my hand through my hair, I attempted to get it to dry faster. "I've got plans I can't cancel."

The silence on the other end of the phone told me her head was spinning. "A girl?"

"No," I lied.

"You're lying to me, Athanasios."

Rolling my eyes, I grabbed the cologne and did a quick spray. Kilyn mentioned how good I smelled in the cooking class Gus and I went to. That night I went and bought another bottle of Creed. The shit isn't cheap, but the way it made her eyes flare was enough for me to drop a few hundred dollars for an extra bottle.

"Mama, why do you think I'm lying?"

She huffed into the phone. "I don't think, Athanasios Adrax Drivas, I know you're lying. What is her name?"

"It is not a girl. It's business."

"Why don't you want to tell me? She isn't Greek, is she? Please tell me it isn't serious."

I could imagine my mother now. Leaning against the counter, pinching the bridge of her nose as she cursed in Greek. She thought it was okay to curse in Greek, even though all of her children spoke it and knew exactly what she was saying.

"I don't understand why you boys can't settle down with a good Greek girl. I'm not getting any younger. I need grandchildren."

I nearly choked on my own spit. "Grandchildren?"

She started rattling off in Greek how her sister's kids were all married and why her three boys were so selfish.

"You should talk to Thaddeus, Mama. He's been dating a girl for almost three months now."

My mother gasped.

I shook my head and sighed. I threw my older brother under the bus, and for what? So I'd get my mother off my own back. I should have felt guilty about it, yet I didn't. I was somewhat amused knowing Thaddeus would have the wrath of our mother on him tonight.

"Why has he not told me?"

"You'll have to ask him, Mama. I really need to get going. I have a business meeting at ten."

It wasn't really a lie. Okay, it was, but whatever. I'd make it up to her and go and spend the entire day with her tomorrow.

"You call me tonight so I can hear your voice, Athanasios. I worry about you. It's been too long. It's time to move on."

My heart ached in my chest. I'd never be able to move on from the loss of Savannah. She was the only love I'd ever known.

"Love you, Mama. I'll try and call tonight. Bye."

"Bye, darling. Love you back."

The phone went dead and I couldn't help but start laughing. If I knew my mother, she was dialing up Thaddeus right now.

MY HAND SHOOK SLIGHTLY AS I reached up to ring Kilyn's door-bell. *What in the hell is wrong with me?*

Before I even hit it, the door flew up, causing me to jump.

"Hey! You're right on time. The doorman let me know you were on your way up!"

I took in the sight before me and smiled. Kilyn was dressed in jeans and a T-shirt that said *I Love This Life—LOCASH*.

Man, it really was her favorite song. The pink Converse shoes tied it all together. Of course, the ponytail finished off the look. She looked so fucking adorable, I wanted to pull her into my arms and kiss the living shit out of her.

Pulling her lip between her teeth, she grinned while she watched me ogle her. I don't think I'd ever seen someone as breathtaking. Her smile had my heart racing and my stomach jumping.

"Am I underdressed? I thought we were just heading up to your cabin. I figured you wouldn't mind if I got comfy."

*Why does that sound hot as hell?*

"No. I think you look adorable."

She frowned and then smiled bigger. "You're easy to please, Mr. Drivas."

Focusing in on those soft lips, I imagined them moving across my body. "Oh, I think you'll find I'm not that easy to please, Ms. O'Kelly. I tend to like things . . . my way."

Her smile grew bigger and more crooked as those green eyes lit up. "Really? Is that a challenge?"

"It could be."

I had to admit I liked the flirting thing we had going on. Kilyn's personality was contagious. She was so damn chipper all the time.

Reaching for a bag, she threw it over her shoulder and walked out of her apartment. "Well then, I hope you're up for the challenge. It will make it all the more sweeter when I get my way."

Jesus, are we talking about sex? I fucking hope so.

The drive up to the cabin proved to be the best hour and a half I'd had in a long time. Kilyn's sense of humor was amazing and she could say the craziest shit with a deadpan expression.

"Have you always used humor to ease tension?"

She stared at me with a serious look. "Is that what I'm doing? Easing tension between us?"

I shrugged. "I don't know. I don't feel tense, actually the opposite. I haven't felt this relaxed in a long time. You bring out something in me, Kilyn."

Her face blushed the most beautiful rose color. The way it caused her eyes to stand out had me wishing I knew what to say or do to make her blush like that all the time.

"Well, I could say the same thing about you, Thano."

I slowed down and put my signal on before pulling into the long driveway that led to my private paradise. A part of me felt guilty Savannah wasn't here for me to show her first, but having Kilyn here felt . . . right. That was the only way I could explain it.

"This driveway is amazing." Her hands came up to her mouth as she gasped when the cabin came into sight. "It's beautiful, Thano! I cannot wait to see the inside!"

With a chuckle, I pulled up and parked. I could hear the excitement in her voice and it made me happy. She was out of the car before I even had my door open. With her bag thrown over her shoulder, she quickly ran up the stairs and walked around the wraparound porch.

"This is amazing! The view is the most beautiful view I've ever seen."

My chest swelled with pride. I had known the moment I pulled up and saw this spot that it was the one.

Spinning back to me, she smiled. "I already have an idea."

Lifting my brows, I asked, "You do?"

"Yes!" she squealed as she grabbed my hand and pulled me to the back of the house.

"Imagine a flagstone patio down there. With a pit, table and chairs, and some amazing, yet low maintenance flowers because you won't always be here to take care of them. Oh my gosh, it will be your heaven on earth!"

I chuckled at how practical Kilyn was even in her excitement.

Walking all the way around the wraparound porch, she turned and said, "Let's see the inside. My head is swimming with ideas."

The wind picked up out of nowhere and we both turned and looked west.

"Did you check the weather before we came up here?" she asked.

My heart dropped. Fuck. I was so excited about spending the day with Kilyn I forgot to check the weather.

When I didn't answer right away, her face dropped. "You didn't, did you?"

# eleven

## Kilyn

THANO STOOD THERE STARING AT me with a blank expression. "How could you forget to the check the weather?" I asked.

He frowned. "Did *you* check it?"

I narrowed my left eye and shot him a look. "Why would I check it?"

"Oh, I don't know, Kilyn. Maybe because you were headed up to the mountains?"

Folding my arms over my chest, I slowly tilted my head and glared at him. "Call me old-fashioned, Thano, but I was kind of leaving that up to you since you invited me up here and even mentioned a storm coming in."

He threw his hands up. "It doesn't matter who checked the weather."

"You mean who *didn't* check the weather."

If looks could kill, I was pretty sure I'd be on the ground. "Fine. I fucked up and didn't check the weather. Let's get in; the temperature is already starting to drop."

It was then I noticed he was right. And the wind had picked up even more.

"Wait. I thought it wasn't supposed to move in until later tonight?"

Thano unlocked his door and walked inside. I followed him in and smiled wide when he turned on the lights. It was an open canvas and I couldn't keep the flood of ideas at bay.

Designing wasn't always what I wanted to do. At one point in my life, I wanted to follow my dreams of singing. Of course, that all changed after Peter. Everything changed after him.

"Let me turn on the weather radio. Can you pull up the weather on your phone?" Thano asked while he walked toward the massive kitchen. For a few moments, I was lost in the beauty of the dark granite countertops, natural stone backsplash and the most beautiful copper oven vent I'd ever seen.

"If you can't get a signal, I have Wi-Fi. The password is mountain."

Thano's voice snapped me out of it. I was pretty sure I had drool dripping from the corner of my mouth. I quickly reached up and wiped for good measure.

"I have a signal," I said, pulling up the weather. It sat there and spun. Thano searched everywhere for the weather radio.

Itching to get some ideas drawn out, I put my phone down and pulled out my pad and drawing pencil. "I'm sure it's fine, Thano. The storm wasn't supposed to move in until later. It's probably just the winds before it."

Thano was saying something from upstairs, but I totally tuned him out while I walked into the massive living room. The stone fireplace was breathtaking and would be the focal point of the room.

"Want a fire? It's a bit chilly in here."

I nodded. "A fire would be amazing." Looking up, I took in the tall ceilings and exposed wood beams. "This room is amazing."

"Thanks," Thano replied with a smile.

I walked around in a circle. "What kind of feel are you looking for in this room?"

With a shrug, he stared at me with a blank express. "Warm and inviting?"

"Is that a question or a statement?"

The way he was looking at me had my heart melting into a puddle on the beautiful hardwood floors. "Um, well, I heard it on a show my mother was watching on HGTV."

Trying like hell to hold it back, I busted out laughing. "Thano! Seriously, how do you see this room?"

His smile widened as he tossed one more log into the fireplace. He put two fire starters in and lit them both before shutting the screen and making his way over to me. When his hands landed on my hips, I swallowed hard and tried like hell to keep from panting like a dog in heat.

"Why do you think you're here, ladybug? I have no fucking clue how I want this place to look. Like a cabin in the mountains and not a bachelor pad like my apartment. Nothing girly, but something that will make your heart stop when you walk in here and look at it."

It felt as if a hundred-pound weight was on my chest. Did he mean to say when I walked in here or when any girl walked in? *Jesus, it's getting hot in here.*

"May I ask you something?"

He winked and replied, "As long as it has nothing to do with what my vision is for this room."

I let out a nervous chuckle. "No. It doesn't."

"Then go for it."

Pulling the corner of my lip in with my teeth, I chewed on it for a few seconds before releasing it and asking, "Why do you call me ladybug?"

He dropped his hands from my hips and took a step back. I instantly missed his warmth.

"What?"

He almost seemed surprised by my question, as if he hadn't even realized he was doing it.

"Don't get me wrong, I really like it. I've never had anyone call me anything other than my name, but why ladybug?"

Thano's face turned white as a ghost. "I didn't even realize I was calling you that."

Pinching my brows, I pulled my head back. "Really? You've called me that a number of times."

He ran his hand through that dark hair of his. The way it left it a hot mess had my lower stomach pulling with desire. What I wouldn't give to run my own fingers through it.

"I was curious why ladybug that's all. I swear, I don't mind."

Thano turned and walked to the back door. He opened it and stepped outside. Clearly, me asking him upset him. I decided to give him a few minutes alone and headed upstairs. Since it would be a guestroom, I would keep the décor simple, yet rustic chic. If Thano's parents ever came to stay, I'm sure his mother wouldn't want dead animals hanging off the wall in her bedroom.

Chewing on the end of my pencil, I wondered if Thano hunted. I'd need to ask. I could totally see an elk mounted on that fireplace downstairs.

As I moved about upstairs, measuring and making some rough drawings, I couldn't shake the way Thano reacted when I asked him about the pet name. I was wishing I had kept my mouth shut seeing as it sent him outside.

When it seemed like he was going to stay out there longer, I headed back downstairs and found the master bedroom. When I stepped in I sucked in a breath of air. The large king-size bed was smack in the middle of the room.

"He said he had a mattress here. This is a work of art!" I mumbled as I walked up to the large four-post oak bed. It had more of a rustic feel to it and that told me a ton about Thano's style. It was bold and beautiful, yet had a bit of a romantic feel to it. Turning to my left, I saw the one chair he said he had. With a smile, I ran my hand along the arm. Thano had a thing for old school charm. The chair and bed had a very French chic flare to them.

I scanned the room and smiled when the perfect color of paint popped into my head. There were three doors in the room. Any one of them led to the master bathroom. It was almost like a game, what was behind the door!

The first door I walked up to was the winner. I figured with its placement it had to be the bathroom. What I hadn't figured was what I was going to find in said bathroom.

"Holy. Shit."

My hand came up over my mouth. Straight in front of me was the biggest window I'd ever seen. A giant oval tub sat in front of it. Closing my eyes, I pictured soaking in the tub, looking out over the mountain range. Of course, the only thing that would make it better was if Thano was soaking in there with me.

"Oh, for Christ's sake. Stop it, Kilyn. Seriously, I need to get laid."

Once I was able to pull my eyes from the view, I noticed the two beautiful vanities with their copper sinks. "Beautiful," I whispered as I ran my fingers along the stone countertops.

"Yes, you are."

Jumping, I slammed my hand over my chest.

"Shit! You scared me, Thano."

He smiled but it didn't reach his eyes. It was the first forced smile I'd ever seen from him.

"Um, this window! Wow."

It was a poor attempt at a conversation, but I was at a loss as to why his eyes were filled with such sadness.

"Yeah, that was my idea. I'm kind of a bath guy and I love the view so I asked for a big window."

Every nerve ending in my body tingled when he mentioned he liked baths. "Well, from one bath lover to another, good call."

I stepped into the massive shower that could easily fit four people in it. Two rain head faucets hung down, and a handheld faucet hung on the wall.

"You could seriously have some fun in this shower," I said with a chuckle before realizing that I said it out loud.

*Shit.*

Thano leaned against the counter and nodded. Okay, this was getting awkward.

Stepping out of the shower, I made my way past him and back into the living room. I only had the room above the garage to look at next.

I turned to ask him where the steps were to the bonus room and shut my mouth quickly. Thano was staring at me and I wasn't sure if it was a good kind of a stare or a bad one.

"I'm sorry about earlier. I'd like to explain my reaction if you don't mind."

I grinned softly as I lifted my shoulders. "It's totally fine, you don't owe me any explanations."

Oh, God. Maybe that was what he called the girl he loved who broke his heart. That would totally suck big time. I needed to wrap this up so we could head back.

"I only need to look at the bonus room, and then I'm done and we can leave."

The way he looked at me, you would have thought I told him his favorite dog died. His eyes fell to the floor before he turned and started walking down a hall.

With a quick peek behind a door, it revealed the laundry room. Good. I was about to ask if he put it in the garage. That would suck during the winter.

The set of stairs were tucked behind the laundry room with another door leading outside to a covered walkway that lead to the garage.

"So you're thinking you'd like to have your office up here?" I asked quickly sketching out the room.

"When I was little, my favorite thing to do used to be going to my grandmother's house."

I stopped what I was doing and turned to look at him.

"She loved being in her garden. She didn't speak much English, so when my brothers and I were little, our parents talked to us in both English and Greek. We quickly picked up both. Our grandmother, though, if she knew a word in English she would speak it. One day I was standing there and about ten ladybugs landed on me. I was in heaven."

With a light chuckle, I imagined the scene in my head.

Thano cleared his throat and shook his head. I swear, it looked as if he had tears in his eyes.

"Anyway, I guess when you said I was calling you ladybug, it threw me. I've never called anyone by a pet name."

I smiled. "Well, maybe I remind you of your grandmother?" Oh, gesh. I just compared myself to his grandmother. Well, if I was looking for sex from him I killed any chance of it.

*Gesh, Kilyn. Stop talking.*

Tossing his head back, Thano busted out laughing. At first I chuckled along with him. But when he kept laughing, almost to the point where he was holding his side and wiping tears away, I got pissed.

"What is so funny?"

Walking up to me, Thano cupped my face with his hands, causing me to hold my breath. "Kilyn, you are nothing like my grandmother."

Jetting my lip out in a pout, I went to talk when Thano ran his thumb across my lips and shook his head.

"If you reminded me of my grandmother, I wouldn't be able to do this." Pressing his lips to mine, I quickly got lost in the kiss. There was something about them that swept me off my feet and left me breathless. I'd never in my life experienced those feelings before. I could get used to it.

When he finally pulled back, I sucked in a rush of air. Thano leaned his forehead against mine and closed his eyes. "What are you doing to me, Kilyn?"

My throat grew thick as it hit me all at once. I was falling for Thano. I was falling hard.

"I could ask the same thing," I mumbled.

His lips kissed my forehead while he intertwined his fingers with mine. "Let's head back downstairs to the main house; it's getting cold in here."

Not saying a word, I let him guide me back down the stairs and through the house. I had a very strong feeling Thano was the dominant type. Both in and out of bed. Yet, he did it in such a caring way, so much so that I was slowly letting my guard down. Inch by inch I lowered the wall and let him climb a little more over it.

Would I be able to let it down completely?

I had no idea. All I knew was, for the first time since Peter stole my innocence, I was ready to open my broken and fragile heart up again.

I prayed Thano would guard it.

## twelve

### Thano

MY HEART WAS POUNDING AS I led Kilyn over to the fire-place. "Let me go grab some pillows from the bedroom."

She barely nodded her head as she looked into my eyes. It was like I was looking into a mirror. Her eyes wore the same nervous look as mine. There was something else in them. Sadness. I wanted desperately to know why that sadness was there. She tried hard to hide it, but it was always there.

Releasing her hand, I quickly walked to the master bedroom and grabbed the pillows off of the bed before walking to the closet. For some reason, I brought up extra pillows and blankets the last time I stayed and I was thankful I did.

As I walked back into the living room, my phone and Kilyn's went off with a warning.

I stopped walking as a feeling of dread washed over my body. Dropping everything to the floor, I reached into my pocket and pulled out my phone.

WEATHER WARNING.
A WINTER STORM WARNING HAS BEEN ISSUED FOR YOUR AREA.

Glancing up, I couldn't help but notice the panicked look on Kilyn's face. "Maybe we should head out."

My eyes darted over to the fire I had made. "The fire. I can't leave until it goes out."

She nodded while chewing on her lip. "Let me hook up to your Wi-Fi and pull up the weather."

Reaching for the pillows and blanket, I headed over to the fireplace and spread them out on the floor. First thing on the list was furniture.

"Oh, Thano. Look!"

Kilyn handed me her phone and all I saw was snow covering the area we were in. We both looked out the window. "When in the hell did it start snowing? We were just out there!" I said as I rushed over and threw the door open. The wind was blowing like crazy.

Kilyn walked up next to me and asked, "Do you think we can beat it if we leave after the fire goes out?"

"We're going to try."

A gust of wind blew and all I heard was a loud crack and then the sound of a tree hitting something. Kilyn screamed and slammed her body into mine. "What in the hell was that?"

Wrapping my arm around her, I brought her back into the house and shut the door. "I'm not sure. We need to try and get this fire out so we can get the hell out of Dodge."

Kilyn and I raced around the house looking for anything to fill up with water. I'd clean out the damn fireplace later. We needed to get home before this stuff stuck.

Fuck. Why in the hell did I bring my car and not my truck?

Kilyn came back down from upstairs and shook her head. "There's nothing. Usually the builders leave trash somewhere."

"They cleaned up yesterday since nothing else needed to be done. Shit." Pushing my hand through my hair, I let out a frustrated sigh. "Wait. I have a bucket in the garage."

Racing out the side door, I came to an abrupt stop at the sight before me.

"Holy shit."

"Oh no," Kilyn mumbled from behind me. "There's a tree . . . on your pretty sports car."

Closing my eyes, I pulled my phone back out and hit Thad's number. It rang five times before he picked it up.

"You better have a damn good reason why you're not here with us. Mom is hounding me and Nicholaus about grandchildren."

I shook my head and sighed.

"Did you hear me, Thano? Grandchildren!"

"Listen, Thad, I need your help."

He laughed. "Fuck you. I need your help! Maybe you didn't hear me. Grandchildren."

Glancing over to Kilyn, I watched as she turned and headed back into the house. No use in trying to put the fire out now. We were stuck.

"Thad! A tree fell on my car and I'm stuck up at the cabin."

"What? Why in the hell are you up there? Didn't you check the weather? A storm is blowing in."

Rolling my eyes, I pushed out another breath of air. "Yes. I know. The last time I checked the weather it wasn't supposed to be in until later tonight. It blew in earlier and Kilyn and I are up here. We can't leave because my car is crushed. Is there any way you can come and get us in your truck?"

"Um . . . yeah. How bad is it up there?"

"It's getting worse, but the snow isn't sticking yet. I think you can make it fine; it's getting out of here that has me worried if the snow keeps falling like this. And bring something to eat just in case. There is nothing in the house."

"Wait, what do I tell Mom and Dad? They're going to ask."

Staring at my car, I moaned. "I don't care what you tell them, just come get us."

"I'm on my way."

Dropping my hand to my side, I slowly shook my head and cursed under my breath for being so stupid.

"Thano? Maybe we should add more wood to the fireplace."

Her voice snapped me out of my daze. "Right, I'll grab more."

——— ♥ ———

AFTER HAULING IN MORE WOOD and piling it next to the fire, Kilyn and I both looked at each other. "Do you think your brother will make it?"

Not wanting her to worry, I flashed her a smile. "Hell yeah. He goes hunting all the time up in the mountains and has driven in worse than this."

She barely grinned as she nodded her head. Plopping on one of the pillows, she stared up at me. "Do you hunt?"

Sitting next to her, I stared into the fire. "I used to go a lot when I was kid."

"Did you grow out of it or something?"

I turned to look at her and my breath caught. She had her legs pulled up to her chest with her chin resting on her knees. My chest ached as I looked at her. I don't think I'd ever seen anyone so beautiful, and that thought alone filled me with guilt. I used to think Savannah was the most breathtaking woman . . . but Kilyn . . . she stole the very air around me.

Lifting my hand up, I pushed a piece of her dark hair behind her ear. "Omorfiá sas eínai áthiktos."

Her eyes lit up with desire as I spoke to her in Greek. Why I did it, I had no clue. I have only ever talked to my family in Greek. Maybe it was because I didn't want Savannah to hear the things I desperately wanted to say to Kilyn.

Lifting her head up, she tilted her head and asked with the cutest damn smile ever, "What did you say?"

I fought within myself to lie or tell her what I really said. In the end, I wanted her to know.

"Your beauty is untouchable."

Swallowing hard, her lips parted slightly. Her eyes sparkled with a happiness I desperately wanted to see every time I looked at those beautiful green eyes.

"No one has ever said anything so beautiful like that to me before."

My heart hurt knowing she hadn't been loved like she deserved to be. If I wasn't careful, I was going to start falling for her. If I hadn't already.

"That's a shame; you deserve to be treated like a princess."

The sparkle in her eyes vanished before she turned and looked into the fire. For a few moments she was lost in another world. One that I instantly knew was unkind to her.

"I'm sorry I got us stuck up here," I finally admitted.

With a lighthearted laugh, Kilyn dropped her legs and sat criss-cross. "Yes! A man who can admit when he has done wrong. God, it is so refreshing."

With a huff, I shot her a look. "Don't get used to it. It happens less than you think."

Her beautiful smile was back. "Really? Are all Greek men stubborn?"

"Yes. And demanding. Controlling. Plus, we're always right."

The crooked grin across her face made me happy. I was glad to know I was able to pull her from the thoughts that made her sad.

"Always right, huh? You weren't right in this situation."

I brushed off her words with my hand. "I was excited to show you the place and it slipped my mind."

She attempted to hold back a wider grin. "So you're not only easy to please, you're easily excited as well. This might not work in my favor after all, Mr. Drivas, if you can't control that."

My body instantly reacted to her flirting. What in the fuck does this girl do to me? I wanted her more than ever now, but I also had the need to prove her wrong.

Moving quickly, I pinned her to the floor and pressed my hard cock between her legs. Kilyn gasped, but promptly wrapped her legs around me, pulling me in closer as we both let a soft moan slip from the back of our throats.

Grinding against her pussy, I stared into her eyes as they widened with excitement. "Trust me when I say I have no problem controlling that area . . . Ms. O'Kelly."

With a smirk, she responded, "Maybe you should prove it."

My thoughts were scattered. I wanted to make love to her, yet I knew the moment I did everything would change. If I let more of Kilyn in, that meant letting go of Savannah a little more.

I did the only thing I could think of. I kissed her. When she laced her fingers in my hair and tugged, I pressed into her harder. It felt like I was in high school again, dry humping my girlfriend and trying like hell to see if I could make her come between the layers of clothing that separated us.

Things quickly began to heat up as our kiss turned frantic. Reaching up under her shirt, I pushed her bra up and pinched her nipple, eliciting a whimper from her lips that traveled through my body straight to my cock.

"Fucking hell, Kilyn," I spoke as I kissed down her neck, pulling her shirt up and taking her nipple into my mouth. Her back arched while she whispered my name.

I needed to slow down. If I kept this up I'd have her pants down and my cock buried inside of her soon.

"Wait. Thano . . . wait."

I barely heard her as I continued to suck and bite on her nipple.

"Thano!" she cried out, causing me to stop and quickly pull back.

"I'm so sorry. I didn't mean to . . . shit."

Jumping up, I adjusted myself and looked at her lying there, panting as she pulled in one deep breath after another.

She sat up, pulled her bra and T-shirt down, and then reached up for my hand. Giving it to her, she pulled me back down to sit next to her.

"No, it's okay. Things were getting a bit hot and heavy and before we got carried away I wanted to make sure we both wanted this. I mean. I want this. Believe me when I say I really, really want this."

Her face flushed with the most beautiful rose color. "But, I think we needed to slow down. I'm not very good with frantic and rushed."

A look of sadness moved across her face but was gone as fast as it came. "I don't even know if you have a condom."

Feeling heat move across my face, I shook my head. How could I be so fucking stupid? I was ready to make love to her and I didn't even have any protection.

Lifting my hand, I placed it on the side of her face. "I'm so sorry, ladybug. The last thing I'd ever want to do is hurt you. I got caught up in the moment and I lost control. It won't happen again."

She looked down and then back up into my eyes. "Don't say that. Please don't say that."

"What? That it won't happen again?"

With a slight smile, she nodded. "I'm not the kind of girl who sleeps around, Thano. Matter of fact, I'm really not that experienced at all. I've been with two guys, and trust me when I say there was nothing earth-shattering about either. But with you, I'm so drawn to you. I can't sleep at night because you haunt my dreams each and every time I close my eyes."

She swallowed hard and closed her eyes briefly before capturing mine again. "You consume my thoughts night and day and that is something I'm not used to. So please don't say you won't do that again, because I want you more than I can even begin to tell you."

My heart felt like someone had a vise around it. With each word she spoke, it closed tighter as she said what I had been thinking for days.

Getting on her knees, she moved closer to me. Her lips pressed against my neck before she moved them up and whispered, "I want you, Thano."

Grabbing onto her shoulders, I pushed her back to look at her. She was surprised by my action and I knew she thought I was stopping her. Far from it. I was about to tell her I wanted her too, when the doorbell rang.

When she frowned, I knew what I had to do. Pulling her to me, I kissed her. Softly. Barely pulling back from her lips, I said, "I want you too, Kilyn. Very much."

Now there was a banging on the door. "That must be, Thad."

Kilyn nodded and stood with me. Pulling in a deep breath, I looked her over to make sure she was okay. "I'm sorry," I whispered as I kissed her on the forehead and turned to head to the front door.

Unlocking it, the door flew open and Thad and Phoebe came barreling in. Both of them started brushing off snow and I was silently thanking the builder for talking me into a tile entrance and not wood.

"What the fuck took you so long to answer?" Thad said, shrugging off his jacket and hanging it up on the coat rack I had installed for the workers.

Phoebe walked up and kissed me on each cheek. "Hey, Thano. Hope you don't mind I tagged along."

With a forced smile, I shook my head. "Of course not."

Thad had met Phoebe a few years back at one of our cousin's weddings. Why he hadn't introduced her to my parents was beyond me since they had been dating for a while. She was the perfect fit for Thad. Plus she was Greek. My mother would love that little bonus. Her dark-brown hair was pulled up in a sloppy bun on the top of her head and her makeup was, of course, heavy as usual. She was a cute girl and didn't need all that shit caked on her face, but who was I to judge.

I watched as Phoebe walked up to Kilyn and introduced herself. "Hi, I'm Thad's girlfriend, Phoebe. You are?"

Rolling my eyes, I made my way over to them. "Always the direct approach. That's Phoebe," I mumbled.

Kilyn smiled and extended her hand. "Kilyn O'Kelly. I'm ah—"

Before I had a chance to even stop myself, I blurted out, "The interior designer I hired to fix up the cabin."

Thad and Kilyn both looked at me with disappointed looks on their faces. Thad shook his head while Kilyn stared at me with a look of disbelief. Here, not more than five minutes ago, I had her tit in my mouth and now I was introducing her like someone who worked for me.

Forcing a smile, Kilyn replied, "Right. The interior designer."

I walked up and stood next to her. I could almost feel the anger rolling off her body. "Well, I mean that's not all, we're friends as well."

"Oh . . . because that made it all the better, Thano," Thad mumbled.

Phoebe looked between all three of us with a confused expression. "So wait, are you friends, dating, the decorator? Because the fire, the pillows, and blanket on the floor scream more than just the decorator and more like friends with benefits, perhaps?"

Kilyn took a step away from me and turned to Thad. "So can we leave?"

His face dropped. "I don't think so. We barely made it up here. The state police were shutting down the road that leads up here. It's snowing like crazy. I think we're all going to be stuck up here until they can plow the streets."

Kilyn's face fell. "You mean we're stuck up here tonight?"

"Maybe for more than one night." Turning to Phoebe, he wiggled his eyebrows. "Good thing I brought food and a blow-up mattress!"

My heart dropped. We were stuck up here and it was my fault. Not to mention Kilyn kept stepping further away from me.

I'd have to worry about what I said later. Right now, we had to figure out a plan. "I'm going to walk over to the neighbors. Maybe they have a way out of here since they live up here."

"Thano, I already said they closed the road. We barely made it past them before they closed it. There's no getting out."

Kilyn wrapped her arms around her body and frowned as she rubbed vigorously to warm herself up.

"Are you cold?" I asked walking up to her and wrapping my arms around her. She melted into me and relief rushed through my body. She wasn't that mad about my fuck up. It was then I realized how cold it had gotten in the cabin.

Phoebe smiled. "I'm going to guess Kilyn is way more than just the interior designer."

Glancing over at my brother and his girlfriend, I smiled as Kilyn buried her face into my chest. "I'm freezing."

"Shit. You didn't even bring a jacket, did you?" All she had on was a T-shirt and jeans.

Phoebe jumped up from where she was sitting in front of the fire. "I've got an extra jacket, but why don't we just turn on the heater?"

Kilyn and I looked at each other and busted out laughing. "Well, hell. Why didn't we think of that?" I said walking over to the thermostat.

Turning the heater on, I held my breath until it turned on. At least we had one thing on our side.

I held up my hands and called out, "We have heat!"

It wasn't more than ten seconds later and the power to the whole cabin went off.

Kilyn let out a frustrated moan and said, "We had heat."

Things were not looking good.

# thirteen

## Kilyn

PHOEBE AND I SAT AND stared at the fire in silence. Thano and his brother decided to hike over to the closest neighbor. Even though Thad brought food, it was like a bag of chips, candy, and Pop Tarts.

"So how long have you and Thad been dating?" I asked, breaking the awkward silence.

With a warm smile, she said, "We've dated on and off for about two years. We've been dating pretty solid for the last six months, though."

My eyes widened in surprise. "Oh, wow."

When she shrugged and looked away, I wanted to ask why their relationship was an on and off one.

"You'd think after two years he'd want to take the next step."

"Marriage?"

She laughed. "No! Not even. I'd take a full time commitment and meeting his family. I mean, I know Thano and Nicholaus, but I haven't met anyone else. My own family is beginning to nag me about getting married and having kids."

Wrinkling my nose, I asked, "Really? How old are you?"

"Twenty-three. Almost. Another week."

Wow. I'd have to ask Thano how old Thad was. I was guessing

thirty or so. I couldn't really understand the whole parent pressure thing since mine weren't around. "That seems kind of young to be thinking of settling down and having kids."

She threw her head back and laughed. "You're not Greek. You probably don't have a mother breathing down your neck every time she sees you, whispering 'tick tock the clock is running.'"

I couldn't help but laugh. "No, I'm certainly not Greek. My parents passed away when I was fourteen."

Her smile fell. It was always the same reaction from people when I told them my parents died. It was that look of pity. I hated it.

"I'm so sorry, Kilyn. I wouldn't have said that if I had known."

With a sincere smile, I reached over and squeezed her hand. "It's okay. You couldn't have known."

She pulled in a breath and blew it out. "Here I'm bitching about my nagging mother and . . . damn. Change of subject. How did you and Thano meet?"

Just his name caused my body to react. Biting on my lower lip, I grinned. "A few weeks back. We bumped into each other at a bar. Talked for a few minutes and the next day he was at my best friend's cooking class. Ever since then, it seemed like we kept running into each other. He ended up coming to my office looking for an interior decorator and he had no idea it was my business."

Perking up, Phoebe pulled her knees to her chest and wiggled her eyebrows. "Fate has been throwing the two of you together."

Was that what was happening? With a chortle, I shrugged. "Maybe. Or it was all a string of coincidences."

She shook her head while pinching her brows together. "No. There is no such thing as a coincidence."

"You don't think so?"

"Nope. If you were to ask my Yiayia, she would tell you fate is throwing you both together. Of course, then she would find out you're not Greek and say fate screwed up."

Laughing, I couldn't help but feel a connection with Phoebe. I liked her. "So is it important with your heritage to marry Greek?"

Phoebe stared at me like I had grown two heads. "Was Eros the

Greek God of love?"

My eyes drifted up in thought, I tried to recall when we studied Greek mythology. "Um . . . yes! He was!" I called out in excitement.

"There's your answer. Marrying Greek is huge. Not really so much with our generation, but with our parents and grandparents it's still very big. But with my generation steering away from it, it is slowly becoming more accepted . . . kind of."

I stared at my hands as my chest ached.

"It doesn't matter to Thano if you're Greek or not, Kilyn. Trust me."

Lifting my eyes, I forced a smile. "Oh, it's nothing like that anyway. I'm a long way off from worrying about that."

She gave me a look like she wanted to say uh-huh sure.

The door opened, saving both of us from the direction this conversation was going. We both jumped up, Phoebe rushing to Thad's side. "I was beginning to worry!" she exclaimed.

Thano glanced over to me and smiled. Returning the gesture, I walked up and took a few bags out of his hands. "Good thing my neighbor is into all the prepping and shit. He had food and plenty of lanterns for us to use for light."

I placed the bags on the counter and pulled out granola bars, protein bars, dried milk, which caused me to shudder, and a few other boxed items along with hot dog buns.

Holding up the buns, I furrowed my brows. "Hot dog buns?"

Thad laughed and opened up a small ice chest that had hot dogs, some mustard, and cheese in it. "Dinner!" he exclaimed.

Phoebe jumped and clapping her hand. "Oh my gosh, we can cook them over the fire!"

You couldn't help but smile at Phoebe's excitement.

Thad smiled and said, "If we can find a stick. Bundle up, baby. Let's go exploring outside."

Thano walked up and looked at me with those dark green eyes of his. "Lift up your arms."

Something in his voice had me doing what he said almost automatically, which was not like me at all. My lips opened and I wanted to argue, but a small part of me was wishing he would pick up where he left off.

When he held up a sweatshirt, I started laughing. Looking up as he put it on, I closed my eyes and welcomed the warmth of it. My stomach dipped as I was overcome with the smell of Thano's cologne.

Oh dear God. I'm keeping this thing.

"I had it in the trunk of my car and somehow I was able to get it open enough to reach in for it."

I loved that he thought to look in his car for something for me to wear. I wasn't used to a man actually caring about my well-being.

"Lucky me," I whispered, as I lifted it to my face and took in a deep breath while Thano turned and started unpacking the rest of the food.

Phoebe and Thad were in the living room laughing about something. I couldn't help but feel a tinge of jealousy. It was clear Thad cared deeply about Phoebe. The way he loved on her made me swoon.

"They've been dating off and on for a few years."

Peeking up, I watched as Thano watched the interaction between his brother and Phoebe.

"That's what she told me. Why have they not committed to one another?"

I was prying, but I couldn't help my curiosity.

Thano shrugged. "Not sure. I think it's the age difference to be honest with you. Thad says Phoebe is immature."

For some reason, I got very defensive of poor Phoebe. "She's twenty-two. What does he expect?"

Holding up his hands in surrender he said, "Hey, don't shoot the messenger. I honestly don't know why he isn't committing to her. All I know is he has fun with her, and maybe that's all he cares about right now."

With a smirk, I examined his face carefully. "What about you? No girl ever stole your heart enough to settle down?"

When his face turned white, I knew I had asked the wrong thing. I had totally forgotten he mentioned someone briefly before.

"I'm sorry," I quickly added. "That's not any of my business. I'm sorry I asked."

Spinning around on my heels, I dashed over to Thad and Phoebe before Thano could utter a single word. From the look on his face, I was positive there was a girl out there who had stolen his heart and broke it. And that knowledge had my chest aching and my head spinning.

"Who wants to play a game? We can play charades!" Phoebe exclaimed.

Thad moaned as I laughed and said, "I'll play!" I tried to sound more excited than I really was. The last thing I wanted to do was play a silly game, but if it passed time and it kept me from reliving the stupid mistake I just made with Thano, I'd play.

"Okay!" Phoebe said with a clap of her hands. "We need paper."

Thad snapped his fingers and pretended to pout. "Oh, darn it. No paper. Looks like we'll have to pass on the game we played in high school."

Phoebe's smile vanished and my heart broke for her. Although I kept it to myself, I had a notebook in my bag.

"I thought it was a fun idea to pass the time, Phoebe."

Peeking over at me, she gave me a weak grin before sitting in front of the fire. "Thanks, Kilyn."

I stole a glance toward the kitchen only to find Thano staring at me. Quickly looking away, I watched as Thad added more wood to the fire.

"We should probably bring in more firewood from the porch before it gets covered in snow," Thano said walking up behind me. I could feel the heat coming from his body and I fought like hell not to look at him. My head and the ache between my legs were starting to argue with each other. One wanted me to keep my distance from Thano, the other wanted more.

So much more.

Thad threw another log in the fire before looking over to Thano. "We'll stack some wood by the master bedroom door."

"Are we all sleeping in there?" Phoebe asked.

Thad and Thano both snapped their heads over and looked at her. I tried like hell to hide my smile. Obviously Thad had no desire to have a slumber party with his brother and I knew why. He planned on getting lucky tonight.

Thano's reaction didn't surprise me either. I knew he wanted me as much as I wanted him. I wasn't so sure, though, he would be doing anything with his brother here. Especially with a girl who was, clearly, not Greek and no condom.

"No, baby, we'll sleep in the guest room upstairs. It has a fireplace too."

With a wide smile that said she was more than happy with that arrangement, Phoebe said, "Yay! This is like a scene from a romance book! Couple gets stuck in cabin during a storm."

Rolling my eyes, I stared at the fire. Claire and Phoebe would get along great with their stupid romance books. None of it was real. At least, it wasn't for me.

"What's wrong, ladybug? You don't like romance books?"

Ugh. This guy was hot one minute and cold the next. I was starting to get whiplash with his mood swings. "No. I don't," I said as I continued to stare at the crackling wood.

Thano sat next to me and bumped my shoulder. "Why not?"

I moved my head and looked directly into his eyes. "Because life isn't like that. It's not filled with love and flowers and the guy rushing in to save you. Real life is filled with heartache, disappointment, and moments you'd do anything to forget about it."

Something moved across Thano's face. His eyes mirrored my sadness I was sure. We both knew that heartache. The only difference between us was he loved the woman who broke him. I hated the man who broke me.

Slowly turning back to the fire, I forced the tears at bay.

He'll never make me cry ever again.

Never.

## fourteen

### Thano

*I*STOOD AT THE BACK window and watched the snow continue to fall. Kilyn's phone was about dead, but she had called Claire to let her know what had happened so she didn't worry about her.

My mother had called about an hour ago. I knew I should have let it go to voicemail, but I answered it like a stupid fool. Thad had, of course, told my parents about the cabin I had built. Then he went off and told her I was trapped up here . . . with a girl.

I cringed as I thought back to my conversation with her a few hours ago. I had to go outside so Kilyn didn't hear me.

❤

"YOU'RE WITH A GIRL. I knew you were with a girl. Didn't I say I knew there was a girl?"

Sighing, I pulled the hood from my sweatshirt up and over my head. "Mama, there is no girl. Kilyn is an interior designer. She's also a friend."

"That's not a Greek name. What is that?"

Swallowing hard, I mumbled, "Irish."

"What? What was that? I didn't hear you."

"Irish, Mama. She's Irish. Kilyn O'Kelly is her name and she is just a friend."

I could hear my mother saying something to someone before coming back on the line. "Why? Why do you do this to your mother? What did I do to deserve the heartache my boys give me?"

"Mama, it's freezing outside. I'll call you tomorrow when I know more about the roads after this storm."

"You be a gentleman, Athanasios. No funny business with the Irish girl. They have bad tempers you know."

Rolling my eyes, I let out a gruff laugh. "I love you, Mama. I'll call you tomorrow and please don't worry."

"We aren't finished talking. You will come by the house when you get back. Straight here. No sex! If you do, you wrap your stick!"

I was positive the look on my face was one of horror. "I've got to go, Mom."

Hitting End, I tried to erase the last minute of that conversation.

"HEY, PHOEBE AND I ARE heading up stairs. I've got the fire going good in both bedrooms."

Looking at my brother, I smiled. "Shit. How long have I been standing over here?"

He shrugged. "Long enough for Kilyn to fall asleep and me to start the fires. You've got to stop getting lost in your own head, Thano."

My eyes darted over to the fire. Kilyn was snuggled up under a blanket sound asleep.

"I'm not lost. I know exactly where I am, and I'm not ready to let anyone else in here with me."

Thad frowned and shook his head. "Then I suggest you let Kilyn sleep in the bedroom and you sleep out here. I get the feeling she's been hurt before. The last thing she needs is for you to fuck around with her emotions because you don't have your own shit together."

I opened my mouth to respond back when I shut it again. I knew he was right. The right thing for me to do would be to leave her alone.

But I didn't want to.

Placing his hand on my shoulder, he wore a concerned expression. "It's time to move on, Thano. Savannah would have wanted you to move on."

Swallowing hard, I nodded my head and hit the side of his arm. "Thanks, bro. I'll see you in the morning."

I watched as Thad headed upstairs. He carried one of the blankets my neighbor had given us and a couple of pillows.

My eyes drifted back over to the sleeping beauty in front of my fireplace. A part of me didn't want to move her; she looked so damn cute.

Walking into my bedroom, I pulled the blanket back from the bed. The fire was roaring and wouldn't need any wood added to it for a while.

I blew out a deep breath of air and headed back out to the living room. Reaching down for Kilyn, I picked her up and carried her to my room. I tried like hell to ignore the knot in my stomach when she wrapped her arms around my neck and nuzzled her face into my chest.

When I laid her on the bed she whispered my name. The sound of it off her lips had my stomach dipping. I dropped to my knees and watched her sleep. Gently moving a strand of her dark hair from her face, I smiled as I took in her beauty.

My heart ached as I tried like hell to fight the feelings I was developing for Kilyn. She was so full of life, yet behind her eyes I saw such sadness there. I wanted to make it disappear, but how could I when I myself carried the same sadness.

The fire cracked as I watched her sleep. Each breath she took had me wanting her more. With every whimper she made, another piece of my wall tumbled down. What would it be like having her wrapped in my arms? Would she be the one to finally wake my heart up?

The energy in the room changed when she opened her eyes. A slow smile played across her face as I fought to breathe. In that moment the world faded away and the only thing that was heard was the beating of our hearts.

"Thano," she whispered as she sat up. Our eyes stayed locked on one another. When she reached for her T-shirt and pulled it over her head, I took in her breathtakingly perfect body. Reaching my hands up, I unbuttoned her jeans and held my breath when she stood. She hooked her thumbs and slid her pants down, leaving her dressed in only her bra and panties.

Still on my knees, I placed my hands on her hips. A rush of goose bumps covered her body, causing me to smile. She sucked in a breath of air when I kissed her right above her panty line.

"Oh, God," she whispered.

I fucking loved how my touch affected her so much. Moving my index finger lightly along her panty line, I looked up and watched the way the light of the fire bounced off her face. I wanted to memorize every look she made when I touched her.

Slowly, I pulled her panties down. My heart was pounding against my chest and I was positive Kilyn could hear it.

Her breathing increased, and I swear I had to fight off the urge to throw her leg over my shoulder and taste her pussy.

I'd save that for later, now I wanted to feel what it was like to be inside of her. Thad looked at me like I was nuts earlier when I pulled him off to the side and asked if he had any extra condoms.

"Bro, I have a whole damn box in the glove box of my truck."

I swear, I wanted to kiss him on the lips when he handed me two.

Placing another kiss on her stomach, I stood slowly. My eyes landed on her chest as it heaved with each breath she took. Lifting my head, our eyes locked.

Kilyn slowly ran her tongue over her lips, preparing for me to kiss her. And damn it if I didn't want to kiss her.

Lightly running my finger over her chest, she gasped and then whimpered softly.

Leaning over, I kissed her chest and slowly made my way to her neck. Placing gentle kisses as I moved, I pushed her hair behind her shoulder. With my lips against her ear, I whispered, "Breathe, ladybug."

The rush of air that left her mouth had my dick jumping. I reached behind her and unclasped her bra. There was never a moment in my life that I longed for more than this one. Seeing Kilyn standing before me naked and ready for me to make love to her was something I wanted etched in my memory forever.

The bra dropped to the floor as I took a step back. Her first reaction was to cover herself. I gently took her hands and slowly shook my head. "To soma sas eínai téleia."

The crooked smile on her face made my stomach feel like I was on a thrill ride. "What did you say?"

My eyes took in her body with hunger and lust. Cupping her face in my hands, I gazed into her seductive eyes. "Your body is perfect."

The flush across her cheeks had me falling even more for her.

I wanted nothing but her in my head and heart tonight. "Kilyn, tell me what I want to hear."

Her lips parted while her eyes frantically searched my face. "I want you."

My hand moved to her lower back, pulling her body flush against mine. "Tell me what you want me to do."

Her eyes penetrated mine and all I saw was desire. There was no sadness in them at all. Swallowing hard, she whispered, "I want you to make love to me."

My eyes closed and I took in a deep breath. Every woman I'd been with since Savannah I had fucked. There was no love making involved. You only made love to someone if you loved him or her. But with Kilyn . . . I wanted to make love to her.

Slowly.

Passionately.

My heart began to beat faster. Was I falling in love with Kilyn?

"Thano?"

Her voice pulled me back from the darkness. "Lay on the bed, ladybug."

For a moment she paused before she did what I said. Reaching into my pocket, I pulled out the condoms and placed them on the bed. I quickly got undressed while Kilyn watched my every move, all the while rubbing her legs together. She was turned on and I could see she wanted me as much as I wanted her.

Pushing my pants down, my cock sprung out. Kilyn sunk her teeth

into her lip and moved her hand between her legs. It was the hottest
fucking thing I'd ever seen.

Reaching over, I grabbed her hand and shook my head. "The first
time you come is going to be with me inside of you."

Closing her eyes, she whispered, "Dear God, you're killing me."

Not being able to contain my smile, I crawled onto the bed and
pushed her legs apart. "I want to go slow. Memorize everything that
makes you feel good."

Her head thrashed back and forth as she grabbed the sheets. "Slow
is good. But a hurried up slow is even better."

Damn this girl. She had somehow managed to sneak into my heart
and I wanted more than anything to keep her there.

Lifting her leg, I gently placed kisses on her thigh. "Oh, God. Faster
slow. Faster slow!"

Smirking, I moved across her pussy, just enough for her to feel my
hot breath and lift her hips for more. Placing my hands on her hips, I
held her down. I wanted her to stay still so I could tease her a bit more.

"No," she whimpered.

"Please. Don't!"

I glanced up, but kept my hands on her, holding her body down.

"Stop!" she called out as she tried getting away from me. I quickly
sat up and moved away from her.

She was breathing so heavy I thought for sure she was having a
panic attack.

"Please don't, Peter. Please," she softly cried.

My heart dropped as I realized she was being taken back to a bad
memory.

"Kilyn, it's me," I said as I reached out for her. She dragged in a
deep breath and stared at the fire.

"I'm so sorry if I scared you, I didn't know, ladybug."

When she looked at me, it about killed me. Fear was not only on
her face, but in her eyes as well. When the single tear slipped down her
cheek, I quickly moved to her side and wrapped her in my arms. Her
body trembled. Reaching for the covers, I pulled them up and over us as
she melted into my side.

"It's okay, baby, it's okay. I swear, I would never hurt you."

She slowly nodded her head and barely responded with, "I know."

I wanted desperately to ask her who Peter was. Whoever he was, I wanted to fucking kill him.

When Kilyn finally fell asleep the sound of her breathing relaxed me almost immediately. As my eyes grew heavier, I made a promise to myself that I would never again see that look of fear in my Kilyn's eyes ever again.

Never.

## *fifteen*

### Kilyn

MY EYES OPENED AND THE first thing I saw was Thano. My chest fluttered as I watched him sleep. It didn't take long for the memory of earlier to resurface. Closing my eyes, I silently cursed Peter for invading my world.

Snapping my eyes open, I focused on Thano's breathing. Smiling, I let the peacefulness of it settle my thoughts. The way he reacted earlier and held me in his arms caused another piece of that wall to crumble to the ground.

The moonlight danced across his face and I was totally swept away from my reality. The only thing that mattered right now was this man and how desperately I wanted to be one with him.

With a smile spread across my face, I decided we needed to pick up where we left off, but this time I was taking the lead.

Reaching over carefully, I turned on the lantern and lit the room up enough to see everything, but not enough to where I thought it would wake him. Grabbing the one condom that remained on the bed, I slid it under my pillow. I slowly moved my hand under the sheet and found Thano's semi-hard dick. Wrapping my hand around it, I gently moved up and down as I watched his brows pinch together and a low moan form in the back of his throat.

My lower stomach pulled with such desire I swear I wanted to crawl on top of him and sink down without even worrying about a condom.

Claire would kill me if she knew I had unprotected sex. With an evil grin, I got an idea.

Opening the condom wrapper, I put the condom in my mouth and attempted to repeat what Susie Walker did with a banana and a condom when Claire and I were at her sixteenth birthday party.

I'd never in my life put a guy's dick in my mouth. This could turn out to be bad. Very bad.

Slipping under the sheet, I positioned my mouth and went for it.

Thano's body jerked as he moaned. If I do this and that asshole slept through all of it, I'll be really pissed.

"Fuuuck," he hissed as his hand laced through my hair and his other hand threw the sheet back to see what I was doing.

Clearly, I wasn't very good at this and ended up having to use my hand. Thano didn't seem to mind one bit.

Crawling on top of him, I captured his eyes with mine. "Are you sure?" he asked.

My chest fluttered with how caring he sounded. "I'm very sure," I replied with a smile that had him flashing his beautiful smile back at me.

His hands went to my hips while I slowly sank down on him.

"Jesus, you're big."

When he laughed, I swear it rolled through my body and heated it even more.

Slowly working him in inch by inch, I leaned down and sucked his lower lip into my mouth, gently biting on it. His moan went straight to where my desire was slowly building.

Lifting up to pull him out some, he grabbed my hips and shook his head as he lifted up, pushing himself deeper inside of me, causing me to let out a gasp.

God he's so big. I'm not going to be able to walk for a week.

With a smirk, I reached between my legs and played with my clit as I sank onto him, allowing his dick to fill me completely. It was heaven. Pure heaven. I'd never felt like this before in my life.

I slowly moved my hips until I got the friction I was looking for. If I kept playing with my clit, I was going to come. My hands moved slowly up my body until I found my nipples.

Thano's eyes darkened with lust and I could feel he wanted me to go faster, but this was my show.

Dropping my head back, I moaned. My hand found that sweet spot between my legs as I played with it again.

"Jesus, you look beautiful touching yourself, ladybug," Thano panted out.

Bringing my eyes back to his, I placed both hands on his chest. I quickly learned to love his pet name for me and I swear every time he called me it I was turned on even more. I moved faster, but not too fast. It was slow. Steady. A rush I'd never in my life experienced.

Thano gripped my hips harder and began pumping, instantly building the orgasm I had been trying to hold off.

His eyes piercing me, he spoke in Greek. "Me trelaíneis."

I had no idea what he said, but it was my undoing. My entire body shook as my orgasm hit me so hard, I swear I saw stars.

"Thano," I cried out before he had his arms wrapped around me with his mouth swallowing my cries of ultimate pleasure.

It felt as if it lasted forever. When I finally slowed my movements, he masterfully rolled us and hovered over me. "That was beautiful, ladybug. Absolutely beautiful."

My head was spinning. I was still throbbing when Thano began moving inside of me.

"Oh, God," I panted out. He was doing something that was the most magical thing I'd ever experienced. I was going to come again. I'd never in my life had an orgasm during sex and now I was about to have two back to back.

"What are you doing to me?" I panted as he smiled.

His mouth moved to my neck. "Does that feel good, baby?"

I swore I could feel it in my toes. "Yes. Please don't . . . don't stop."

Not even caring how I sounded, I was desperate for this orgasm.

His lips were next to my ear where he whispered, "I don't want you to come again yet, ladybug."

My eyes widened in shock. *What? Is he insane?*

"What!" I whimpered.

I began to move my hips but he pressed down harder on me. For a one quick moment I panicked as he pinned me, but when he looked into my eyes, I knew I was okay.

"Are you okay?" he asked as he slowed down some.

Frantically nodding, I replied with a gasp, "Yes!"

"You feel so good, Kilyn. I've never—"

He stopped talking and buried his face into my neck as he seemed to lose his control. What was slow and steady turned into Thano pulling back and grabbing my hips. He pulled out and pushed back in so hard and deep, I cried out.

That was it. He was hitting the spot over and over with each thrust into me and I loved every single second of it.

"More!" I whispered.

"Kilyn, baby . . . come for me now."

My eyes rolled to the back of my head as he pushed in and did something with his hips, causing me to slam my hands over my mouth and cry out as the orgasm rippled through my body. Something happened between the two of us in that moment as we both came together. Thano pushed in deep, his body shaking as I felt myself squeeze around his dick. When he stopped moving, he buried his face into my neck again, gasping for breath.

My arms wrapped around his neck while I tried to take in air. Once we both had our breathing under control, Thano looked up and into my eyes. I was very aware that he was still inside of me. I could feel his dick twitching and, for some reason, it made my stomach drop that he hadn't wanted to pull out right away.

His eyes searched my face . . . as if he was looking for something. With a smile, I placed my hand on the side of his face. "I've never experienced anything like that before."

His face lit up while he lifted his eyebrows. "Two orgasms?"

I wasn't sure why I felt the need to share it with him, but I did. "I've never had an orgasm during sex before . . . let alone two."

Thano's smile faded some, before it grew into a wide smile.

Leaning over, he gently kissed my lips and pulled back some.

"Kilyn, I need you to know that was one of the most amazing moments of my life. I don't think I could ever put it into words what making love to you felt like."

My heart slammed against my chest.

Then I remembered his whispered words in Greek. "What did you say to me earlier? In Greek."

He let out a nervous chuckle. "I have no idea why I keep talking to you in Greek."

I smirked before giving him a wink. "Because you know it turns the girls on!"

Thano was still inside of me, resting his body on his arms. He slowly shook his head. "I've never talked to anyone but my family in Greek before. Not even Savannah."

Savannah. That must be the girl who broke his heart.

I frowned. It was suddenly very awkward with him bringing up another girl while his dick was still inside of me.

Clearly, he saw my reaction to him saying another girl's name. He quickly pulled out and jumped out of the bed. Slipping the condom off, he tied it in a knot and threw it in the trash can he had sitting in the room. He let out a deep sigh and began moving into the bathroom as I sat up.

"Wait. You didn't tell me what you said."

When he turned and looked at me, I sucked in a breath. His face wore an expression of . . . regret. I wasn't sure if he regretted bringing up this Savannah girl or making love to me.

Clearing his throat, he barely said, "I said you drive me crazy."

And just like that, he turned and walked into the bathroom, turning on the shower. Pulling my legs up, I no longer felt that warm happy bubbly feeling I felt five minutes ago. Fighting back the tears in my eyes, I closed them and counted to twenty. I needed to get my emotions in check.

"Kilyn, did you want to hop in the shower?"

My eyes snapped open and anger raced through my body. I scrambled out of the bed and wrapped the sheet around my body. Walking into the bathroom, I expected him to still be in the shower. When he wasn't, it felt like I had been slapped across the face. It would have been so romantic to have had him stay in there.

If he was trying to send me a message that what just happened was a mistake, I got it loud and clear.

He frowned when he saw me wrapped in the sheet. I stood frozen in one spot while he dried off with a towel he must keep here for when he stays the night.

"Um . . . I only have one towel."

Lifting my chin and squaring my shoulders, I dropped the sheet. Thano's eyes took in every inch of my body before I turned and stepped into the shower. The only thing in the shower was a bar of Irish Spring soap. Rolling my eyes, I quickly scrubbed my body and then used it to wash my hair.

Peeking out of the shower curtain I saw he had left the towel and lantern for me. After shutting off the water, I reached for the towel and dried off in record speed. It was freezing in the house.

When I stepped out of the shower, I ran my hand over the steamed up mirror. Staring at my reflection I was overcome with a sense of sadness.

How could such an amazing moment be ruined by the mention of one name?

He regretted sleeping with me.

How could I have been so stupid to let my guard down and let him in? I should have known better.

Pulling in a deep breath through my nose, I slowly blew it out. Spinning on my heels, I walked into the bedroom only to see Thano sitting on the bed. He had lit another lantern so the bedroom was lit up. I quickly found my clothes and got dressed.

"Wh-what are you doing?"

"I'm getting dressed, what does it look like?"

"Why?"

I slipped on my T-shirt and shook my head as I looked back at him. "I can't do this."

He drew his head back and gave me a confused look. "Do what?"

"For years, I built a fortress around my heart. You're the first guy

I've ever let my guard down with. The first one I've opened my heart up to, and I feel like all I'm getting is whiplash with you. One minute you're whispering romantic things to me in Greek and then—"

Looking away, I fought to regain my composure. I wasn't going to let him bring me to tears. No guy would ever do that to me again.

My eyes caught his stare and I was positive I saw something in those eyes that I've longed to see in a man's eyes, only it was gone as soon as it came.

My chest tightened and I felt sick to my stomach. "And then you're looking at me like you just made the biggest mistake of your life."

Thano jumped up and walked toward me. I held up my hands. "Stop. Please don't come near me. I don't think I can resist you when you touch me." My chin trembled as I looked down and swallowed hard.

*Get it together, Kilyn.*

"Your heart is camouflaged and I don't know how to read it." Looking back up at him, I barely said, "One minute you're warm and the next you're cold. Maybe I'm not supposed to be the one to read it."

He shook his head. "Kilyn, I . . . I'm not sure I'm ready yet for you to have a piece of my heart."

And there it was.

The final blow to my already fragile heart. I forced a small grin. "And here I thought, maybe, we both shared a moment together."

"We did," he said with an urgency in his voice.

"I've been through too much shit in my life and maybe . . . maybe I was wanting something that just wasn't there."

He shook his head, "No. Kilyn, if you would listen to me for a minute."

His doorbell rang and we both looked out. I was dressed and he wasn't.

Taking the light, I said, "I'll see who it is."

"No, wait," Thano said as he frantically searched for his clothes.

Quickly making my way out of his room, I needed to put distance between us. Opening the door, I breathed a sigh of relief as I saw a state trooper standing there.

He smiled, as he looked me over. "Ma'am, just checking to make sure everyone and everything is okay. I see you had a tree land on your vehicle."

"Oh, um . . . yes that is Thano's car. He owns the cabin."

"The storm has already passed and they are working on the roads to clear them, so you should be able to leave by morning."

I glanced over my shoulder and saw Thano walking toward the front door.

"And the power?" he asked.

The trooper nodded his head. "Crews are working on it now. I'm actually heading back down the mountain."

"Is there any way you could take me to Manitou Springs?"

It was out of my mouth before I even realized I was thinking it.

"What?" Thano said. "Kilyn, what are you doing?"

Not bothering to look at him, I stared at the trooper. He looked between the two of us.

"Is everything okay here, ma'am?"

"Yes. Everything is fine; I'm feeling rather claustrophobic. I don't think I can wait until morning."

Thano walked up next to me. "Jesus, Savannah. What in the hell are you doing?"

My head snapped over as my mouth dropped open. My entire body shook from head to toe. "My name is Kilyn. Not Savannah."

Thano's face turned white. "I . . . I didn't mean to call you that. I swear, Kilyn."

Turning back to the trooper, I looked at him with pleading eyes. "Please, can you take me home?"

When the single tear rolled down my cheek, he nodded.

I quickly slipped on my Converse sneakers. Thano stood there the whole time, not uttering a single word.

Before I stepped out into the frigid cold, I looked at him. "I'll have your drawings ready by Wednesday."

He opened his mouth to speak, but nothing came out. I hadn't realized until that moment how much I had longed for him to put up an argument. For him to beg me not to leave.

Another stupid tear slipped from the corner of my eye. Quickly wiping it away, I forced a smile.

"Goodbye, Thano."

The trooper started for his truck as I followed.

By the time I got to the car, I lost all control of my emotions and began crying. When the trooper opened the door to the back seat, he lightly took a hold of my arm. "Are you sure everything is okay?"

I nodded. "The only thing that's wrong is I was foolish enough to open my heart up again. He didn't do anything to hurt me, I swear."

He didn't say a word. Just a small head nod as he held the door open for me to slip in.

The trip down the mountain was nerve wracking and probably the longest drive of my life. By the time I got home, a small amount of snow covered the streets. With the streets empty and the lights shining on it, it almost looked magical.

"Are you okay, Kilyn?"

During our drive, I made friends with Trooper Joe. He was married, with three boys, all under five. His wife was his best friend and they had been high school sweethearts.

"I am. Thank you so much, Joe. I'll never be able to repay you."

He walked me up to the door and flashed me an adorable smile. "Nonsense. It's my job to help people."

My phone vibrated in my hand, but I didn't dare look at it.

Joe nodded and turned to leave as I unlocked the main door to my apartment building.

"Hey, Kilyn?"

Glancing over my shoulder, I asked, "Yes?"

"Give him a chance to explain. He looked like his whole world collapsed when you walked out of his house."

*I doubt it.*

With a forced smile, I nodded. "I will. Night, Joe."

"Good night, Kilyn. Good luck with everything."

I watched as he walked back to his Chevy Tahoe. "Be careful!" I called out. Not really caring that it was almost five thirty in the morning and I was yelling out.

When my phone vibrated again, I lifted it to see Thano's number. My finger hovered over the answer button. When it stopped ringing, I slipped it into my back pocket and made my way into the building.

## sixteen

### Thano

I STARED OUT THE WINDOW while my mother went on and on about someone coming over for dinner. It had been almost a week since I'd talked to Kilyn. She had emailed me the plans she drew up for the cabin. When I called her office, Kasey told me Kilyn had taken a few days off and wouldn't be in until next week. If I needed anything, Claire should be able to help.

"You're a million miles away, Athanasios."

Lifting my head up, I smiled at the sight of my grandmother. "Yiayia, look how beautiful you look."

She made a spat sound three times on herself before reaching her arms out for me. "When am I going to get some great-grandchildren? I'll be dead soon, I'd like to meet them, you know."

I held back a smile and kissed her on the forehead.

"You see, Mama, I told you. He is stubborn. He wants to see me suffer."

Rolling my eyes, I glanced outside to see Thad walking up with a group of people. "Who is that with Thad?"

My mother clapped her hands and cried out, "They're here! Quickly, Athanasios, walk your Yiayia into the dining room and help her get seated."

My grandmother pulled her arm from mine and shot my mother a dirty look. "I'm not dead yet. I can walk myself to the food."

Turning to me, she asked, "Have you been eating? You look too thin. Come to me tomorrow, I'll make you a good old-fashioned Greek dinner." Leaning in closer, she whispered, "Your Mitera doesn't cook as well as I do."

Peeking over to my mother, she hadn't heard her mother dissing her. Deciding to go along with her, I nodded. "Sounds good, Yiayia."

We both walked into the dining room as everyone else was piling in. Thad caught my eye and I swear he looked like someone had kicked him in the balls.

He walked up to me and said, "Mom's friends. From Greece. I just picked them up at the airport. Heads up, the one in red . . . she's your betrothed."

My head jerked back. "What the fuck?"

Everyone turned and looked at me. I swear, if my mother was able to shoot daggers from her eyes, I'd be dead right now.

"Athanasios, your mouth. Do I need to wash it out with soap?"

The girl in red looked at me and smiled. She was pretty. Very pretty, but I wasn't the least bit interested in her.

"Sit, sit! Let's eat!" my mother called out as the group didn't even have a chance to be introduced.

By the time the food was served, I was introduced to my mother's best friend's family. Seeing as this was the first time I'd heard of this best friend, needless to say, I was a bit surprised to learn that her youngest daughter, Karen, and I used to play endlessly when we were younger.

"So you lived here in the States until moving to Greece ten years ago?" I asked.

Agatha nodded. "Yes. When my father-in-law needed help with the family's restaurant, my husband was quick to move us all back to Greece."

Nicholaus looked bored out of his mind and kept looking at his watch. "Got somewhere to be, Nicholaus?" I asked with a smirk.

Before he could answer, my mother replied, "Nonsense. He is

looking forward to tonight with you, Athanasios."

Nicholaus and I both sat up straighter and said together, "Tonight?"

My mother smiled as she glanced over to my father. He looked like he would rather be sitting in front of the TV watching football. "Did you not talk to the boys?"

He rolled his eyes. "For the love of all things good, can you let them be?"

I stole a look over to Thad. He shrugged but smiled. He had finally brought Phoebe home to meet my parents the other day. I knew he only did it to get our mother off his back. Strut a pretty Greek girl in front of our mother and she was satisfied, for the time being.

"Nonsense. I want my boys to find happiness."

"Oh, shit," Nicholaus mumbled.

I couldn't help but notice how Karen was staring at me. I wonder if she got the memo this wasn't the late eighteen hundreds and marriages were no longer fixed. Leaning over to Nicholaus, I whispered, "If you can cause a distraction, I'll grab my truck and we can hightail it the hell out of here."

He chuckled and whispered, "Okay, but is it bad that I am actually attracted to Hadley? It's been a while since I've gotten fucked."

Turning to him, I shook my head. "Are you kidding me?"

"No. I'm not. She's pretty, Mom is throwing her at my feet, and I'm tired of jacking off in the shower."

"You'll lead her on, asshole. What happens when Mom starts talking marriage?"

Nicholaus laughed. "Jesus, Thano. I'm talking about fucking the girl for one night. What in the hell are you doing talking marriage?"

"You can't take Mom's best friend's daughter out and then fuck her and expect she is going to be okay with that."

"Who? Mom?"

Rolling my eyes, I hit him on the leg. "No! Hadley. She's the one who isn't going to be okay with it."

Nicholaus reached for his glass of wine and took a drink, but not before he winked at Hadley and she blushed. "Oh, trust me. She's going to be fine with it. So will her little sister, Karen. You can practically smell the horniness coming off of both of them."

I fell back into my seat as I pushed my hand through my hair. When I looked across the table at Karen, her eyes were lit up while she ran her tongue slowly over her lips.

I quickly looked away. *Oh, shit. I'm so screwed.*

THE MUSIC FELT LIKE IT was pounding inside my head. Nicholaus and Hadley had hit it off almost immediately. Of course, they also made out in the backseat of the truck the entire ride over to the club. At one point, I swore they were fucking with the way she was sitting on his lap.

"Will you dance with me, Thano?" Karen asked with a pout.

My muscles tensed. "Maybe in a bit."

She looked disappointed. "I really don't want my sister to have all the fun tonight."

I could easily take this girl back to my apartment and fuck the shit out of her.

The problem was, I had zero interest in her. The only way to cut to the chase was to ask her what she wanted from me.

"What exactly are you wanting from me, Karen?"

She tilted her head and pressed her lips together. Walking up to me closer, she ran her finger across my chest. "Sex. Lots and lots of sex while I'm here before my mother drags me back to Greece."

I laughed and shook my head. "Then you're with the wrong Drivas brother. You should have gone out with Thad."

Her smile dropped and was replaced with a look of anger. "I knew it. My mother said you probably weren't over your fiancée dying, and she was right. What a waste of time. The only reason I went along with this is because all my mother does is tell me I need to find a good Greek boy to marry. Ugh. I just want to get laid. Maybe Hadley will share Nicholaus."

My eyes widened in surprise.

Well, okay, then.

Laughing, I used my hand and made a sweep across the crowd.

"Well, if you want to get laid, there ya go. Have at it."

Turning, I walked up to Nicholaus and shoved my keys into his hand. "If you're into threesomes, Karen is open for it."

My brother's face lit up. "Fuck yeah. Where in the hell are you going?"

"I'll take a cab home. I'm over this shit."

SITTING IN THE LOBBY OF Kilyn's office, my knee bounced as I waited for Claire. When she cleared her throat, I jumped up.

"Claire, it's good seeing you again."

She lifted one eyebrow and managed to narrow her other eye. I don't think I'd ever seen anyone pull that off before. It for sure made her scary looking as hell.

"I wish I could say the same thing, but seeing as you made my best friend take off for a week and not tell a soul where she was going, I think I'll pass on the friendly gestures."

Kicking at nothing on the floor, I nodded. "I deserve that. I was wondering if I could talk to you, though. Please."

Glancing over to Kasey, she said, "Send my calls to voicemail unless it's Kilyn and don't tell her the ass . . . I mean . . . don't tell her Thano is here."

Ouch. I was starting to second-guess me coming to talk to Claire.

I followed her into a meeting room where she shut the door and motioned for me to have a seat.

I did and waited for her to sit. When she didn't, I dragged in a deep breath and decided to get right to it.

"Who is Peter?"

Her face turned white as a ghost.

"I'm sorry. What?"

"Peter. Who is Peter?"

Swallowing hard, Claire sank into a chair and covered her mouth. The tears in her eyes caused my heart to start racing.

Shit. Now I really wanted to find this guy and beat the hell out of him.

Opening her mouth to speak, her voice cracked a few times before she was able to talk. "Why are you asking?"

I moved about in my seat for a second. "When Kilyn and I were up in the cabin, we um . . . we made love."

She pinched her brows together. "Yes, I know. I also know you acted like you had made a mistake after you fucked her and then you called her by someone else's name."

My heart physically ached thinking that Kilyn thought I regretted being with her. I had no damn excuse as to why I called her Savannah except for maybe having just said her name earlier.

Cracking my neck, I tried not to let my anger show. If Kilyn had only given me a chance to talk to her, none of this bullshit would be necessary.

Standing, I looked directly at Claire. "First off, I do not regret making love to Kilyn. That's what we did. Made love. I didn't fuck her, as you saw fit to say. We made love. It was amazing. She was amazing. She is amazing. I have . . . issues I've been trying to work through."

Claire let out a gruff laugh. "You don't say. Well, newsflash, Thano. Kilyn has issues too, but she wouldn't lead you on and then drop you."

Scrubbing my hands down my face, I let out a frustrated sigh. "That's something for me to talk to Kilyn about. Not you. Sorry, Claire."

She glanced over my shoulder and smirked. "Well then, here's your chance."

Turning around, my breath caught at the sight of Kilyn standing there.

"Kilyn," I whispered.

With a soft smile, she looked from me over to Claire. "Sorry I left without telling you where I was going. I needed some time to clear my head."

Claire stood and made her way over to Kilyn. "It's totally not okay, but I'm glad you're back. Where did you go?"

"My parents' summer place."

With a knowing nod, Claire kissed Kilyn on the cheek. "Want me to stay?"

When her eyes met mine, I saw something in them. Something that gave me hope I hadn't fucked things up too badly.

"No. It's okay."

Peeking over her shoulder at me, Claire used her two fingers and motioned that she was watching me. I couldn't help but chuckle. I loved seeing how close the two of them were.

When Claire shut the office door behind her, Kilyn made her way to the very opposite side of the room and sat down at the end of the table. I slowly sat and we were both soon lost in one another's eyes.

Kilyn finally broke the silence. "Why are you here?"

I knew what I was about to do might push her away from me, but I was ready to take that chance.

"Who is Peter?"

Her face turned white like Claire's had.

When her breathing picked up I had to force myself not to jump up and take her into my arms.

Glancing down to the table, she swallowed hard and then cleared her throat. "Peter is Claire's brother. When my parents died, I went to . . . um . . . I went to live with Claire and her family. I had no other family. My father's parents died years ago and my mother was estranged from her family."

My heart ached inside my chest. I wanted to comfort her but I knew she needed her space as she retold her story. She played with a spot on the table as she continued to speak.

"Claire and her family were all I had left. My parents named Claire's parents as my legal guardians if anything was to ever happen to them. I moved in with them almost immediately. I was fourteen and little did I know my nightmare wasn't only going to be my parents dying."

# seventeen

## Kilyn

MY HANDS WERE SHAKING AS I let the memories race back into my mind. Thano looked pale. I could tell he was forcing himself to stay seated and not rush over to me. That comforted me a small bit.

"What do you mean?" he asked.

"Everyone treated me like I was a part of the family. Claire and I shared a room for the first year I lived with them. Then her father got a promotion at work and we moved to a bigger house. My parents' estate was tied up in probate and all of it would go to me at twenty-three. There was a small amount of money that was given directly to Claire's parents, but they insisted on setting it aside for me."

I couldn't help the small smile that spread across my face. "Kim and Scott, that's their names, they honestly treated me like their own child. It still blows my mind to this day what they did and continue to do for me."

"They sound like wonderful people."

Looking at Thano, I nodded my head. "They are."

I shook my head and blew out a breath. "After Scott got the promotion, I was able to have my own room. It seemed like once we moved, things changed between Peter and me. I'd, of course, always had a crush on him. You know . . . your best friend's older brother. He was almost two years older than Claire and me and was always watching out for us. Protecting us."

With a weak smile, I looked back at the small chip in the table and started running my finger over it again. "Peter used to tell me how beautiful I was and that someday when I got older, he'd show me how much he loved me. He was going to be my knight in shining armor. The one who would save me from the bad dreams I still had about my parents' accident. Little did I know, at the time, he would become my worst nightmare."

Peeking up, I saw Thano make a fist. He was probably already guessing what happened.

"What did he do to you, Kilyn?"

Years of therapy helped me to get past the betrayal of Peter's trust. It helped me to understand I wasn't at fault. There were moments, though, I found myself standing in the shower scrubbing my body to get his smell off me before I realized it really wasn't there. I was at the point in my life I could talk about it if I had to. But one question from Thano and I was on the verge of breaking down.

My chin trembled before I closed my eyes and counted to twenty. Opening them again, I looked directly at him. *Tackle it head on, Kilyn.*

"When I turned sixteen, Peter took me out to dinner. He said he wanted to show me off to everyone. I was finally old enough for him to show me how much he loved me." I slowly shook my head. "I was stupid and naïve and believed every word he said to me. I had no idea what he meant when he kept saying that. Scott went out of town for his new job often. He was supposed to be gone for two days. That night, Peter came into my room. I remember sitting up in bed and asking him what he was doing. He locked the door and gave me a smile. My heart leapt in my chest because he handed me single rose."

I looked out the window and pressed my lips together. "To this day, I can't stand to look at pink roses."

Thano continued to watch me, not saying a word.

"I was dressed in nothing but a T-shirt and panties. When I got out of bed to take the rose, Peter looked at me like he had never looked at me before. It was like he was seeing me for the first time. He took my arm and pulled me to him. He kissed me and, at first, I liked it. But then he got rough. He bit my lip so hard it started to bleed."

Anger moved over Thano's face.

"When I told him to slow down, he said he was sorry, it was just that he wanted me so badly. It was then it all hit me. He wanted to have sex with me. I told him I wasn't ready for that but he said I was. I was so scared. He pushed me down onto my bed and quickly unbuttoned his jeans and pulled out a condom. He told me if I yelled out, Claire and his mother would think I was a whore for having him in my room. I didn't know what to do. I wanted to yell out but I had gotten out of bed to take the rose. In my mind, I instantly thought I invited his thoughts by getting out of bed. But I also knew Claire knew me better than that. I'd never let a boy in my room. I got confused as to why I didn't tell him to leave when he first came in."

Thano shook his head. "No, Kilyn."

"I was so lost in my thoughts, I didn't realize what was happening until he ripped my panties off. I started to push him away, but he put his hand over my mouth and then used his other hand to hold my hips down."

Thano stood up, causing the chair to fall back and me to jump at the sound. "That motherfucker."

"He tried like hell to get it inside of me, but I fought him with every ounce of strength I had. I thought if I fought long enough, he'd realize what he was doing. But then he got mad and grabbed me so hard, I began crying and stopped moving. When I stopped moving, he eased up on his grip, but he still held me down."

Closing my eyes, I shook my head. "It hurt so bad I just laid there. I guess he thought I was either enjoying it or I had given up the fight. When he moved his hand from my mouth, I screamed as loud as I could. I heard someone try to open my door and so did Peter. He quickly covered my mouth but I kept trying to scream. The next thing I knew, the door busted open and Scott rushed in. He saw Peter on me and pulled him off of me. He threw him to the floor and that was about when

Claire and her mother walked in." My voice cracked as I rubbed my hands over my arms to warm myself up from the instant chill in the air.

"Jesus, Kilyn. I'm so sorry, ladybug."

My eyes snapped up to his. "Claire and her parents had to testify against Peter. It took me a long time to forgive myself for having to have them put their own son and brother in jail."

Thano walked around the table towards me. "He deserved it."

Slowly standing, I nodded. "I know that now, but at sixteen it was harder to accept."

Stopping right in front of me, Thano put his hand on the side of my face. I allowed myself to feel the warmth of his touch as I gently leaned against it for a moment before stepping back from him.

"So, now you know my story. I don't let it define who I am, yet I did allow the hurt and betrayal to keep me from opening my heart up to another. At least until you. I live life to the fullest, enjoying every moment I'm given. I won't lie and say I don't have moments of weakness because I do. I think you saw that when I left your cabin."

Thano nodded slowly, lost in his own thoughts.

"Now it's my turn. Who is Savannah?"

I imagined his face looked exactly like mine did when he asked about Peter. My heart raced as I waited for him to tell me.

"She was my fiancée."

My hand went to my stomach and I instantly felt sick. That wasn't what I was expecting and I was stunned by how that news made me feel.

He grinned slightly. "Actually, she was my high school sweetheart. My parents were not thrilled I was dating a girl who wasn't Greek, but I loved her and I didn't care. I asked her to marry me when we were in college. My mother was upset with me, but Savannah had such a way about her, she won my mother over." He let out a soft laugh. "That's not entirely true. My mother was upset with me, but finally stopped arguing with me."

I didn't want to know the answer to my next question, but I asked it anyway. "Did you get married?"

His shoulders dropped and he shook his head. "She was walking down the aisle and collapsed."

My hand instantly came up to my mouth as I sucked in a breath of air.

Oh. My. God.

"She had a heart attack and died. Right there at the church. In front of everyone. We found out she had a heart defect that no one knew about."

Dropping my hand, I let my tears fall freely. I could hear the pain in his voice and that killed me.

"I'm so sorry, Thano."

He looked up at me, his eyes filled with tears. "I promised her my heart and I'm not sure I can give it to anyone else."

My mouth fell open as I searched for something to say. "When I'm with you, I forget all the pain. I forget Savannah."

Reaching out for the chair, I grabbed it to keep myself standing. My legs felt as if they were about to give out on me. "When we made love, I'd never experienced such emotions, not even with Savannah. I never whispered things to her in Greek. I never called her ladybug. With you it's so . . . different."

Quickly wiping my tears away, I tried to make sense of what he was saying to me. I was beyond confused. One second he was telling me he couldn't give me his heart and the next he was telling me how different it was with me. My head was spinning.

"I didn't tell you the whole story about the ladybug. My grandmother told me ladybugs were drawn to pure love. True love. When I realized I was calling you ladybug . . . it freaked me out."

Furrowing my eyes together, I forced myself to talk. "Why? Because I couldn't possibly be the one you loved?"

I was lost between feeling so incredibly hurt by his words and angry as hell because he was denying what was right in front of him.

He looked at me with a blank expression. "I loved Savannah."

Swallowing hard, I asked, "And you can never love again? Is that what you're saying to me, Thano? You can never find another love like that . . . or God forbid something even more. Something deeper? Because I thought I was so broken by Peter I would never be able to trust someone enough to love them. I opened my heart up and I started falling in love with you. So you're telling me you could never love me?"

"I'm not sure about anything right now, Kilyn. I know I can't stop thinking about you. I can't stop thinking about that night we made love and that confuses the hell out of me."

Standing, I looked directly into his eyes. "Well, let me be clear on one thing. I am not Savannah. I will never be her nor do I ever want to be compared to her. I've lost a part of me as well, Thano. The only difference between us is I have chosen to move on with my life where as you have chosen to stay in the past. I won't let myself get hurt by you or anyone else."

He narrowed his eyes as if I had said the most insane thing ever. "I don't want to hurt you. That is the last thing I'd ever want to do, Kilyn."

Forcing my tears back, my throat and lungs burned. My chin trembled and I had to fight to keep the room from spinning.

Looking down, I watched as my tears fell and landed on the floor. I lifted my head and forced myself to speak.

"But that's where you're so wrong, Thano. Because you just did. More than you will ever know."

His eyes widened as a pained expression took over his face. Taking a step closer to me I held up my hands to stop him. A sob escaped from my pressed lips. "No. Please don't touch me."

"Wait. Kilyn, don't do this."

"I'm sorry, Thano. I can't play second to someone else. I'm falling in love with you and the only way I can keep my heart guarded is by letting you go."

A tear slipped from his eye and slowly rolled down his beautiful face. "Please don't do this."

Taking a step forward, I reached up and softly kissed his lips. "I hope you find what you're looking for."

Thano shook his head.

Quickly making my way around him, I headed to the door. My heart was pounding in my head so loud I could hardly hear myself think.

As I reached for the door, Thano grabbed me and spun me

around. His eyes pleading with me to stay. "Don't do this. Please, Kilyn. I . . . I . . . shit."

His hand pushed through his hair as he let out a string of curse words.

"Fucking hell, please stay. I need to figure this all out. I'm confused that's all."

My chest heaved as I tried to contain my feelings. I wanted more than anything to fall into his arms and tell him I would wait. I'd wait forever for him to realize he loved me and not some ghost. But that wouldn't be fair to either of us. I'd always second guess who he truly loved. There wouldn't be a day that would pass where I wouldn't wonder if I was just someone he settled for.

Lifting my chin, I gave him a weak smile. "If you really wanted me to stay, you wouldn't be confused, Thano. You would have told me how you felt about me without even having to think about it."

His eyes filled with tears while I reached my shaking hand around my back and found the doorknob. My body felt cold as I turned it. Opening the door, I walked as fast as I could away from the only man I'd ever loved. Possibly the only man I'd ever truly love.

## eighteen

### Thano

FROZEN.

Kilyn quickly walked away as I stood there watching her like the fucking idiot I was. Frozen in place, unable to move.

Her words swam in my head causing it to throb with each breath I took.

*"If you really wanted me to stay, you wouldn't be confused, Thano."*

Those words replayed over and over as I stood there looking at an empty hall.

"What did I do?"

Pushing both hands through my hair, I wanted to scream out. I wanted everyone around me to feel the same pain I was feeling.

I let her walk away. The one woman who moved me like I'd never been moved.

My ladybug.

Shaking my head, I turned and stared out the window.

My ladybug.

Was Kilyn my true love and not Savannah? I loved Savannah so much. Or did I love the idea of Savannah? Closing my eyes, I was taken back to the night I told my parents I asked Savannah to marry me. It was my father and I alone on the back porch.

*"Do you love this girl, Athanasios, or is it a first love crush?"*

*Staring at my father, I was dumbfounded. "Not you too, Dad. You're start-ing to sound like, Mom. Yes, I love her and no, it's not because she was my first love. I want to be with her."*

*He lifted his left eyebrow and gave me that knowing look. The one that said he knew more than me. "You sure you're not hell bent on being with her because your mother is against it?"*

*My heart skipped a beat. I had never lied to my father and I wasn't about to start. Swallowing hard, I forced a smile. "That may have been the reason I first started dating Savannah."*

*"Really? The foundation of your relationship was started on deceit."*

*"That's not the reason now. I fell in love with her and I want to be with her."*

*Walking up to me, my father placed his hand on my chest. "In here, Athanasios, that is where true love starts. It starts with your breath catching the first time she smiles at you. Your chest will tighten and then warm with the sound of her voice from across the room. The desire to be near her will over-whelm you. Your heart will actually feel as if it has been torn in two when she sheds a tear. That, my son, is love. True love."*

Opening my eyes, it hit me like a brick wall. I loved Savannah with all my heart. I knew that without a doubt. But none of those things ever happened when we first met. I thought she was beautiful, she gave me her undivided attention and knowing she wasn't Greek gave me a rush. Every time we were together it was a damn fucking rush.

With Kilyn, her not being Greek never even entered my mind. I was drawn to her immediately. Her smile made my breath catch in my throat every damn time. Her laughter gave me hope; my desire to be near her was constant. When we made love at the cabin it felt as if we were one. It was the most amazing moment in my life. Talking to her in Greek, calling her ladybug . . . I never did any of that with Savannah. The first time I made love with Savannah we were both drunk and it was prom night. I didn't even really remember it.

The guilt swept over my body instantly as I turned and made my way out of the building. My head throbbed as I fought to understand what in the hell was happening to me.

I headed to the only person I knew to go to.

Savannah.

==== 🖤 ====

STARING DOWN AT THE GRAVESTONE, I slowly sank down to my knees.

"Savannah, I loved you. I swear, I loved you with my whole heart."

Scrubbing my hands down my face, I let out a frustrated groan.

"I don't know what's happening to me. My world was destroyed when you left me, but now . . . now I feel like I'm finally coming back to life and it's all because of Kilyn. I feel so guilty because I feel things so differently with her than I did with you, and I don't know what to do with that. Why did you leave me? Why?"

Falling back onto my ass, I rested my arms over my knees and stared at her name. Savannah Lynn Thompson.

Looking away, I stared at a bird that was sitting in a tree. The snow from the storm was already gone and the weather was back to the low sixties. It was a beautiful day.

"It's beautiful out today. You would have loved it."

The bird flew off and I closed my eyes. "I can't move on, Savannah. I've fallen in love with her, yet I can't move on."

"She'd want you to."

My eyes snapped open and I jumped up to see Savannah's brother Sam standing there carrying a bouquet of flowers. My heart stopped for a moment. I hadn't seen him in a few years. I had grown close to Savannah's family when we dated, but after her death we grew apart. He set them down next to the flowers I had brought.

"Don't you think four and half years is enough time, Thano?"

With a sigh, I looked down and kicked at a piece of grass. "Everyone keeps telling me to move on, I don't know if I can."

"Why do you think that is?"

I looked into his eyes. It was the first time anyone had actually asked me that. "Hell, I don't know, Sam. Maybe because she died walking down the aisle and there was nothing I could do. We didn't even get a chance to start a life together."

He never once broke my stare. "Or is it because in a small way, you felt relieved she died and that has filled you with guilt."

My hands balled into fists as anger surged through my body. "Fuck you, Thompson. I loved your sister and wanted to marry her. Why in the hell would I have wanted her to die?"

He let out a soft laugh. "Oh, I know you loved her, and she loved you. But I don't think either one of you wanted to admit you loved each other for the wrong reasons."

I could feel my heart pounding in my chest. His words rattled my entire body.

"What in the hell are you talking about?" I asked.

Sam turned and faced Savannah's grave.

"Thano, I want you to really dig down deep and think about this. The two of you were together since high school and all through college. When you asked Savannah to marry you, was it truly because you wanted to spend the rest of your life with her, or was it because you felt it was your sense of duty? Kind of like right now how you feel like it is your sense of duty to mourn her and not move on. You let the guilt of feeling happy keep you from actually feeling happy."

His words felt like they were a slap to my face. I opened my mouth to argue, but I couldn't. For the first time in over four years, I let reality in.

Sam gave me a weak smile. "It's okay, Thano. You can't beat yourself up over it anymore."

"I loved her, Sam. I really did."

"And she loved you, but even Savannah wasn't sure. The day before the wedding she confided in me. She said she was having second thoughts but didn't know how to talk to you about it. I told her she needed to talk to you before the wedding, but I'm going to guess she never did."

My eyes widened in shock. "She was having second thoughts about getting married?" I shook my head as if it would help the jumbled mess inside of it. Knowing Savannah had the same doubts almost had me feeling relieved as the guilt lessened some. "Wait—my mother said Savannah told her mother she wanted to talk to me."

Sam's expression turned sad. "My mother wouldn't let Savannah share her fears with you. She told her she was being silly and that she needed to push past the fears."

*Oh, God.* I took a few steps back. My heart sank as I looked at Sam. "Do you think that's why she had the heart attack?"

He jerked his face back in shock. "No! Thano, you already know the doctors said she had a heart defect."

I forced the air into my lungs. "But . . . what if the added stress caused something to happen?"

Walking up to me, Sam grabbed onto my arms. "Stop. Thano, think back to the numerous times you saw Savannah complaining her chest was aching. Each time she would give some excuse, almost as if she somehow knew something was wrong. Even I remember her saying something when we were in Cancun on a family vacation, after we went for a walk along the beach. The wedding—you—none of that had anything to do with her dying. Her heart gave out. There is nothing more to it. Stop beating yourself up every chance you get. Thano, don't let your fear keep you from opening your heart again. It's time to move on."

Closing my eyes, I numbly shook my head. "You're right," I barely said as he dropped his hands.

"About?"

I opened my eyes and pulled in a deep breath before slowly pushing it out. I looked into Savannah's brother's eyes and decided I couldn't ignore it any longer. "I was relieved. A small part of me was relieved the wedding never happened. The guilt I've felt over the last four years knowing that has been something I've carried deep inside of me, refusing to ever let that thought back into my head again. The moment I first thought it, I hated myself for thinking it. I loved Savannah and I only wanted to make her happy and give her the life she deserved. I thought by marrying her, I was doing what we both wanted. Now I don't even know if either one of us wanted it at all."

Both of us remained silent for a few moments before Sam finally spoke. "I think you both wanted it in some small way, but if you had gotten married, I honestly don't think you would have stayed married for long before you grew apart. That's the thing about love, Thano. There is love . . . and then there is the love that you can't live without."

Kilyn.

I wasn't sure how long we stood there in silence before Sam finally shook my hand and took off. It was another few minutes before I decided it was time to leave.

"I'll always love you, Savannah. But it's time I forgive myself and open up my heart to someone else. I think you would love Kilyn. She's full of life and so strong." Closing my eyes, I softly said, "I pray to God I didn't mess things up with her."

Feeling a tear slip from my eye, I quickly wiped it away.

With a smile, I whispered, "Goodbye, Savannah."

## nineteen

TWO WEEKS LATER

## Kilyn

WALKING INTO ONION CREEK, I took a deep inhale through my nose. God, something smelled wonderful. I wasn't even sure how I could even think of eating after the Thanksgiving dinner two days ago at Kim and Scott's house. I was still full.

My phone buzzed in my purse, alerting me of a text. Pulling my phone out, my breath caught as I saw his name.

Thano.

*Thano: Got the final drawings. Everything looks great.*

Pressing my lips together, I stopped walking so I could text him back. Surely he had to have some changes.

*Me: No changes? You agree with everything?*

I chewed on my thumbnail as I waited for his response. I made the master bedroom a little more girly than I should have seeing this was a guy's cabin. The shabby chic décor was a bitch move but in the end it actually turned out kind of cute. Cute being the key word.

*Thano: Yes.*

My mouth fell open. That's it? That's all I get is a simple one-word response. Yes.

Feeling the anger build up, I started running my fingers quickly over my phone.

*Me: Really? Did you look at them, Athanasios? REALLY look at them.*

Standing in a small corner off to the side, I waited as I tapped my foot impatiently.

People started coming in for Claire's class and passing me. Each one giving me a warm greeting. It was almost as if they knew I was on the edge of losing my shit.

Five minutes went by before he finally responded.

*Thano: Yes, Ms. O'Kelly. I REALLY looked at them.*

*Me: And that's what you want to go with?*

*Thano: Yes.*

Ugh!

I hit his number and tried to calm my erratic heart down. I knew this was a risk . . . hearing his voice. When I gave him the option of using another designer he said no. All of our communication had been through email or text.

"Hello."

Oh, dear God in heaven. His voice sent my libido into high alert.

"Th—" My voice cracked and I had to clear it . . . twice.

*For Christ's sake! Get it together!*

"Mr. Drivas, I need to be sure you looked at the drawings for every room and sign off on all of them before I okay the work to begin."

"I did."

Closing my eyes, I brought up my hand and pinched the bridge of my nose. *Stay calm, Kilyn. Calm.*

"Your bedroom, Thano. Did you look at your bedroom?"

I heard rustling of papers and then a chuckle. "Yes. I saw the master."

Letting out a frustrated sigh, I replied, "And?"

"Well, my mother liked it, so I like it."

My mouth dropped to the ground. "It's nothing like what you asked for."

"Then why did you draw it up that way if you thought I wasn't going to like it?"

Slapping my hand to my forehead, I shouted, "Because I wanted you to say you didn't like it!"

"Why?"

I went to talk and nothing came out.

Why did I do that? Oh. My. Goodness. What am I, in high school playing games?

"Well . . . I um . . . I wanted to make sure you were really paying attention to the designs and not agreeing for the sake of agreeing."

Thano cleared his throat. "I would never do that. This is where I hope to live permanently someday, I want it to be the way I want it."

My heart jumped to my throat. Someday he'd be making love to another woman in the bedroom I designed. Some Greek bitch would be cooking up a storm in my dream kitchen.

Yes. I had to admit it to myself, I designed Thano's kitchen with my dream kitchen in mind. I got personal with a job. Very personal.

"Well, I hope when it's done you'll be happy."

"I'm sure I will be."

The silence was almost too much to take.

"Was there anything else you wanted to talk to me about, Ms. O'Kelly?"

My heart felt as if it were physically breaking all over again. "No. Oh, um, yes. Since you approved the plans Claire will be contacting you about when the workers will be there to start work."

"Claire? Why not you?"

I wiped the tears from my cheeks and faced the corner. The last thing I wanted was for people to see me crying. Trying to sound as normal as possible, I choked out my words.

"Claire usually handles this stage of things since her husband is the contractor we use. I'll be sure to have her send you her cell phone number should any . . . should, um . . . should any problems, um."

Squeezing my eyes shut, I cleared my throat. "Should problems arise."

"Kilyn, are you okay?"

I shook my head and pressed my lips tightly together as I covered my mouth with my hand. If only he knew how badly he broke my heart.

Dropping my hand, I whispered, "I'm fine. I have to go."

Hitting End, I pushed my phone into my back pocket and counted to twenty.

Now that that was over, I needed to concentrate on moving on. I'd already quit the gym where Thano worked out and I gave my notice to move from my apartment. I was going to stay with Claire and Blake until I found another place.

I did everything differently from what I normally did, and that included not going to my favorite coffee shop in Manitou Springs. The fear of running into Thano was almost becoming obsessive.

Claire's voice from behind me caused me to jump. "Hey, are you okay?"

Opening my eyes, I spun around and forced the fake smile I had mastered at sixteen years old.

"Yep! I think I'm coming down with something and I needed a few minutes. Are we ready?"

She nodded her head and gave me an inquisitive look. "Are you sure you're okay?"

Wrapping my arm around hers, I laughed. "Yes. I promise I'm fine."

"Okay, well, let's go. We have a huge group of rowdy women out there. I think it's some kind of party."

My smile grew to a sincere one. "Oh, how fun."

As we made our way back to the kitchen, I glanced over to the small group of women and smiled. Then my heart stopped. One woman looked directly into my eyes and I swore I'd seen those eyes looking at me before.

I closed my eyes and shook my head to clear my thoughts. I bumped directly into Claire. "Oh, sorry," I said as my face heated.

Giving me a probing look, I held up my hands and said, "I'm fine. I thought I saw someone and I wasn't paying any attention."

Claire lifted her eyebrows and tilted her head as if she was trying to size me up.

Leaning closer to her, I softly said, "Can we just get this going? I'm fine."

"You've been crying!" she said louder than she meant to.

I let out a nervous laugh and looked out as twelve pair of eyes stared at me.

Scanning them, I couldn't help but notice the one lady with the familiar eyes giving me a concerned look.

Okay, well, I could try and play this off or I could be honest. Shrugging my shoulders, I let out a gruff laugh. "I opened my heart to a guy and he broke it. There. I said it. Now let's get to cooking!"

I reached over and hit play on my iPod. My favorite song by LOCASH started and I did a spin and danced while Claire laughed and the rest of the ladies gave me a clap.

The only one who wasn't clapping was the older woman. I did my best to avoid her eyes as Claire began to tell everyone what we would be cooking today.

"We always start with a healthy smoothie to make for us to drink while we cook."

I picked up the pre made smoothie Claire must have made before she came searching for me, and took a drink. Choking, I curled my lip and gasped. "Holy crap! What's in this thing? It's awful!"

Claire glared at me as the room erupted in laughter.

"I won't be making that," one of the older ladies said from the group.

Covering my mouth with my hands, I shrugged.

Plastering on a smile, Claire began speaking. "For those of you who would like to make this immune boosting smoothie, ignore Kilyn. It contains Swiss chard, mustard greens, avocado, papaya and rolled oats. Oh, and pumpkin seeds!"

I stared at Claire. And it wasn't just me . . . everyone was staring at her. "Yeah, I think I'm going to side with Kilyn on this one."

Turning, I noticed it was the older lady who said it. She looked at me and winked.

Returning her smile, I mouthed, Good choice.

Claire put her hands on her hips. "Does anyone want to make it?"

No one said a word.

Clapping my hands, I said, "I have two bottles of a Merlot I've been dying to share! Wine is good for your heart . . . right, Claire?"

She wore a scowl on her face but soon let out a chuckle. "Fine, a glass of wine for everyone."

I quickly ran and grabbed three bottles, I said two, but I had a feeling I would be polishing one off on my own.

"Now, this evening we have a wonderful group of women who said they were referred to us. They are here spending the day with each other as they celebrate Katerina's fifty-fifth birthday!"

Everyone clapped, me included. Katerina was the woman who had the familiar eyes. She almost looked like . . .

My eyes widened. No. There was no way.

"Since they are all of Greek heritage, I thought we would do a Greek entrée and dessert."

My head snapped over to Claire as I felt my chest tightening. *Oh, holy shit. This is not happening.*

I stared down at the food Claire had put out. What in the living hell was this shit?

"Today we'll be making spanakopita, which is a Greek spinach pie. For dessert, it will be Greek honey cake. We'll start with the cake so it can bake while we make the spanakopita."

I'm almost positive I was staring at Claire with a *what the fuck* expression. When she gave them instructions on how to start the cake, she walked over to me and pulled me to the side. "I'm sorry. I wanted to give you a heads up but you got here last minute, and then when I saw you in the hall, well, it slipped my mind."

"It slipped your mind! It. Slipped. Your. Mind? Thano's Greek. He destroyed my heart. Did I mention he is Greek? How many Greek men have I gone out with? Oh, let me think." Lifting my eyes up, I acted like I was thinking before shooting her a look. "That's right. There's only been the one!"

She nodded. "I know this, and that's why I was trying to give you a heads up. But Katerina called and said it was a group thing. I don't know what I was thinking. I thought it would be fun to make something Greek for them. Plus, the other people in the class will love this!"

I peeked over my shoulder and watched as Katerina and the other Greek women corrected the other students on how they were mixing the ingredients. "She looks like Thano," I whispered.

Claire looked at her. "There is no way. Don't all Greek people look the same?"

I shot my head back and looked at her. "What? That's so rude!"

"Well, I don't know! Come on it's ruder to be over here whispering off to the side."

I followed her hesitantly. Taking a deep breath, I headed down to see who needed help as Claire stayed at the front and went over the instructions. The next thing I knew, Katerina was up with Claire. She had taken over the instructions and I couldn't help but laugh when she took complete control over everything.

Standing in the middle of the group of Greek women, I totally forgot about Thano. Which was weird since I was submerged in all things Greek. These women were powerful, strong-minded, beautiful women. And funny as hell.

"So, Katerina, what made you pick these dishes?" Claire asked.

With a huge smile, she replied, "Oh, that's an easy question to answer. They are my youngest son's favorite dishes."

Claire smiled as another girl in the crowd asked the next question. "I've heard about Greek men! What's his name and is he single?"

Everyone laughed, including me. When I looked back up, Katerina was staring directly at me. Her green eyes seemed to be penetrating right to mine.

"His name is Athanasios, and you'd have to ask him if his heart is taken or not."

It felt as if all the air had been sucked out of the room. The glass dish I'd been holding in my hand slipped and fell to the floor.

Shattering everywhere as I felt my legs go weak and I whispered, "Thano."

## twenty

### Thano

"SO, HOW LONG ARE YOU going to walk around pouting?"

Glancing over to my brother, Nicholaus, I screwed my face up. "What are you talking about?"

With a roll of his eyes, he pushed out a frustrated breath. "Thano, it's been a month since you and your little Irish girl hooked up."

"Don't call her that."

"Is she not Irish?"

Blowing out a breath, I watched as the cold air made it look like smoke.

"So are you ignoring me now, Thano?"

Turning to him, I replied, "No. I thought we came up here to hunt. I haven't been elk hunting in forever and all you want to do is talk about if Kilyn is Irish or not."

"Is she?" Nicholaus asked in a hushed voice.

With a frustrated moan, I put my gun down. "Yes. Yes she is Irish, Nicholaus."

Trying to hold in his laughter, he replied, "Mom's going to be pissed!"

My heart felt shattered thinking of Kilyn. "I don't care what Mom thinks. It doesn't really matter anyway; I fucked things up with her."

"So, make it right."

I stared out over the mountains. It had snowed a bit and everything was covered with a light powder of white. It was so peaceful and beautiful. A part of me wanted to stay up here, hidden from everything. "I don't know if I can."

"Do you love her, Thano?"

Not even having to think about it, my response was natural. "Yes. I mean, I don't know how fast you can fall in love with someone, but I know I was falling in love with her. All I think about is her. When I close my eyes I see hers. Hell, I don't even feel complete knowing I won't see her each day. It's like something is missing."

"Jesus, dude. You've got it bad. Must be that luck of the Irish thing."

With a light chuckle, I shook my head. "None of that matters to me."

"So go after her. What's the problem?"

Looking at my older brother, I frowned. I'd always been close to both my brothers. They may act like jerks sometimes, but they had hearts of gold. "She thinks I'm in love with Savannah and that she'll always be second best to that."

"Is she right?"

The guilt was still there, but it was slowly slipping away day by day. "No. It's the opposite. When I was with Kilyn, she brought out emotions I'd never felt before. My body craved her in a way I'd never experienced before."

Nicholaus nodded his head. "Not even with Savannah?"

"Nope, not even with her. Hell, I even found myself saying things to Kilyn in Greek. I never once uttered a word to Savannah in Greek."

Nicholaus chuckled. "Damn, dude, that was the first thing I discovered with women. You speak to them in another language and those panties are falling to the floor."

I wasn't going to argue with him on that. By the look in Kilyn's eyes, I knew it turned her on even more.

"So, what are you going to do?"

With a shrug, I looked back out as I grabbed the gun. "At first I thought I would give her time. But yesterday I found out she left the gym we both worked out at and her business partner and best friend let it slip that she was also moving. She's doing whatever she can to put distance between us."

"That sucks, dude."

It did suck. But I knew in my heart Kilyn was the one. I felt it deep in my soul. "I don't want to rush with this. I need her to know that I'm one hundred and ten percent committed to her and that Savannah is my past." With a slight smile, I nodded my head. I was going to fight for her. Fight with everything I had in me. "My future only belongs to Kilyn."

My brother stared at me for the longest time before he scrunched his face up. "What the fuck dude . . . when did you turn into a pussy?"

With a chuckle, I pushed him on the arm. "Fuck off, asshole. You're jealous because I have not only the good looks but the words for the ladies."

"Please. I've gotten more pussy in the last year than you have in your lifetime."

Narrowing my eyes, I asked, "And that makes you happy?"

"It certainly makes my dick happy. Who wants to argue with a happy dick?"

"Uh . . . your unhappy heart?"

Lifting his gun, he aimed and smiled. "At least I'm not the one who has to tell Mom you're in love with an Irish girl."

When he fired the rifle, I turned and watched the elk drop right on the spot. I wasn't sure how in the hell that thing didn't hear us talking . . . or maybe it did and couldn't of cared less.

Glancing my way, he flashed me a smile and winked. "Looks like it was my lucky day."

"HOW DO YOU LIKE EVERYTHING?" Claire asked as she stood in my kitchen with Blake.

I glanced around my finished cabin. Everything was perfect and, in some small way it, felt like a piece of Kilyn was in every room.

"It looks great. Is um, is Kilyn not going to be here today?"

Claire looked away. "Um. Normally she would be here but—"

The doorbell rang and Claire breathed a sigh of relief as I made my way over to answer it. When I opened it and saw her, my heart skipped a beat and my stomach dipped.

"Kilyn."

With a forced smile, she stood a bit taller. "I'm sorry I was late. I wasn't sure I would be able to make it."

Feeling like an idiot for standing there, I opened the door wider and motioned for her to come in. After a moment of hesitating, she walked in. She quickly smiled from ear to ear as she took in the finished cabin.

"Claire and Blake are in the kitchen," I said.

I followed her as she walked around the corner and into the kitchen. When she gasped, I smiled. Claire had made the off comment that the kitchen was exactly like the one Kilyn had wanted for her own house someday. I knew then that Kilyn had put more into this design than she would ever admit.

"It's beautiful. Blake, your guys did a great job as usual."

Blake grinned. "Well, they had a good plan to work off of. Are the colors what you envisioned? I know sometimes they can look different once they're up and in the house.

Kilyn shook her head. "No, they're perfect. Exactly how I imagined it."

After quickly touring each room, Kilyn walked back into the kitchen with a satisfied smile. "Everything looks perfect."

Turning to me, she asked, "Are you happy with everything, Thano?"

I wanted desperately to say no, I wouldn't be happy until she was in my arms.

"Totally. Everything looks amazing."

*Pussy.*

The front door flew open and instantly I felt my chest tighten when I heard my mother's voice. She rushed into the kitchen followed by my grandmother, Aunt Maria, Sophia, and finally my father.

Turning to look at Kilyn, I pinched my eyebrows together in confusion when I saw the horrified look on both her face and Claire's.

My mother came to a stop and looked directly at Kilyn.

It was so quiet you could hear a pin drop. Oh, and maybe my heart about to pound right the fuck out of my chest.

"Kilyn! Claire! Come . . . come, come and give me a hug."

My jaw dropped to the ground as I watched my mother engulf both girls in a hug.

"You look beautiful, Kilyn." Turning to my grandmother, she asked, "Doesn't she look beautiful, Yiayia."

Oh, no. No. No. No.

My grandmother walked up and spit on Kilyn, causing her to let out a small yelp and jump back.

"Did she just spit on her?" Blake asked in a whispered voice from behind.

Slowly nodding my head, I replied, "Not really. They make the sound of spitting."

"Tell me that's a Greek thing, dude, or I'm not sure how I feel about your family's treatment toward Kilyn."

I couldn't help but let out a small chuckle. "Totally a Greek thing."

Blake chuckled and said, "Priceless. Look at their faces. Kilyn looks like she's afraid to move."

My mother held onto Kilyn as she asked, "So, are you practicing on that dish?"

*Dish?*

Kilyn risked peeking over to me before her eyes snapped back over to my mother. "Um . . . I am, actually."

"Ah . . . see, even the Irish are smart when they want to be. You drink too much, but you can be smart."

*What in the fuck?*

"Mama, um, how . . . do you know . . . wait . . . what's going on? What dish are you talking about?"

My mother waved me off with her hands. "I want to taste your honey cake when you have it perfected. Now, I want to see this house Kilyn decorated for you, Athanasios. Show your family around."

Oh, dear God. My mother sought out Kilyn. Why? Was she forcing Kilyn to cook Greek food? I knew I should not have mentioned her to my mother. She used her evil ways to track her down.

"Athanasios? Are you going to stand there like a bump on a log or are you going to show me the house?"

"You've seen it," I mumbled.

Narrowing her eyes, my mother took a step closer to me as my father cleared his throat.

"Here we go," he said under his breath.

"Is that how you're going to treat your Mitera after I climbed the mountain to see your little project?"

My face constricted. "Climbed? You drove up here with Dad."

"And what about your Yiayia? She'll die before she ever gets back up here again."

My grandmother nodded her head. "I will. Who is hungry? I have some pita bread in my bag."

Everyone turned and looked at her as she pulled out the bread.

Blake lifted his hand, "Oh! I'll have some. I love pita bread."

Yiayia smiled and handed the bread to Blake as Claire stared at him with a look of pure shock.

Pushing my hand through my hair, I let out a frustrated moan.

"Katerina, let me show you around since I know all the colors and everything." Kilyn said with a smile.

My mother grinned as my grandmother walked up to Kilyn. "I want to see the master bedroom where the babies will be made." Turning to me she narrowed her eyes. "That is, if I live that long at the rate Athanasios is going."

Kilyn looked at me and I saw the sadness in her eyes.

Once they walked off, I turned to my father. "Dad, why do you just stand there and let her talk?"

He looked at me like I had grown two heads. "Athanasios, let me tell you something about women. Both of you come closer to me," he said motioning for both Blake and me to get closer.

"You pick your battles. This was one I wasn't ready to fight because trust me, by the end of the day she'll give me at least ten other reasons to argue with her."

My shoulders slumped over and I dropped my head. "Dear Lord in heaven, please help me," I whispered. Looking back up at my father, I asked the one thing I wasn't sure I wanted to know the answer to.

"How does she know Kilyn?"

Letting out a roar of laughter, my father sat down on one of the stools at the kitchen island. "You come home one day and tell your mother you're falling in love with a girl and her name is Kilyn. Oh, and by the way she's not Greek and she is designing my house. You practically threw the girl into the lion's den with your own hands. You mentioned meeting her at the Onion Creek place. Your mother is smart. She did some research."

"Oh, no."

With a smirk, he replied. "It was the whole lot of them. Your mother, Aunt Maria, your other Aunt Maria, your Aunt Agnes, Sophia, your cousin Sophia, and I believe your cousins Angie and Maria were there."

Blake turned and looked at me. "Do Greeks believe in recycling names or something?"

With a stony expression, I stared at Blake as he replied, "What? It is a legitimate question!"

Putting my attention back on my father, I asked, "Did Mom say or do anything to let Kilyn know she was my mother?"

"That you would have to ask your mother, but if I had to put money on it I'd say she did."

"Fuck!"

"I'll wash that fucking mouth of yours out with soap young man if you curse like that again."

Blake laughed. "But you said—"

Holding up my hand, I cast a warning to Blake. "Don't. Just leave it."

Hearing my mother's voice grow closer, I said a silent prayer she hadn't messed things up even more with Kilyn.

They walked up and my eyes bounced around looking for Kilyn.

My mother walked up to me and kissed me on both cheeks. "Kilyn slipped out the side door. Said she had to get back into town to meet with another client. Very nice, your Irish girl. Very smart with the colors too."

I was positive my mother saw the look of pure disappointment on my face.

"Yeah. She is."

Blake and Claire were the next to excuse themselves. This was it. I had no other excuse to have Kilyn here. I had her right in my reach and I let her slip away.

Again.

# twenty-one

## Kilyn

THE DOOR TO MY OFFICE flew open as I let out a scream and slammed the book I was reading shut.

"Whatcha reading?"

Glaring at Claire, I shook my head. "Did you forget how to knock?"

With a smirk, she sat down and propped her feet up on my desk. "You didn't answer me."

I leaned back in my chair and inspected her carefully. She was up to something. "Well, you didn't answer me either."

"Nope, I asked first."

Letting out an exasperated sigh, I sat up. "For Christ's sake, Claire, what do you want?"

"I want to know what you're reading and then I want to know why you felt like you had to sneak out of Thano's house yesterday. You left me with Katerina and . . . what was her name? Yeeyaw? Heehaw? Shit, it was something like that."

With a shocked laugh, I asked, "Are you serious? Why did I sneak out? The whole tour his grandmother kept mentioning Thano having babies. His mother must have mentioned a dozen times about me being Irish and not to mention she knew who I was when she came to the cooking class, Claire! Do you understand that? She came to check out who the evil leprechaun was going after her precious Greek god son!"

Claire sat there with a screwed up face. "Did you just call yourself a leprechaun?"

Adjusting in my seat, I looked out the window. "It was the first thing that came to my mind."

When she busted out laughing, I couldn't help but do the same.

We laughed so hard we had tears running down our cheeks. Every time I tried to say something, I laughed harder.

"I'm. Going. To. Pee. My. Pants!" Claire gasped.

The light knock on the door had us both looking up. I jumped up with a start, causing Claire to lose her balance and fall out of the chair.

The guy standing on the other side of my office was drop dead gorgeous. Not as gorgeous as Thano, but he was for sure easy on the eyes.

"Excuse me, Ms. O'Kelly?"

"Yes," Claire and I said at once. I quickly shot a look over to Claire who let out a nervous chuckle.

"Sorry. She's Ms. O'Kelly and I'm totally going to excuse myself."

The guy flashed a smile and a dimple on each cheek appeared. Claire turned to me and dropped her mouth open as she mouthed. Holy shit!

Walking around my desk, I met him half way as he entered my office.

"I'm Kilyn O'Kelly. May I help you?"

"Dale Conner."

Hmm, even his name was dreamy. Then it hit me. "Oh my God. Mr. Conner's son! I'm so sorry, Mr. Conner. I totally forgot we had that shopping trip booked. When your father called me yesterday to say you were stepping in, it totally slipped my mind. Please forgive me."

It was then I noticed he was still holding onto my hand. Lifting it to his lips, he smiled as he kissed the back of my hand. "Trust me, Ms. O'Kelly, you have nothing to apologize for. The fact is, I was dreading this afternoon until I realized that I get to spend an afternoon with the most beautiful woman in Colorado."

My face heated as he looked at me with hungry eyes. Maybe this was what I needed to put a little more distance between Thano and me.

"Why, Mr. Conner, flattery will get you everywhere."

He lifted his eyebrows and softly replied, "Let's hope."

Swallowing hard, I tried to remember this was a client and this stupid flirting was bound to get me into trouble. Especially since deep down inside I knew I didn't want to do what he clearly wanted to do.

It was time to ease up on the flirting and kick it more into professional mode.

"Well," I said releasing a breath and smiling. "Let's concentrate on picking out some fabric swatches and paint colors."

"Then afterwards, dinner?"

Pressing my lips tightly together, I forced a smile. "Let's just get through the afternoon shall we?"

THE NEXT THREE HOURS HAD me laughing for the first time in almost a month. Dale was not only handsome, but funny as well. We had a ton in common and it turned out he was an art major and worked for an art gallery in Denver. He even loved the opera.

"So what made you interested in art?" I asked as we strolled through Acacia Park.

With a wide grin, he replied, "Probably my mother. She loves anything to do with art. She's a painter, and I remember sitting when I was little and watching her paint. I thought it was the coolest thing ever to watch her take a white canvas and add the most beautiful things to it. Flowers are her favorite thing to paint."

"I love painting, but I'm afraid I'm not that good at it. Now give me a room to draw out and I can do that no problem!"

Dale laughed. "Have you always wanted to be a designer?"

I may have been enjoying myself, but I was not opening up with Dale like I had Thano. "Yep. Pretty much. I'm a tad bit boring."

"So, how about dinner?"

Searching desperately for my body to tell me I was attracted to Dale, I chewed on my lip. A part of me was screaming to just go have dinner and enjoy the company of a good-looking man. The other part of me was screaming out Thano's name.

"Where did you have in mind?"

His eyes lit up, but I held up my hand. "Strictly business. That's it."

He pretended to pout but nodded his head. "For now. We'll see if I can change your mind by the end of dinner."

I instantly didn't like the over confident and smug way he thought he was going to get me to change my mind.

He called for a taxi and held the door open for me. The next thing I knew we were pulling up to the Blue Star. It was a tapas bar I'd been to a number of times. The moment we walked in, something in the air changed. Goose bumps raced over my body and I swore someone was watching me.

Dale motioned for me to follow the waitress. When he placed his hand on my lower back, I quickly picked up my pace so his hand fell away.

My gaze bounced around the bar. I couldn't shake the feeling someone's eyes were on me.

I took a seat and set my purse on the chair next to me.

"Would you like to pick out the wine, Kilyn?"

Still looking around, I completely ignored Dale.

"Kilyn? Are you even with me?"

Snapping my eyes back to him, I grinned and said, "I'm sorry. I had the strangest feeling someone was watching me."

Dale looked around and then put his attention back on me. "That's because the most beautiful girl in the room walked in. All eyes were on you."

There went my cheeks heating up again. "Anyway, what were you asking?"

"Wine?"

"Please, you pick," I responded as I reached for my purse and took out my phone. I sent a quick text to Claire to let her know I was having dinner with Dale. When she didn't answer right away, I pulled up my email. When there was nothing there from Thano, I cursed myself for hoping there would be.

Who was I kidding? Thano was stuck in the past and I was walking around reading books about the Greek culture and trying like hell to figure out why his grandmother spit on me three times. I finally got the answer today in the book I had bought at Barnes and Noble.

"You're lost in thought."

Making myself smile, I shook my head. "Sorry. I've got a lot on my mind with projects and such."

We quickly got lost in an easy conversation. I had to admit, Dale would be easy to date and he was probably good in bed. Not as good as Thano, but I'm sure he would be okay.

Looking away, I closed my eyes. Jesus. Am I really now settling for some guy so I can forget Thano?

My breath caught in my throat and I opened my eyes. His green eyes pierced mine almost immediately.

"Thano," I whispered.

He was standing with his best friend Gus and two women.

Placing my hand on my stomach, I tried to keep down the sick feeling I had growing.

He's on a date.

He's moved on.

When he glanced over and looked at Dale, his eyes turned angry. Was he really going to be upset that I was out with someone when he had some bleach blonde on his arm?

Fuck that.

Looking away, I focused back on Dale. "So, how often to you come to Colorado Springs?"

Taking a drink of his wine, he placed it back on the table. My heart was racing as I felt Thano's eyes on me. That's why it felt like someone was watching me. Thano had seen us walk in.

"I try to come at least once a week to help my father. This family cabin is important to him. Family is actually important to him. He wants a place we can all get together and spend holidays and such with."

Smiling, I tried like hell to ignore the burning feeling my body felt from Thano's stare. I took a chance and glanced back over to them. They were still standing; it appeared Gus's date had spilled her wine. I hope it got all over Thano's stupid tan pants that looked so damn good on him.

When he smiled at me, I looked back to Dale.

"Well, I hope that we can make it a place your family will feel at home in."

"Oh, I don't doubt it. I've seen your work. I'm really impressed, especially since you really haven't been in business for all that long."

Reaching for the wine, I tried like hell to keep my hand from shaking.

"Are you okay, Kilyn?" Dale asked with a concerned look on his face.

"Um, yes. I think I need to use the ladies room though for a minute, if you'll excuse me."

He stood when I stood and I couldn't help think that was very sweet of him. I took the long way around to the restrooms so I wouldn't have to walk near Thano and his date.

Once I made it into the restroom, I sucked in a few deep breaths. My phone buzzed in my purse.

Pulling it out, my heart dropped to my stomach when I saw Thano's name.

*Thano: Who is the guy you're with?*

My eyes widened and I was positive my jaw hit the ground.

"Are you fucking kidding me? How dare he!"

Tapping angrily on my phone, I replied back to his text.

*Me: A client. Who's the bleach blonde? Your latest ladybug?*

After I hit send, I covered my mouth. "Oh, God," I whispered. "Why did I say that?"

I waited for ten minutes and Thano never replied back. I couldn't blame him. What I said was cruel and I knew it.

With a frustrated moan, I dropped my phone back into my purse and covered my face with my hands. Screaming into them, I dropped them back to my side and counted to twenty.

Opening my eyes, I decided it was time to cut this dinner short. Dale would be upset, but I'd tell him I was not feeling well all of a sudden. After all, I'd been locked away for ten minutes in the restroom.

I reached for the bathroom door and walked out, only to be grabbed by the arm and dragged down the hall by Thano. He slammed me up against the wall and looked into my eyes.

My chest was heaving as I tried like hell to pull in air. He was piercing my gaze with his dark angry eyes, and holy hell was it turning me on.

"What in the fuck did that mean?"

I knew what he was talking about, but for some reason, I egged him on. "What did what mean?"

"My latest ladybug? Do you really think I go around picking up women and having sex with them?"

Lifting my chin, I replied, "I don't know. Do you? For all I know you've already whispered in her ear in Greek. Maybe telling her how beautiful she is."

Thano hit the wall next to my head, causing me to let out a small scream. I'd never seen him so angry. The funny thing was, I wasn't the least bit afraid because I knew he would never hurt me. If anything, I was the one who hurt him with my comment.

"Do you have any idea how torn apart I've been, Kilyn?"

Searching his face, I looked back into his eyes. "No. If you were so torn apart, why haven't you . . ."

I looked away.

"Why haven't I what?"

Peering back at him, my voice was angry. "Called me, Thano. Reached out in some way to let me know you were so torn apart. For all I know, you've been completely fine. I mean, you're on a date, so you must not be that torn apart."

"It's Gus' sister."

Pinching my eyebrows together, I asked, "What?"

"The girl I'm with, it's Gus's sister. Both of them are his sisters. They just got into town and Gus asked if I wanted to come along. I've known them since they were little."

*Oh, hell.*

"Well, that doesn't matter because you have done nothing to reach out to me so—there!"

He pulled his head back. "So there? What are we, in middle school, Kilyn?"

I sunk my teeth into my lip and tried like hell to come back with one of those witty replies that always seem to escape until twenty minutes later when it hits me.

Lifting his hand, he pushed a piece of hair behind my ear. "I've missed you so much, ladybug."

My eyes closed and I fought like hell to keep my tears back.

His lips moved across my neck, causing my entire body to tremble. "I miss you in my arms, Kilyn."

I slowly shook my head.

"Even if you haven't missed me, please say you have. I think it would kill me if you told me something else."

Opening my mouth, I tried to force myself to talk, but my throat burned as I tried to keep my emotions at bay.

When his lips moved up and pressed against my ear, my knees went weak. I reached for his arms and held on with all my might.

"I've missed your laugh, ladybug. The way you make me feel like I'm the only person in the room when you talk to me. I need to feel your lips pressed against mine or I may go crazy."

The small hallway was beginning to spin. "Please tell me you'll give me another chance. I want to show you how much I love you so badly."

A small sob slipped from my lips as I pulled my head back and searched his face. "Wh-what?"

"Let me make love to you tonight. Please."

*Oh, dear God, yes.*

What happens to me when this man is near me? I'm left defenseless when I'm in his arms.

"But, what about Savannah?"

Cupping my face within his hands, he stared at me with such intensity I held my breath waiting for his words. "Look into my eyes, Kilyn."

I did what he asked. His green eyes were bright as the sun. The sadness and darkness I saw in them before was now gone.

"She is my past and you are my future. We both have scars, Kilyn, but I know they will fade in time if we're together."

He grabbed my hand and placed it on his chest. "You're the only woman who has ever truly been here. Right here in my heart. Without you, I'm nothing. With you, I'm hundred percent complete. You have moved me out of the darkness and into the light and, I swear, I will spend the rest of my life showing you how much I adore and love you."

Every nerve ending in my body tingled as my heart rate quickened. With a soft expression, I whispered, "If you say something to me in Greek I'm pretty sure you will be guaranteed to have me in your bed tonight."

The smile that spread across his face caused me to giggle.

Leaning over, he brushed his lips lightly over mine and whispered, "Se agapó."

My lower stomach pulled with desire. "Wh-what did you say?" I asked against his lips.

He slowly kissed along my jaw until I felt his hot breath against my neck. When he nipped at my earlobe, I moaned. There was never a moment in my life where I was so turned on.

"I said . . . I love you."

## twenty-two

### Thano

KILYN PRACTICALLY MELTED INTO MY body when I whispered in her ear that I loved her. Her body shook as she gazed lovingly into my eyes.

With a beautiful smile, she softly said, "I hope you know you just changed the whole game."

With a chuckle, I winked. "And you know I'm playing for keeps, right?"

Her eyes sparkled and practically lit up the dark hallway. "What about me not being Greek? I still haven't perfected that damn honey cake thing your mother said was your favorite."

Laughing, I pressed my lips to hers. With her arms wrapping around my neck, we quickly got lost in each other.

I barely heard a male's voice clear his throat. Pressing myself into Kilyn, she moaned into my mouth and it took everything out of me not to take her right here.

"Um . . . excuse me? Kilyn?"

Breaking our kiss, she whipped her head to the side. "Dale. Oh, gosh, I totally forgot all about you."

Ouch. Not what any guy wants to hear under any circumstances.

With a frown, Dale asked, "Am I interrupting something?"

Not really knowing where this guy thought he was going to get with Kilyn, I decided to make a statement loud and clear.

"Yes, me getting back together with my girlfriend."

Kilyn looked back at me, her mouth gaped open. We never really were officially dating so I'm sure my declaration came as a surprise, and I hoped like hell she didn't get upset with me.

When she slowly smiled, I knew I was in the clear.

"I see. So does this mean our dinner is being cut short, Kilyn?"

Cutting in before she could say something, I laughed. "Hell no. Why don't the two of you join us? My friend Gus's sisters are in town and I'm sure they would love for someone new to join our group."

Dale looked at Kilyn and then back to me. "Sure. Why not. I'm not ready to call it an evening yet."

Lacing my fingers with Kilyn's, I lead them both over to our table. "Gus, Casandra, Lacy, this is Kilyn and one of her clients, Dale."

Casandra and Lacy both eye fucked the hell out of Dale and I knew he was no longer my problem. "Client?" Lucy asked.

"I'm an interior designer. Dale's father has a house in the mountains I'm decorating."

Casandra perked up and patted the seat between her and Lucy. Dale quickly took it.

"Ah . . . I'll grab our drinks," Kilyn said as she watched Dale completely become engrossed with Gus's sisters. Gus, of course, did a quick hello and focused back in on the girl at the next table.

"I'll help you," I said, placing my hand on her lower back and following her over to the table. Grabbing Dale's drink, I motioned to let the waitress know Kilyn and Dale were now joining our table.

Kilyn chuckled as we made our way back. "I'm pretty sure we could drop the drinks off and slip right on out without anyone noticing we're gone."

Wiggling my eyebrows, I asked, "Is your work with Dale done?"

She flashed me a seductive smile. "Yep."

We set the drinks down and I grabbed a few twenty-dollar bills out of my wallet and tossed them onto the table.

Taking Kilyn's hand in mine, I practically dragged her out. "Did you drive here?"

"No, my car is still at the office. Did you?"

Reaching my hand, I waved for a taxi. "No, Gus drove."

I could practically feel the desire pooling off of Kilyn. The sooner I got her back to my place the better.

Once the taxi pulled up, I held the door open for her as she slipped in. Giving him my address, I quickly pulled her over to me and pressed my lips to hers.

When my phone started ringing, we both groaned. Pulling it out of my pocket, I rolled my eyes when I saw it was my mother.

"It's like she has hidden cameras everywhere."

Kilyn giggled as she settled in next to me. God it felt good having her with me.

"Hey, Mama."

"Athanasios, your father needs you to come over and help him with this bookshelf."

"Now?"

She made a tsking sound and said, "Yes, now. Thaddeus and Nicholaus are not answering their phones. You father is going to kill himself if you don't come help."

I silently cursed my brothers. "I'm kind of in the middle of something; can I come over tomorrow and help him?"

My mother started yelling at my father in Greek as Kilyn covered her mouth and laughed.

"Tomorrow? Tomorrow I could be dead!"

Oh, Lord. Now she sounds like Yiayia. "Mama, I seriously don't think you'll die before Dad gets the bookshelf up."

"You don't know that, Athanasios. No one can predict these things. What are you doing that you are so busy you can't come help your father?"

I knew I was about open up Pandora's Box, but what the hell.

"I'm on a date."

Kilyn's hands dropped to her lap while her mouth gaped open. "Thano!" she whispered.

For the first time in a long time I did the unthinkable.

I silenced my mother.

"Did you say you were on a date? Dimitris! Your youngest son is on a date."

I could hear my father saying something in the background but I couldn't make it out.

"Praise the heavens above. Bring her to me."

My eyes about popped out of my head. "What?"

"Now. Bring me this girl so I can see who has captured my son's heart."

"Um . . ." Turning to Kilyn she wore a look of horror on her face. She slowly shook her head.

"Um . . . Mama, we sort of had plans and I'm not sure we can change them."

"Have you eaten?"

"No . . . I mean, yes! Yes, we ate."

Just then Kilyn's stomach growled. She laughed and my mother heard her.

"Awe! Your stomach tells the truth. I'll put a little something on; it won't take long. I'll see you in about thirty minutes."

Feeling a sense of panic wash over me that I was losing control of this conversation, I called out, "Wait! We can't, Mama! You've already met her!"

Pulling the phone from my ear, I stared at it.

"She hung up."

I turned to look at Kilyn. Her mouth was open as she stared at me. "I don't know whether to laugh or cry."

"Same."

With a long drawn out moan, I dropped my head back against the seat. "I fucked up. Again."

"What happens if we don't go?"

"She will call my cell over and over as she drives to my apartment. If I'm not there I wouldn't be surprised if she turns on the tracker. I'm almost positive she has one on each of her son's phones."

Kilyn laughed while taking my hand in hers. "She's going to find out sooner or later. We might as well get it over with."

She began looking over her body.

"What are you doing?"

"Seeing if I have anything I really love on before your mother or grandmother spits on me."

I stared at her for a few seconds before I lost it laughing. "What makes you think they'll spit on you? And they don't actually spit, anymore. They just make the noise."

She lifted her eyebrow. "Says you. If either one of them compliments me, I get spit on. I've been reading up on Greek superstitions and all of that."

My heart jumped as I looked at her. "You have?"

With a sweeter than sweet smile, she nodded. "I have."

Slipping my hand around her neck, I pulled her lips to mine and kissed them. When I pulled back some, I searched her face. "You have no idea how happy that makes me."

Without taking my eyes off of her, I told the taxi driver we had a change of plans and gave him my parents' address.

It didn't matter if my parents loved or hated Kilyn. I had nothing to prove to them and, although I wanted their approval, I didn't need it.

Kilyn's eyes dropped to my lips as she licked her own. "I have to be honest with you, Thano."

"Please always be honest with me, ladybug."

Lifting her eyes to mine, she scrunched her nose up in the most adorable way and said, "I'm scared to death for your parents to find out about me."

With a lighthearted laugh, I put my arm around her shoulders and pulled her to me. "Somehow, I think it's going to be okay."

"How do you know?"

I shrugged and said, "Because my mother already likes you."

"She doesn't even know me."

"That's not true. She has met you a few times. And that whole thing with her and her posse showing up at the Onion Creek Gardens, that was totally planned."

Kilyn pulled back some to look at me. "It was?"

"Yep. I had told my mother about you. She started piecing things together and took it upon herself to go check you out."

Now it was her turn to let out a moan and drop her head back. "Oh, dear God. Thano, I made such a fool out of myself that day. I totally messed up the dishes and I dropped something and broke it. Oh, God! This is bad! This. Is. So. Bad."

My heart felt so full and I was surprised I wasn't the least bit worried about the wrath of my mother. Pulling Kilyn onto my lap, I lifted her chin and looked into her eyes. "This is not bad. This is you and I finding our way back to each other. I don't think it was a coincidence you and I running into each other all those times. We were meant to be together. Even if I couldn't see it at first, I've always known it in my heart. All we have to do is show up, eat some food, help my father with some bookshelf and then I'm taking you home and making love to you all night."

She lifted her eyebrows. "All night, huh?"

I gently kissed around her face. "All night."

"Is that a Greek thing . . . the stamina?"

I could feel my body heating as Kilyn squirmed about in my lap. "Hell, yes, that's a Greek thing."

Sinking her teeth into her lip, she smiled big. "I think I'm going to like having a Greek boyfriend."

"Oh, baby, trust me. There are so many things about having a Greek boyfriend you're going to love."

Pushing her ass against my hard dick, she winked. "Starting with this?"

A low growl came from the back of my throat as I whispered against her lips. "Me trelaíneis, Kilyn."

# twenty-three

## Kilyn

I HAD NO IDEA WHAT Thano whispered and I didn't care. I was too lost in his kiss to care about anything. The way he made me feel was unlike anything I'd ever experienced before.

The kiss was broken much sooner than I would have liked as the taxi driver cleared his throat. "We're almost there, sir."

With a pout, I slipped off his lap and sat next to him as Thano chuckled. Reaching into his wallet he pulled out money. When the taxi pulled up to what I was guessing was Thano's parents' house I stared out the window.

Holy. Shit. The house was amazing. It was beautiful.

"Thanks so much," Thano said to the driver as he slipped out quickly and reached for my hand.

"Do I look okay?" I asked.

Thano laughed. "They've seen you before up at the cabin."

Tilting my head, I narrowed my eyes at him. "Well, up at the cabin we hadn't been sucking face and your hands weren't all up in my stuff."

"Your stuff?"

I hit him on the chest and dragged in a deep breath. Thank goodness I wore dress slacks today. Checking to make sure everything was in place, I looked up at him and nodded.

"I'm ready."

"You say that now."

Thano placed his hand on my lower back and began guiding me to the front door. Stopping. I frantically looked at him. "What do you mean?"

"Nothing, ladybug. Let's get this over with."

My heart began beating harder and I felt like I had just run in a marathon. I started sweating, my breath was labored, and my legs felt like jelly.

This was such a bad idea.

*Was that my pulse I felt in my throat? Oh, Christ.*

By the time we got to the top step, the massive wood door flew open.

Katerina stood there with a smile on her face. And behind her were all the women from the day they came to the Onion Creek Gardens.

"Are your parents having a party?" I asked in a hushed voice.

Thano chuckled and pushed me in front of him. He was feeding me to the lions.

Walking up, I dragged in a deep breath and smiled. Katerina looked me over and stepped to the side along with everyone else.

Thano followed closely behind me as we walked into a massive foyer. I didn't dare look around . . . what if that was rude in the Greek culture?

Damn it! Why didn't I buy that other book? Why didn't I finish reading the one I bought?

Thano's mother shut the door and walked up to me. No one said a word.

"She isn't Greek," someone whispered as Thano clasped his hand in mine.

When my eyes met Katerina's, something happened. I wasn't sure what it was, but I knew it was good.

Placing her hands on my arms, her face grew into a wide smile.

"Thank the heavens above it's you he brought home!"

My eyes widened with a dazed look. A rush of adrenaline tingled through my body as I turned to look at Thano. He wore the same expression I was positive I had. Looking back at Katerina, I opened my mouth to say something but nothing came out.

"Are you feeling okay, Katerina?" someone asked from behind her.

"I am feeling wonderful! My Athanasios is in love and with the beautiful Irish Kilyn!"

I cringed and waited for the spitting to happen but it didn't. The rest of the room was in total shock. Too stunned to commence with the spitting.

Grabbing my hand, Katerina pulled me into the house as we made our way into a huge dining room. My eyes about popped out of my head when I saw all the food.

"Jesus, Mama. When did you cook all of this?"

Katerina shot Thano a dirty look before turning back to me. "Kilyn, you sit here with Yiayia. Athanasios, you sit on her other side."

Thano and I did as his mother said. When I sat down, I turned to Thano's grandmother. She gave me a polite smile, but then said, "You're not Greek."

I smiled nervously, as I replied, "No ma'am, I'm not."

"You're the Irish girl."

Deep breaths. Deep. Breaths.

"Yes, Yiayia, this is Kilyn."

"Oh! Yiayia is grandmother!" I blurted out. Why was that now just hitting me?

Everyone turned and looked at me.

Katerina leaned over to, whom if I remembered right, was her cousin Maria and said, "The Irish always were a little slow."

Maria nodded her head. "It's all that beer they drink. Does something to the brain cells."

I turned to Thano and leaned closer to him. "They do know I can hear them, right?"

He smiled. "Oh, they know."

With a nod, I replied, "Just making sure."

The next thing I knew, every kind of Greek dish was pushed my way. Even if I tried to pass over it, Yiayia was spooning some onto my plate.

"You're too skinny. Now, Katerina, she could stand to drop a few pounds, but we need to get some meat on you for the babies."

I glanced down at my already overflowing plate and swallowed hard.

My head popped up.

*Wait. What? Babies?*

Good Lord what was all of this food? I picked up a skewer that had the most delicious looking food on it.

"Souvlaki," Thano said. "It's pork tenderloin and veggies."

My mouth began to water when I realized I hadn't eaten since morning and I was starving. Using my fork to slip the food off the skewer, I took a bite and was instantly in heaven.

"Ohmygawd," I whispered.

Thano wiggled his eyebrows and took a huge bite of something that looked like a pastry-filled delight!

He pointed to it and said, "It's basically chicken in a patty."

I dug into that next dish. It was better than the pork.

*Shit. I'm going to gain twenty pounds just from this dinner.*

Katerina handed me a dish and said, "Moussaka. Get a good helping of that. It's Athanasios' favorite."

Doing as she said, I took a generous helping and then took a bite. Holy crap. It was like lasagna but ten times better.

"Have you ever had Greek food before, Kilyn?" Dimitris asked.

Shaking my head, I replied, "No. I mean I've had a Gyro before and what Katerina cooked at cooking class that day, but that's about all."

He gave me a warm smile. "My Katerina is a good cook. She can teach you."

Thano grabbed my thigh and squeezed it under the table causing my entire body to enflame.

I turned to Katerina only to see her watching me intensely. "I'd love that very much."

Her face turned up in a full-fledged smile. I was instantly reminded of my own mother and all the times I helped her in the kitchen.

More food was passed around as Thad and Nicholaus showed up. The look on their faces when they saw me sitting at their parents' table was priceless. There was so much chatter and everyone talking at once that I had a hard time keeping up with everything.

When Katerina stood, she announced she was clearing the table for dessert.

"Oh, no," I whispered. There was no way I could put anything else in my mouth.

I glanced around and realized I had been thrown in with the family and no one was really introduced.

"So, should you introduce me to everyone?" I asked Thano in a hushed voice.

"Um . . . if we could get them all to shut up I would. I'll give you a run down on who is who. Over there next to my father is my cousin Maria. Next to her is her husband Nick. Their daughter Maria is next to him. Then we have cousin Sophia, cousin Angie and her twin sister Maria."

I lifted my eyebrows. Wait. Was that three Maria's?

"Then you've got my mother's sister Agnes and her daughter Sophia and her son Thanos."

"Like your name?"

Thano shook his head. "No, his name is just Thanos. There is an s on the end."

"Oh," I mumbled. Just when I thought I was getting it.

"You've got my cousin Angelo and his wife Christine and their little girl Marianna."

My head was spinning. Looking at Thano, I asked, "Why are there so many duplicate names?"

He shrugged. "I guess Greeks like to name their kids after one another."

Katerina and one of the Marias came walking out each carrying a dish.

Thano's mother looked at me and said, "We've got baklava, galak-toboureko, loukoumades, and chocolate cake!"

Chocolate cake! That I knew!

When it was all placed on the table, my mouth watered but my pants forbid me to eat another bite. That was until Yiayia started putting it all on another plate for me, declaring I hadn't eaten enough.

"Are all Irish girls so small?" Sophia asked as she pushed the chocolate cake my way.

"Well, um . . . I'm not really sure."

Everyone stopped and looked at me. Dimitris moaned and mumbled, "Here we go."

Katerina placed her hands on her hips and wore a serious look on
her face.

"Does your family not get together for holidays? Like Saint Patrick's
day?"

I couldn't help it; I giggled as I looked around at all of them. When
I saw they were serious I looked at Thano who was currently shoving
what I think was the loukoumades into his mouth.

"Oh, well, um . . . my parents died when I was fourteen and I had
no other family. I moved in with my best friend's family and they are
a . . . well, an um . . . a blended family of I think Italian, German, and
something else."

I honestly had no clue what Claire's heritage was and I totally made
that shit up on the fly.

Tears filled Katerina's eyes as she asked, "You lost your parents at
fourteen?"

With a slow nod, I was almost afraid to open my mouth to speak
again.

The next thing I knew I was being hugged by every female that was
in the house and walked outside to take a tour of Katerina's garden.
Looking over my shoulder, Thano stood there with a huge grin on his
face and powdered sugar on his cheek.

Thad and Nicholaus stood on either side of him. When all three of
them lifted their hand and waved I wanted to scream out for help.

Those bastards!

I was being led away by a Greek mob and I wasn't sure I would
survive.

## twenty-four

### Thano

"DUDE, YOU'RE REALLY GOING TO let them whisk her away like that?" Nicholaus asked.

I couldn't help but chuckle at the horrified look on Kilyn's face. "She'll be fine. Better to let her see what she is getting into now."

My father walked up and stood next to me and sighed. "You do know Yiayia is currently assessing your girlfriend's stomach. She's probably trying to see if her Irish vessel is capable of carrying a Greek child."

Letting out a roar of laughter, I popped another loukoumades into my mouth. Walking up to the window, I watched as Kilyn smiled and laughed while she and my mother walked toward the gardens. "What do you think of her, Dad?"

"I think she is a lovely girl and I can see how much you care for her by the way you look at her. And she you."

Feeling a warmth spread through my chest, I looked at him and then back to Kilyn. "I do. I love her."

My father remained silent next me. "You think it's too soon, don't you?" I asked.

"Who am I to think anything. The heart feels what the heart wants to feel. I am glad to see you have put the past where it belongs and you have moved on. The bigger question is . . . does this girl love you enough to put up with this family?"

Thad and Nicolaus both laughed behind us. "Aunt Maria is already saying Kilyn is out for Bampas' money."

My father huffed next to me. "Nonsense. I'm sure Kilyn's parents left her a comfortable inheritance. He was a very successful man."

Pinching my eyebrows together, I turned and faced my father. "How would you know that?"

He continued to look out at Kilyn and my mother.

"I knew him. Worked with him often to be exact. He was one of the top cardiac surgeons in the nation. He was coming back from a conference he spoke at in Canada when the private plane they were flying in crashed. I knew they had a daughter, but I had forgotten what her name was until that day up at the cabin."

"Why didn't you tell me?"

With a shrug, he looked at me. "Would it have made a difference?"

"No. It wouldn't have at all." Looking back out at Kilyn, my heart ached for her. I couldn't imagine losing my parents at such a young age and then to go through what she went through.

"I bet she'd like to know you worked with her father, though. She really never mentions her parents at all. I didn't even know he was a doctor."

Slapping me on the shoulder, he grinned. "I will when the time comes. Let's not overwhelm the poor girl all in one day."

"THANK YOU SO MUCH FOR the lovely evening, Mr. and Mrs. Drivas."

My mother waved her hands in the air. "Nonsense, just because you are dating my Athanasios doesn't mean you have to be so formal. You will call us Katerina and Dimitris. And then after the wedding, Mama and Bampas."

Kilyn's jaw hit the ground.

"And that is my cue to sweep you away from the madness before they ask me to impregnate you here on the spot."

Now her face turned white. "Wh-what?"

Hitting me on the chest, my mother said, "Nonsense, we have to have the wedding first, then we talk babies."

"Oh, my," Kilyn whispered pressing her hands to her face.

With my arm slipped around her waist, I guided Kilyn out the door and to the waiting taxi. Finally, I was going to get her home and have my way with her.

It wasn't even five minutes and she was out cold with her head resting on my shoulder. Never in a million years would I think I would love something as much as I loved the sight of Kilyn sleeping next to me.

When the taxi pulled up to my apartment, I handed him cash and told him to keep the change. Kilyn must have been exhausted because she never woke up. Not even when I placed her in my bed.

After watching her sleep for almost an hour, I stripped out of my clothes and took a hot shower. I didn't even have to turn around to know she was standing there. When her hands touched my back I felt goose bumps erupt over my body.

Closing my eyes, I held my breath as she wrapped her arms around me and peppered my back with soft kisses. Each time whispering my full name. Turning around, I let my gaze roam across her beautiful body. Cupping her face with my hands, I leaned down and pressed my lips to hers as hot water cascaded around us.

It started off slow and sweet. Each of us taking our time as our tongues danced together. Moving her around, I pressed her against the shower wall, deepening the kiss. Her hands moved up while her fingers laced through my hair. When she grabbed it and tugged, I knew she wanted more.

My hand moved down her body and between her legs where I slipped two fingers inside of her.

Moaning, I moved them slowly while she pressed her hips to me . . . silently begging me for more.

Breaking our kiss, I moved my lips along her neck as she softly whispered my name again.

Pulling back, I looked her in the eyes. "I don't have a condom, baby."

I could see the conflict in her eyes. We'd only been together once, and it wasn't fair of me to ask her to do anything she wasn't comfortable doing.

She swallowed hard. "I'm on the pill."

Pushing a piece of wet hair from her face, I smiled. "I've never had unprotected sex, Kilyn."

Her eyes widened in surprise. "Never?"

Shaking my head, I kissed her lips. "No. I've always worn a condom when I've had sex."

"Savannah?"

"Always. She never wanted to be on the pill and insisted I wear a condom every time."

The smile that spread across her face had my knees shaking. "So this would be the first time for both of us?"

I frowned as I thought of Peter. Kilyn must have seen it because she started to chew on her lip. "He wore one. At least he did that."

"I'm so sorry, ladybug."

She shook her head. "How do you say kiss me in Greek?"

With a huge grin, I said, "Fíla me."

Wrapping her arms around my neck, she smiled and said, "Fíla me, Athanasios."

Lifting her up, she wrapped her legs around my waist. Leaning her against the wall, I pressed my lips to hers. There was nothing slow or steady about the kiss. It was frantic and needy.

Our moans echoed in each other mouths. Pulling back, I gasped for air. "Are you sure?"

Nodding her head, she replied, "I've never been so sure of anything in my entire life. I want you. All of you with nothing between us."

My heart slammed against my chest as I lifted her and slowly pushed in. My eyes about rolled to the back of my head it felt so fucking good.

"Shit," I mumbled as I buried my face into her neck coming to a still. If I moved I was going to come.

Her fingers mixed with the hot water running down my back as she lazily ran them over my skin. "Thano," she whispered.

I couldn't even look at her my emotions were everywhere. I wasn't confused and I didn't feel guilty, it was the opposite. I'd never felt more complete in my entire life. As if all these years I've been waiting for her. Pressing my lips to her ear, I barely was able to speak. "I've never . . . felt anything . . . so amazing."

"Please move. Oh, God . . . I need you to move!"

It needed to be slow, but somehow I knew the second I moved it would be anything but slow.

"I don't want to hurt you, ladybug."

She pulled back, forcing me to look into her eyes. "How would you hurt me?"

I wasn't going to hide what I wanted with Kilyn. When it came to being with her I wanted it both ways. I wanted to make love to her endlessly, but I also wanted to hold her down and fuck the living shit out of her. With her past, I didn't want that side of me to scare her.

Honesty was what I promised her.

"Kilyn, I want to fuck you. Hard and fast."

Her eyes blazed with a fire I'd yet to see.

With her mouth opened slightly, she lifted the left side of her mouth into a smile. "Mr. Drivas, do you like to get a little naughty?"

My cock was throbbing inside of her. "With you, I do."

Licking her lips, she lowered her head as her cheeks turned red. "Will you always tell me if you're going to do . . . I mean if you want to pin me down in any way I need you to tell me first."

My expression softened. "Oh, ladybug, I'd always tell you, I swear."

"I don't have a lot of experience, Thano."

"Baby, I haven't been with that many women. With you though . . . I want to . . . explore. I want to play."

"I want that too."

Pulling out of her some, we both sucked in a breath. "Promise you'll tell me if I hurt you."

Nodding her head frantically, she panted out, "I will. I'll tell you, I swear."

My eyes fell to her soft lips. Leaning over, I sucked her lower lip into my mouth as she let out a whimper. Slowly pulling out, I pushed in harder. Kilyn gasped and dug her fingers into my skin.

"It's okay. I have to get used to your size, but don't stop. Please, don't stop, I want this so badly."

And like that, it was as if a switch had been turned on. I moved at a hard fast pace. Kilyn's hips soon moved in the same rhythm as we got lost in each other. The sounds of our bodies hitting filled the bathroom.

"Oh, Christ! Kilyn!" I called out. I wanted her to come with me inside her but I wasn't sure if she would. Trying like hell to hold out I watched while her eyes widened.

"There. Oh, God, Thano! Yes!"

Her mouth crushed against mine as I felt her pussy squeezing down on my cock. That was all it took for me to explode in one of the most powerful orgasms I'd ever experienced.

"Ah . . . I'm coming," I shouted out in euphoria. It was so beyond amazing I couldn't hold it in. Letting out a deep moan, I poured my cum into her body.

When I felt like she had pulled the last drop out of me, I wrapped my arms around her body tightly and softly said, "My sweet beautiful, Kilyn."

This woman had saved me. Pulled me from the deepest darkest corner and brought me back to light. I'd never be the same again.

Her lips pressed against my neck as they moved along my jaw and finally to my lips where she smiled a beautiful smile.

Carefully lifting her off of me, I reached for a washcloth and cleaned every inch of her body. When I touched between her legs she hissed.

"Are you sore?"

Her face turned red again and it wasn't from the hot shower. "Yes. But it's a good kind of hurt."

With a chuckle, I kissed above her, causing her to moan. I'd have to make sure to leave her alone for a day or two. The last thing I'd want to do is hurt her more.

I quickly washed off as she watched me. Reaching for the water there was a knock on my bathroom door.

Kilyn and I both froze.

"Athanasios? Are you almost done?"

Both our eyes widened in horror as Kilyn covered her mouth and sank down to the floor.

"Athanasios! Can you hear me?"

Kilyn started hitting me on the leg. "Answer her before she walks in here!" she whispered.

"Yeah, Mama. Give me a second."

Turning off the water, I reached down and helped Kilyn up. We both quickly dried off. Wrapping the towel around her, Kilyn spun in a circle.

"Where should I go?" she whispered.

With a quick glance around, I looked at the window. Kilyn hit me in the stomach. "No!" she hissed as she motioned to the fact that she was wrapped in a towel.

I pointed to the closet where she quickly rushed in.

My hand pushed through my hair as I took a few deep breaths. If my mother heard anything I'd never be able to look her in the eyes again.

Squaring off my shoulders, I drew in one last gulp of air and opened the door. Searching my room quickly, I didn't see her. "Mama?" I called out.

"I'm in your living room."

I let out a frustrated sigh and said, "Let me get some clothes on."

When I finally made my way to the living you, she sat on the sofa staring at me.

Before I even had a chance to open my mouth she said, "Masturbating is a very normal thing, Athanasios."

My mouth fell open as I stared at her.

Holy fuck.

What was worse? My mother catching me having sex . . . or my mother thinking I jacked off in the shower?

Either way, this was not good.

## twenty-five

### Kilyn

AFTER THANO LEFT THE BATHROOM, I dashed out of the closet and into his room. Shit! My clothes were in the bathroom but I wanted to hear why his mother was here. Seeing one of Thano's T-shirts, I slipped it on.

What in the world was his mother doing here? Was this a common thing for her to just show up?

Oh. My. Gawd!

What if we had been in the bedroom having sex and not the shower? She would have walked in on us. I already felt like I was walking on the edge with her.

"Masturbating is a very normal thing, Athanasios."

Taking a few steps back, I slammed my hands over my mouth to keep my laughter in. She thinks Thano was masturbating in the shower!

Tears were forming in my eyes as I fought like hell to not lose it. I could only imagine Thano's face right now.

"What?" he practically shouted.

"It's not the first time I've caught one of my boys in the act. It's perfectly normal . . . ask your father."

Stumbling back to the bed, I grabbed a pillow and buried my face in it as I laughed my ass off.

"Mama! Really I don't need to hear this and I wasn't masturbating!"

My head lifted as my eyes widened.

*He wouldn't.*

"Athanasios, please, I understand I was young once."

Thano moaned and I covered my mouth again.

"It's not like that."

"She's a very beautiful girl, that Kilyn."

I couldn't help the smile that spread across my face.

"There is no reason to be ashamed that her body makes you feel things."

"Mama! Please stop talking."

Standing, I sunk my teeth into my lip and stood over by the door.

"Now, she could stand to drop a pound or two."

My mouth gaped open as I looked down at myself. What the hell? I weighed a healthy one hundred twenty-four pounds for my five-foot-three body!

"Oh, Jesus Christ," Thano mumbled.

I took a step away from the door when I heard his mother walking.

"You do not use the Lord's name in vain, or I'll put a bar of soap in your mouth."

Frowning, I shook my head. She does realize her son is a grown man . . . doesn't she?

"Mama, I don't know how to tell you this but I'm almost twenty-nine. You can't wash my mouth out with soap anymore and Kilyn is perfect. And why are you here?"

The silence that followed had me chewing on my thumbnail.

I heard Katerina take in a deep breath. "I needed to make sure you were sure this time."

My heart stopped I was positive.

"Sure of what?"

"Kilyn."

Oh. Shit.

"I know with Savannah you were trying to prove a point with her not being Greek. I won't lie and say I'm a bit disappointed you're not with a Greek girl."

"Mama, can we talk about this tomorrow?" Thano pleaded.

"No. I need to know if you are with her for the right reasons. I actually like this girl. She's funny and you can see she has a love for life. Now don't get me wrong, I adored Savannah. She grew on me after a while, but this Kilyn O'Kelly. There is something about her that I like."

My hand covered my chest as I felt it tightening.

"Mama, she's here right now."

Closing my eyes, I shook my head and cursed under my breath. Just when I had the Greek mom on my side he goes off and blows it!

Katerina's voice quivered before she attempted to lower her voice. "Wh-what? Kilyn's here?"

"Yes. She's in my room."

"Oh, dear. So that wasn't you . . . oh . . . I need to sit down."

"Let me go get her."

*What! No! No! No! Don't go get me! Are you insane?*

Spinning around, I scanned the room. Where could I possibly hide? Frantically running around the room, I spied a pair of Thano's sweatpants. I started to put them on when I heard Thano talking again.

My head snapped over to the door when I heard it open. I lost my balance, causing me to stumble and run smack into the dresser hitting my head straight on.

"Kilyn! What in the hell are you doing? Are you okay?"

Thano rushed over to me as I rubbed my head and moaned. "I hit my head."

Kissing my forehead, he chuckled. "What were you doing?"

"Trying to put your sweats on and then I panicked because I knew you were going to come get me and I hadn't gotten all the way dressed."

He placed his hand on the side of my face as I leaned into it. His smile somehow calmed my nerves instantly.

Helping me up, Thano reached down and tied the strings on his sweatpants.

With a sexy-as-sin smile, he said, "You sure look adorable in my clothes."

Feeling my cheeks heat, I looked down. Thano placed his finger on my chin and lifted my eyes to meet his. "Oh, ladybug, how I love you."

My hands came up to his forearms were I balanced my shaking legs. Smiling, I replied, "I love you."

He motioned with his head for us to head out to the living room. Somehow, I knew as long as I had Thano by my side, there wasn't anything I couldn't face.

The moment we stepped out into the living room I braced for one very angry mother to call me an Irish leprechaun-loving whore.

What happened next surprised the hell out of me.

Katerina smiled a big bright smile and clasped her chest. "Oh, thank God he wasn't masturbating!"

=====  ♥  =====

## TWO MONTHS LATER

PULLING THE GLASS DISH OUT of the oven, I smiled.

"That smells so good!" Claire said as she clapped her hands and did a little hop.

I set the glass dish on top of the stove and stared at my creation.

Galaktoboureko.

My heart quickly began to beat faster. "What if I forgot to add something? Does it look like it's supposed to look? Oh, God!"

Claire laughed and pushed me, causing me to stumble slightly. "When did you start becoming such a freak?"

Turning to look at her, I blew the piece of hair that was hanging over my eyes. "Since Thano's mother welcomed me into their very Greek family! Sometimes, I feel so out of place."

"Nonsense, I'm sure they love you, Kilyn."

With a shrug, I jumped up and sat on the stool . . . staring at the Greek dessert I had made for dinner tonight over at Thano's parents' house.

"We've only been officially dating for two months so I don't think we can say they love me. They tolerate me is more like it. And that's only because of Thano. I swear, if his grandmother tells me I could stand to lose a few more pounds as she is pushing food at me I may scream."

With a chuckle, she replied, "It's worth it though right?"

My body warmed as I thought about Thano. "So very worth it. The sex is beyond amazing."

Claire giggled. "I was thinking more along the lines of he makes you happy, you've finally found your happily ever after, you know, something sappy."

My heart squeezed in my chest as I let out a very dramatic sigh. "Thano always tells me I pulled him out of the darkness. He has no idea how much he did the same with me. I honestly never believed I'd find someone I wanted to fully open my heart to."

"I see the way he looks at you. It makes my heart happy."

Looking down, I closed my eyes. "Sometimes I feel like I'm dreaming. It's all happened so fast, and I try so hard not to overthink things, but sometimes I wonder if I deserve his love."

"Hey, look at me, Kilyn."

With a heavy sigh, I lifted my eyes to hers.

"Why in the world would you think you don't deserve his love?"

My lips pressed tightly together as a tear slowly made a path down my cheek. "I see the way he looks at me sometimes when we are making love. I can't help but let my imagination run wild."

Claire frowned, "How does he look at you?"

Shrugging, I responded, "I don't know. Like he wants to do more but he's afraid. I think he is a lot more dominant in the bedroom than he leads on."

She wiggled her eyebrows and said, "Meow. Why does that sound so damn hot? Damn, girl, I'd be all over that shit."

Laughing, I shook my head and looked away as my face heated.

"Oh, no. What are you thinking about?"

Squeezing my eyes shut, I blurted it out. "I let him tie me up last night!"

Claire gasped. "Shut the hell up! You did?"

Opening my eyes, I nodded like a little schoolgirl while I chewed on my thumb. "Yep."

She quickly sat down on the stool next me and gave me a wide-eyed smile. "And? Don't leave me hanging. Did you like it?"

"I was so unsure at first. He started off by only tying one hand and made me hold the other hand up. But once he started and told me I couldn't touch him . . . oh my goodness, Claire. I have never been that turned on in my entire life."

"Oh. Oh, this is good," she said while rubbing her hands together. "What did he do to you?"

"Played."

Her mouth dropped open. "That's all you're going to say? Played how? With his hands? With his mouth?"

"Both!" I said before we both fell into a laughing fit.

We sat there and giggled like schoolgirls as I told her how Thano made me come with just his touch on my body.

Claire dropped her head back. "Oh, God! Why isn't Blake part Greek?" Lifting her hands to the sky, she cried out. "Why? Why?"

Walking in to the kitchen, Blake asked, "Why, what?"

We both jumped up and said, "Nothing."

Blake gave us a disbelieving look while his gaze bounced between the two of us. "What are you two up to?"

Glancing over to the stove, I saw my dish. "Shit! I'm going to be late! I have to go."

Claire jumped into action and grabbed a lid to put over the galakto-boureko and then slipped it into a warming bag.

Throwing my purse over my shoulder, I took the dish and smiled. "Wish me luck!"

"You've got this! They're going to love it!"

With a sinking feeling in the pit of my stomach, I made my way out to my car. Setting the Greek dish down in the passenger seat, I pulled out my phone and sent Thano a text.

*Me: I'm on my way.*

*Thano: Did you make it?*

I let out a sharp breath.

*Me: Yes. I hope I did it right.*

*Thano: You did, ladybug. Don't worry.*

Not being able to help myself, I smiled. I imagined Thano's velvety voice calling me his favorite pet name.

*Me: Leaving Claire's now. Are you there?*

*Thano: Yep! Be careful driving. Love you.*

*Me: Okay, love you back.*

Turning the key, I started my car and headed over to Thano's parents' house.

The entire drive over there I kept giving myself a pep talk. I knew how to cook. I simply followed the directions and made it. How hard could it be?

Shit. Maybe I should have made a test one first and tasted it. What if it tasted like ass?

Oh. God. I could hear Thad and Nicholaus, now, saying it tasted like leprechaun ass.

The urge to slam on my brakes was strong, but before I knew it, I was pulling up and parking. There were a ton of cars.

"What in the hell?"

I watched as a whole family, a husband, wife, and three kids, walked into Thano's parents' house.

Reaching for my phone I hit his number.

"Deep breath in. Deep breath out." Closing my eyes, I counted to twenty.

"Hey, are you here?"

Gasping for air, I asked, "You said it was a family lunch."

"What?"

"Lunch, Thano! You said we were having lunch with your family. In my feeble Irish mind that meant, your parents, your Yiayia, and your brothers. And maybe . . . just maybe if I was lucky . . . one of your brother's would have brought a girl."

"Ah . . ."

Rolling my eyes, my head dropped to the steering wheel.

"Phoebe's here. Does that help?"

I gasped. "Ohmygawd! Are you serious? Thad brought her home?"

"Yeah, and I'm sure she would really love to have you in here since she is the newbie now and not you."

Nodding my head, I squared off my shoulders. "I'm coming in!"

"That's my girl! I'll meet you at the door."

By the time I got out of my car and around to the passenger side, another couple with two young kids walked up. Lifting my hand, I smiled and called out, "Hello!"

They kindly returned the gesture, but kept right on walking.

With shaking hands, I walked up to the door. Thano was talking to the guy I just waved to.

"Man it's been a long time, Marios. How have you been?"

The man laughed. "Busy. Eva is pregnant with twins."

I couldn't but notice how Thano's face lit up. "No Kidding! Man that's great! Congratulations."

When he looked over Marios' shoulder, he flashed me that beautiful smile of his that made my stomach feel like I had a group of dancing butterflies in it.

Slapping Marios on the shoulder, he quickly made his way over to me. With shaking hands, I held up the galaktoboureko.

"You delivered it! It was made by your hands and my mother will love that! Come on she's in the kitchen."

*Please let it be good. Please, dear Lord, let it be good!*

We snaked our way through all the people and finally ended up in the kitchen. It was packed full of women. My eyes widened in shock. Katerina was standing at the stove stirring something in a pot as was Yiayia.

Why were they both stirring it?

I just needed to drop this off and find Phoebe. She was probably hiding out in some corner.

"No! No! You roll the dough out like this! It's all in the wrists."

Turning to my right, I couldn't believe my eyes. Phoebe was wearing one of Katerina's cooking aprons and arguing with Aunt Maria . . . no that was Aunt Sophia . . . I think. Shaking my head to clear my thoughts, I focused back on Phoebe. She didn't need me! And she certainly wasn't curled up in a corner.

"The way I cook it is better. Trust me!" Phoebe called out.

It was then I noticed every single woman in that room was shouting over each other.

"Are they afraid they won't hear each other?" I asked Thano.

He started laughing and rolled his eyes. "Greek women."

With a forced smile, I quickly set my dish down and tried to retreat.

"Kilyn! You made us a dish!" Katerina yelled out.

You could have heard a pin drop.

"Oh, shit," I mumbled as Thano reached for my hand.

I watched Katerina open the pretty blue floral warmer and reach in. She slipped the lid off and raised her eyebrows.

"Our Thano's Kilyn made galaktoboureko," Katerina called out.

One of the Maria's leaned closer to me and made a sound as she sucked in her breath. "That's Katerina's dish."

My head snapped over as I stared at her. "Thano told me to make that dish," I whispered.

Turning back to Katerina, I watched her cut into it as everyone watched.

I could tackle her. I'd easily bring her to the ground. Then I could grab the dish and run. I was on track in high school. I'm a fast runner . . . when I need to be.

When the fork went into her mouth, I held my breath. She closed her eyes and stopped chewing.

With a firm grip, I pulled Thano's arm. "Why did you have me make that dish?" I whispered.

He chuckled and kissed me on the tip of my nose.

"Good. Yes. Very, very good."

I stared at Thano . . . afraid to look at Katerina.

The next thing I knew, I was in her arms as she yelled out. "We'll make her a Greek yet!"

Everyone cheered and I finally let out the breath I'd been holding. When she pulled back, she gave me the brightest smile.

"It's not as good as mine . . . but my Thano will not starve after all!"

"Opa!" Everyone cheered.

I looked around the room with a huge smile on my face, until her words sunk in.

Wait. What?

# twenty-six

## Thano

KILYN STOOD OFF IN A corner for most of the afternoon. I'd really hope that her and Phoebe would have hit it off a bit better, but Phoebe seemed to have melted right in with the family.

Looking across the room, our eyes met and she smiled that bright life-loving smile of hers. My heart raced knowing she was mine.

"Athanasios? It's been forever!"

Turning to my right, I saw Nikoletta. The girl I dated in high school before Savannah. Actually, she was the girl my mother secretly wished to bind me in a marriage contract to, I swear.

"Nik! Wow, it's been what, six or seven years?"

With a wide grin, she replied, "About that. How have you been?"

She wrapped me up in her arms for a hug. When we pulled back and she kissed me on the lips, I was stunned for a moment.

Quickly stepping back, I snuck a peek to see if Kilyn had seen the kiss.

Oh, yeah. She saw it.

She stood there with her mouth dropped open, and if she were any more pissed she would probably bust the beer bottle in her hand.

My attention was drawn back to Nikoletta when she reached for both of my hands. "Oh my goodness, it's so good to see you. When your mother called and invited me . . . well . . . needless to say, I was surprised but happy."

My smile faded some. "My mother invited you?"

"Yes! Just out of the blue." Anger quickly swept over my body as I searched for her. "I mean when I ran into your Yiayia the other day and she told me you were still single I was so surprised. You're even more handsome now than you were in high school."

I was stunned to the point where I was speechless. Yiayia I understood, but my mother? She claimed to like Kilyn so much.

"So are you still in marketing? At least if I remember right, the last time I saw you that's what you did."

With a quick nod of my head, I looked back over to Kilyn. My mother was talking to her.

*What the fuck is going on?*

Turning back to Nikoletta, I tilted my head. "Did my mother happen to tell you I was dating someone?"

Her face dropped. "No. She didn't tell me at all."

She laced her hand around my neck and gave her lips a quick lick. "Maybe we should go somewhere more private so we can talk."

Reaching up with my hand, I pushed her hand away.

"I don't think so, Nik."

"Oh, come on, Athanasios, for old times' sake. I won't tell anyone if you don't. You remember the time in the auditorium at school. Row 7 seat 7. The way my voice echoed through the room as you gave me my first orgasm."

Swallowing hard, the memory hit me like a brick wall. Nikoletta was the first girl I ever gave an orgasm to.

"Yeah, Nik. I remember, but please can you keep your voice down, my parents don't need to know I fingered you in high school."

"Thano?"

I closed my eyes when I heard Kilyn's voice.

She was standing to my left. I wasn't sure how long she had been standing there. Nikoletta didn't bother to keep her voice down at all.

Smiling, I leaned over to kiss her cheek, but she pulled away. My stomach dropped and it felt like a weight was on my chest.

"I'm not feeling well and heading home."

"Um . . . are you sure?"

Kilyn let her eyes roam over Nikoletta before looking at me. "I'm very sure. I don't belong here."

She spun on her heels and started making her way to the front door. Starting to go after her, Nikoletta grabbed my arm. "Let her go if she isn't feeling good. Let's catch up."

My mother walked up with a huge grin. "Nikoletta! What are you doing here?"

Glaring at my mother, I shook my head. How could she pretend to not have anything to do with this? And what in the hell did she say to Kilyn?

"Mama, why would you try to hurt Kilyn like this?"

Her face fell. "What? I don't know what you're talking about, Athanasios. I'd never hurt Kilyn."

Nikoletta placed her hand on my arm, "Athanasios, let's step outside for some fresh air before you say something you'll regret."

My mother looked between the two of us as I pushed my hand through my hair in a frustrated manner. "I thought you liked her."

Her eyes widened in shock. "I do like her! Why would you think I didn't?"

I pointed to Nikoletta. "This is why! You invited an old girlfriend of mine to the family dinner knowing Kilyn would be here. And clearly, whatever you said to Kilyn a few moments ago upset her and caused her to leave."

My mother turned to Nikoletta. "No! I invited her over tomorrow night!"

Pulling my head back, I looked at Nikoletta with a confused expression. She smiled weakly. "Was it tomorrow?"

My mother nodded. "Yes! I specifically said tonight was a family dinner and tomorrow I would love to catch up and talk about your parents and how they were liking Greece."

That's when it clicked. Nikoletta showing up tonight . . . she knew I'd be here.

Placing her hands on her hips, my mother turned to me and glared at me. "And you. How could you think I'd pull something so dishonest and low? How could you think I'd ever hurt that sweet girl? I love Kilyn."

My heart stopped. "What?"

"I saw her standing in the corner and I knew she was feeling out of place. I simply went up to her and told her to join the other women in the kitchen. She was on her way there but said she had something to ask you. So you tell me, Athanasios, was it me who sent her leaving, or you?"

"Mama . . . I'm sorry, I just assumed."

Shaking her head, she gave me a look that actually made my body shudder. "I should smack you on the head and rinse your mouth out with Joy soap!"

She stormed off, leaving me with Nikoletta again.

"I believe you know where the door is, Nik. And please don't bother coming back tomorrow."

The stunned look on her face was priceless as I took her by the arm and helped show her to the door.

After telling my father I was leaving, I tried to talk to my mother but she completely ignored me. I didn't have time for games. I needed to get home to Kilyn.

"All right, Mama, if that's how it's going to be. I'm leaving to go talk to Kilyn. Se agapó."

Lifting her hand in a silent gesture, I quickly tracked down the five people I needed to move their cars to let me out. The faster I got to Kilyn the better.

WALKING INTO MY APARTMENT, I shut the door and tossed the keys on the side table.

"Kilyn?"

Her car was parked in her spot so I knew she was here. I'd finally talked her into moving in with me a few weeks back since she had been living with Claire and Blake. She moved in on Christmas Eve and it was the best gift I'd ever gotten. It was a huge step, but falling asleep and waking up with her every day was amazing.

I headed straight to the bedroom and came to a stop when I saw her packing.

"What are you doing?"

She spun around and all the air was sucked from my lungs. Her face was covered in tears and mascara.

I'd never felt such a deep pain in my heart like I did at this very moment looking at her tear soaked face.

"Baby, no. I swear to you she was my high school girlfriend, and I was as surprised by her actions tonight as you. As soon as you left, I asked her to leave."

She stood there staring at me as more tears came.

"Did you hear me, Kilyn?"

Sitting down on the bed, she buried her face in her hands and sobbed uncontrollably. Dropping to my knees in front of her, I pulled her hands down.

"Talk to me, ladybug. Please talk to me."

Shaking her head, she sucked in a shaky breath and attempted to talk.

"I'll . . . never . . . fit . . . in. Your Yiayia hates me!"

My hands came up as I wiped her black tears away. "No, she doesn't, baby."

She nodded and used the back of her hand to wipe her snot.

Ew.

Gross.

"Yes . . . she does! She told me today not to turn you into a beer loving drunk! Because you know . . . all people from Irish decent are beer-loving drunks. Your mother thinks you're going to starve because I can't cook, but I'm actually a damn good cook! I can learn to make Greek food just as good as them but they won't ever give me a chance. I know they won't. I'll never be good enough."

Hearing her fears had my heart breaking.

"That's not true."

"It is true!" she yelled out. "Do you know how many of your

cousins came up to me today and said they couldn't believe Katerina was okay with you dating me? A non-Greek in the family."

"No, I don't know and I don't care, and neither should you. Some of my family is very old school Greek. I don't care what any of them think."

She stood up quickly. "I do! Today they were questioning me about growing up Catholic. I was scared to death to tell them I haven't set foot in a Catholic Church since I was fourteen! This will be our life forever. Me, always wondering if your family accepts me. Your grandmother thinking I'm not good enough. Your mother thinking I'm starving you. I think your father only likes me because he knew my father." She shook her head and mumbled, "I can't do it."

Grabbing the suitcase, she slammed it shut. "I have to leave. I need . . . I need to think."

The only way to describe the feeling in my chest was to say someone was squeezing the fuck out of my heart.

"What?" I mumbled as I watched her carry her suitcase out of the bedroom.

She can't leave. I'm not letting her leave me.

Reaching for her jacket, she headed to the door. "Maybe I was too hopeful that this would work out. That . . . that we . . . would . . . work out."

My eyes widened in horror. Racing around the front of her, I fought to pull air into my lungs.

"No. Kilyn. Please don't leave. Baby, I can't breathe without you, don't you know that?"

Tears streamed down her cheeks as my heart pumped faster. My eyes searched her beautiful face. "You're the only reason I smile when I go to sleep at night and when I wake up each morning. Your smile can turn the worst of days around and make me the happiest man on earth."

A sob slipped from her soft pink lips. "I don't know what to do. I love you so much, Thano. I've never loved anyone like I love you."

"That's all we need, ladybug."

She closed her eyes tightly and blurted out, "I lied!"

The only thing I could hear was my heart racing like I'd just run a marathon.

My mouth went dry and I forced the words out of my mouth.

Trying like hell to swallow, I finally formed words. "Wh-what did you . . . what did you lie about?"

Her eyes snapped open. God, how I loved this girl. Even with her eyes bloodshot red, she still caused my breath to catch.

"I don't like baklava!"

Wait. What did she say?

Shaking my head, I leaned in closer to her. "What?"

Her head moved from side to side. "I know! I feel terrible about it. I tried. Oh, God I tried so hard, but every time I eat it I want to gag!"

With a smile on my face, I pushed a piece of loose wavy hair behind her ear. When her lip jetted out in a pout, I fell in love with her even more.

"What's your favorite thing to do?"

With a furrowed look, she whispered, "What?"

"Your favorite thing to do with me. Tell me what it is right now."

Her face turned upright into a smile. "When we drive up to the cabin with the windows down and the radio blaring."

"I never would have done that before you, Kilyn. You changed my life. There isn't anything I wouldn't do for you. I'd jump out of a damn airplane if I thought it would make you happy. I'd rather die than have you walk out of my life. Please say you'll stay with me. Please."

Her tears started up again and I wiped them away with my thumbs.

"What about your—"

Placing my lips to hers, I kissed her. I needed her to feel how much I loved her. How there wasn't anything I wouldn't do for her and that our love would get us through anything.

When I pulled back, I rested my forehead to hers. "I had plans for us tonight. Let me take you out. We'll forget about my family, Greek food, all of it. It's only you and me tonight."

Stepping back, I placed my finger on her chin and lifted her eyes to mine.

"Will you go on a date with me tonight?"

With a slight nod, she smiled. "Yes."

My body instantly relaxed. After this, the rest of the night was going to be a piece of cake.

# twenty-seven

### Kilyn

THANO'S EYES WERE FILLED WITH love as he looked into mine.

"Will you go on a date with me tonight?"

My stomach dipped as I responded with, "Yes."

His body relaxed and I hated that my insecurities caused him stress. I wanted so badly to feel like I was a part of his family, but after today I wasn't sure I ever would be.

"Come on, let's go put your suitcase up and get changed."

I probably looked like a mess with all the crying.

Gesh. What was happening to me? I never cried like this.

Thano grabbed my suitcase and took my hand as he pulled me to the bedroom. The only thing I really wanted to do was fall into bed with him and get lost in his eyes.

"Dress warm. We'll be outside. Oh, and wear jeans and sneakers."

My interest was piqued as I lifted my eyebrows. "Okay. Are you going to tell me where we are going?"

With a smirk, he simply winked and pulled a sweatshirt over his head. My lower stomach pulled with desire as I watched him run his hand through his hair.

"Don't look at me like that, ladybug. Come on, get dressed."

I did as he asked and quickly changed. Freshening up my makeup, I made sure to apply waterproof mascara. I had no idea what we would be doing, so I put on thermals as well as a long-sleeve shirt. I'd take my jacket and gloves also, just in case.

"Pack a small bag as well. I think we'll spend a few days up at the cabin if you're able to."

My heart soared. I loved going to the cabin. It held such amazing memories for me. After all, it was there we made love for the first time. We didn't go up there as often as we wanted to, so I jumped at the chance to go. It was just what I needed to clear my head.

"I have a design to do, but I can bring it with me."

By the time we got to Thano's truck, my heart was beating like a racehorse. We never took his sports car up to the cabin. Not after the tree fell on it.

Opening the door for me, he smiled as I slipped into his car. Leaning in, he kissed me on the lips. "Ready for some fun?"

With a giggle, I nodded my head. "Totally ready! Do I get a hint?"

He laughed and tapped the tip of my nose. "Nope."

Shutting the door, I watched him walk around the front of the truck. Even though my head was spinning, I still wasn't sure if this would all work out, I couldn't ignore how much I loved this man. I'd never really loved anyone besides my parents, Claire, and her parents.

Thano jumped in and started up his truck. "Okay, let's go have some fun."

KEEPING MY MIND BUSY WITH smalltalk, I wasn't paying any attention to where we were going as I went on and on about nothing.

"Claire and Blake are trying for a baby."

Thano smiled. "Are they really? Good for them."

Nodding, I felt a tiny bit of jealousy in the pit of my stomach. "Her folks are pretty happy about it. They've been bugging them about it for a while."

"Are you close to her parents?"

"Yes. I mean, they're like my second parents. I know they love me like I'm their daughter."

He reached for my hand and kissed the back of it. "You know my parents adore you, Kilyn."

With a shrug, I looked away.

"Tonight, my mother said she loved you."

Looking back at Thano, I asked, "She did? She really said that?"

With a huge smile, he nodded. "Yep."

It was then I noticed we were at the airport. Anxiety washed over my body as I looked back at Thano. He was pulling into a different part of the airport. The area where private planes were kept.

"Where are you going?" I asked with a nervous edge to my voice.

All he did was turn to me and wink.

Pulling up to a hangar, Thano put his truck into park. "We're here! Come on."

Before I had a chance to even ask why we were at a hangar at the airport, Thano got out of his truck and made his way over to my door. I opened it and slowly got out. Lacing his fingers with mine, we headed over to the three guys standing a few feet away.

"Thano! Damn, man, it's good to see you."

The guy seemed to be the same age as us. His blond hair was a mess, but the only thing you noticed was his sky-blue eyes.

"Saul, it's good seeing you. It's been awhile. How are you doing?"

The man's eyes quickly looked over at me before his attention went back to Thano. "I'm doing good. Still flying people all over the place. Your dad called in a favor for you I see."

My heart began pounding as my eyes drifted over to the small jet that was parked outside of the hangar. Swallowing hard, I tried to speak but nothing came out.

Thano's laugh caused me to look back at the men. "He did. It's a quick flight, right?"

"Oh, yeah. I've already called in the flight plans so we're good to go."

Oh. My. God.

We were flying somewhere. In a plane. In a small plane.

Turning to me, Thano must have noticed the sheer look of horror on my face. And then it hit him.

"Oh, shit. Kilyn, I wasn't even thinking. Baby, we don't have to do this if you don't want to."

My eyes bounced between him and the plane. Whatever he had planned he went to a lot of trouble to plan it. I wasn't about to let my fears stand in the way.

"I'm . . . I'm fine, honest."

His hands cupped my face, bringing my eyes to his intense stare. "We don't have to do this."

Lifting my hands to his, I smiled. "I've flown since my parents' death. It's always been on big planes and not smaller ones, though." With a nervous chuckle, I continued. "I've missed out on some pretty fun trips because I wouldn't fly on a smaller plane. It's a stupid fear."

He barely shook his head. "It's not stupid."

I pressed my lips together and forced a grin. "I want to do this."

The way his thumbs moved across my cheeks had a calming effect on me. "Are you sure?"

"I've never been so sure."

Thano dropped his hands and I instantly missed his warm touch. "I need to get the bags. Wait right here."

I stood there and watched as he grabbed the bags and brought them over to the jet. My heart was racing as I listened to them talking.

There would be two pilots. The flight to Dallas would be short. A car would be there to pick us up.

My hand came up as I rubbed my fingers against my forehead. I was trying like hell to ignore the sick feeling in my stomach, as well as the headache that was quickly coming on.

Closing my eyes, I counted to twenty. This was good. I needed to do this.

I swear I blacked out because before I knew it, we were up in the air and I was gripping Thano's hand so hard it was turning white.

"I'm sorry I forgot, Kilyn. I can't believe I did that."

By the time the plane leveled out some, I was feeling much better. "It's okay. I don't even remember telling you how my parents died."

He looked down and then back up at me. "You didn't. My father did."

I nodded. "So, because of you forgetting, does this mean you're going to tell me where we are going?"

With a laugh, he shook his head. "No. But I know something else we can do."

Wiggling his eyebrows, my mouth dropped. "No! Thano, are you insane?"

"No. I'm thinking we need to relax you. What better way to relax than sex?"

I quickly looked around the plane. There were four large chairs and behind them was a table.

"Whose plane is this anyway?" I asked.

"My Uncle Mitch's. He flies all over the place for work."

Thano smiled and I couldn't ignore my libido screaming at me to climb on top of him. Why did I listen to him and wear jeans?

Standing, I walked back to the table and ran my finger over it. "So, will the pilots be coming out anytime soon?"

"Why? Does talking about my Uncle Mitch turn you on?"

Widening my smile, I placed my finger in my mouth and gently bit down on it. "No, but you do."

His eyes darkened and my body blazed with a fire deep inside. The way he was looking at me had my stomach flipping and flopping with each step he took closer to me.

"Do you want me, Kilyn?"

With a deep breath in, I whispered, "Yes."

"Are you still wanting to leave me?"

My head shook. "No."

"Good, because I'll never stop loving you and fighting for us. Do you understand that, ladybug?"

I found myself holding my breath when he stopped directly in front of me. "Do you?" he asked again. Pushing the breath out, I nodded.

"Say it," he whispered as he dipped his face and buried it into my neck.

Oh. God. I wanted him to rip my clothes off and have him take me up against the table and I didn't give two shits who heard or saw.

"Say . . . what?" I panted.

He chuckled and his hot breath hit my neck, causing goose bumps to erupt over my body. "That you understand."

My eyes closed. "I understand. Thano, I want you desperately."

His lips moved softly across my skin. "Desperately, you say?"

It was becoming harder to stand while my legs grew weak. "Y-yes. Please."

"But you said we couldn't."

Gripping onto his strong arms, I felt his muscles contract under my touch, causing my body to burn with want. "We can. Oh . . . God . . . we can!"

His velvety hands slipped under my shirt and made their way to my breasts.

"I feel your nipples and damn if I don't want to suck on them."

With a force, I pulled him closer to me. "Yes," was all I managed to get out.

"Kilyn, if we do this it has to be fast."

My head dropped back as he moved those magical lips across my neck. "Fast. Okay. Got it."

"Do you? Because, baby, I'm going to fuck you and you're going to be very quiet. Do you understand?"

Oh. Lord. Thano talking like that had my body ready to explode.

"Yes," I panted.

He lifted me and set me on the table as he took a step back and undid his jeans. He didn't have any underwear on, so when he took himself in his hand and began to stroke himself, I thought I was going to come right then and there.

"That's hot," I whispered as I unbuttoned my jeans and slipped back off the table, pushing them down. I couldn't get my sneakers off and Thano clearly grew impatient. He grabbed me and spun me around.

"Put your hands on the table. I'm fucking you from behind."

My heart was racing, and the moment he pushed inside of me, I called out, "Oh, God!"

Thano grabbed my hair and pulled it back. "You have to be quiet."

Pressing my lips together, I tried like hell not to utter a peep as Thano fucked me. It felt like heaven and I knew I would come quickly. I loved this side of him, which still surprised me somewhat.

When my legs began to quiver, I knew I was going to have to concentrate on keeping my mouth shut.

"Baby, you're squeezing down on my cock and it feels so good."

That was my undoing. I came hard while my entire body shook. Trying to keep quiet seemed to intensify the whole experience.

Thano pushed in hard and I felt him grow larger. He made a small grunt and released his cum into me. A wide smile grew across my face as I dropped my head and fought to drag in air.

"Shit," Thano said in a hushed voice.

Turning to look over my shoulder, I stared into his green eyes. "What's wrong?"

"I don't have anything to clean us up with."

With a quick look around, I saw some napkins. Reaching for them, I handed them to Thano as he pulled out and quickly began cleaning me.

I loved how he always put me first in everything.

He slowly pulled my jeans up, turned me to face him, and kissed my lips.

"Hey, Thano, just letting you know we'll be starting to descend here shortly."

Both our eyes widened in horror. My mouth dropped open as a giggle escaped while Thano's mouth grew into a crooked smile. My heart skipped a beat at the sight.

It was right then and there I knew nothing mattered but our love for each other. No matter what was thrown at us, we'd make it through all of it.

Together.

# twenty-eight

## Thano

**M**Y HEART WAS BEATING LIKE I'd just run a damn marathon. When Saul started talking, I couldn't believe it. Then Kilyn started giggling and my heart felt as if it were soaring in the clouds next to the plane.

Glancing over my shoulder, I watched as Saul headed back to the cockpit. When I looked back at Kilyn, she had her hands over her mouth as she tried to keep in her laughter.

"Do you think he saw us?" she asked in a whispered voice.

I shrugged my shoulders. "I don't think so."

She closed her eyes and said, "God, I hope not. That would be so embarrassing if that got back to your father!"

Laughing, I pulled her close to me. "I couldn't care less if it did get back to him. But, it looks like we're members of the mile-high club."

Kilyn wiggled her eyebrows. "I'll be sure to add that to my résumé."

My eyes dropped to her lips. Leaning in, I kissed her gently before pulling back. "How do you feel about flying now?"

When her teeth sunk into my lip and she peered up at me through those long eyelashes, my heart felt as if it had skipped a beat. "I've suddenly grown a fondness for flying."

Throwing my head back, I let out a roar of laughter. I was pissed at myself for making such a stupid mistake with the plane, but if having sex was Kilyn's way of getting past it . . . I was totally okay with that.

"So, what's in Dallas?" Kilyn asked making her way back over to her seat.

Letting out a soft chuckle, I looked at her. "Oh, no. There is no way you're getting it out of me. It's a surprise."

With a pout, she dropped into the seat. "So, wait. If we're headed to Dallas tonight . . . are we really going to the cabin?"

"Nope. I just said that to get you to pack a bag. We're staying in Dallas for two nights."

Her smile practically lit up the entire plane. "I've never been to Dallas!"

"Well, I'm glad I'm the one who gets to take you."

"Me too. And I don't even care where we're going. I'm just glad we're together."

Taking her hand in mine, I lightly kissed the back of it. "Me too, ladybug."

Once we landed, Saul and the other pilot taxied up to a private hangar. Kilyn and I got off the plane and quickly headed to a car that was waiting for us. I don't think I'd ever seen Kilyn so damn excited. She was like a kid in a candy store.

Slipping into the car's backseat, the driver greeted us by name. I don't know how my father did it, but I owed him big time for helping me plan out tonight.

"Mr. Drivas, Ms. O'Kelly. My name is Ted, and I'll be your driver for the next few days. Are you ready to go to your destination?"

With a huge smile and my heart racing in my chest, I replied, "Yes, we are."

I watched Kilyn as she looked out the window. "Dallas is huge! It's so beautiful at night."

"Yes, it is," I agreed.

Kilyn was so busy looking out at everything she didn't even notice we had pulled up at our destination.

"This is my business card, Mr. Drivas. Please call me when you and Ms. O'Kelly are ready to head to the hotel."

Taking the card, I slipped it into my wallet. "Thank you so much, Ted."

My hand took Kilyn's as I gave her a little tug. "You ready?"

Her head snapped around as she looked at me and nodded her head. "Oh, yeah! Totally."

The second we stepped out of the car and she looked at where we were and her eyes lit up, I knew all the trouble and money it cost me to do this was worth it.

When she turned and looked at me, she had tears in her eyes. "A carnival? You flew us to Texas on a private plane to take me to a carnival?"

With a wink, I replied, "That's one reason."

Her little crooked smile swept me off my damn feet. "Are you insane, Athanasios Adrax Drivas?"

Fuck, I loved when she said my full name.

"No. I'm in love."

A single tear slipped from her eye and slowly rolled down her cheek. Lifting my hand, I wiped it away.

Taking her hand in mine, I led her to the entrance. "Come on, they only stay open until one in the morning and we have a lot to do in only a couple of hours!"

I'd never seen Kilyn laugh and smile as much as she did tonight. We played games, rode rides until I felt like I was going to throw up, and ate carnival food until Kilyn thought she was going to throw up.

It was the perfect night.

Well, almost perfect.

Standing in line at the Ferris wheel, I couldn't help but feel nervous. With Kilyn standing at my door only just a few hours ago, ready to leave, I hoped like hell I wasn't about to really scare her off.

"We're up next!" she said with excitement in her voice.

As we approached the ride, my knees felt weak and my stomach was already twisting up in knots. Rubbing my hand across my pocket, I breathed a sigh of relief. It was still there.

Kilyn hopped into the bucket with a wide smile on her face. "My whole body feels like it is tingling!"

Chuckling, I took her hand in mine as we slowly made our way higher as the rest of the buckets were filled with people. When we got near the top, her jaw fell open and she gasped.

"Thano. It's beautiful. Look at all the lights."

I looked out over Dallas and nodded in agreement. "Was it worth the plane ride?"

She turned and looked at me. "This night has been beyond amazing. I don't think you could do anything else to make it any better."

Swallowing hard, I looked into her eyes. "I'm hoping I can."

Her green eyes filled with desire. She opened her mouth to talk when the ride started, causing her to let out a small yelp.

We both laughed as she looked out at everything. "This is amazing. I never really knew they were so tall."

"You've never seen the one up at Pikes Peak?"

She shook her head. "Nope!"

"Well, when it opens, I'll take you. Talk about views."

Kilyn smiled as she settled into my side. We went around two more times when I finally built up the courage to do it. Reaching into my pocket, I pulled out the blue box.

I cleared my throat and took a deep breath. "Ladybug?"

"Mmm?"

"I need to ask you something."

She moved away some and looked me directly in the eyes. "Anything," she said with a slight smile.

I'd never felt this way before. Not even with Savannah. There was something so profoundly different about this moment with Kilyn. Licking my lips to help with my dry mouth, I smiled and spoke with a wavering voice. "I love you so much."

Her face softened and warmth radiated throughout my body from the smile she gave me.

"I love you too, so very much. I'm sorry I freaked out earlier."

"None of that matters. All that matters is you're here with me right now." Looking into her eyes, I let out a breath and whispered, "You're so beautiful, Kilyn."

With a flush on her cheeks, she peered down at her hands.

Opening the box, I took a deep breath and slowly blew it out as I got ready to speak from my heart.

"You're truly the only woman I've ever felt my heart stop for. The thought of not having you in my life is one I never want to ever have again. You are my life. My future."

I held up the velvet box that held the princess-cut diamond. Kilyn covered her mouth with her hands and tried to hold back a sob.

"Kilyn O'Kelly, would you do me the honor of marrying me?"

Her eyes filled with tears and her hands dropped to her lap. Her chin trembled as she looked at the diamond and then back up into my eyes. "Is this really happening? Is this for real?"

Smiling, I nodded.

With a smile as big as the Texas sky, she exclaimed, "Yes! Yes, I will marry you!"

My hand laced through her hair while I grabbed her neck and pulled her lips to mine. There was nothing about this moment I would ever forget.

Not even when the ride stopped moving and we sat stuck at the very top for over an hour before they finally got the damn thing running again.

It was the best night of my life.

# twenty-nine

## Kilyn

*I* WAS FLYING HIGH AS Thano and I walked into the lobby of the Warwick Melrose Hotel. My eyes bounced all over as I took in the beauty of it all.

Reaching for my hand, he laced his fingers with mine as we walked to the front desk.

When we stopped, the young girl's eyes lit up at the sight of Thano. I was used to it now. The gawks and looks from women. Some even had the nerve to flirt with him right in front of me. At first it pissed me off, but in the end I was the one going home with him, so what did it matter.

"Good evening, welcome to the Warwick Melrose."

We both smiled as Thano replied, "Hey there. Reservations for Thano Drivas."

The girl quickly began typing. Her face lit up as she looked between the two of us.

"Yes, Mr. Drivas, I see we have you in our presidential suite."

My head whipped over to look at Thano. He chuckled and said, "No, I think you have that wrong. I only booked a king suite."

She glanced down at her computer again. Shaking her head, she replied, "No. No, I have here you are to be put in the presidential suite. You originally booked the king suite, but someone called and changed it. It also appears your two-night stay with us has been prepaid."

I was positive my jaw was on the ground.

"Does it say who called and changed it?" Thano asked.

She searched on her computer. "Looks like it was a Mr. Dimitris Drivas."

"Pateras," Thano whispered.

Scrunching my nose up, I thought for a moment. I was almost positive that meant father.

The young girl smiled. "So, here is your key, and you also have access to the private entrance around the side of the hotel if you would like to use it."

"That won't be necessary," Thano responded with a small chuckle.

After giving us the key and a map of the hotel and surrounding area, she grinned from ear to ear. "Are y'all here celebrating anything?"

I almost said no before I remembered the ring on my finger. Holding it up, I felt my heart quicken. "Thano asked me to marry him this evening."

"Congratulations! How exciting. Well, I hope we are able to make your engagement that much more special."

Thano looked at me and wiggled his eyebrows. "Oh, I think we have that covered."

THE MOMENT WE WALKED INTO the room, we both let out a gasp. I spun around and laughed. "This is bigger than your apartment!"

The living area was huge and had enough seating for Thano's entire family. Okay . . . maybe not all of them.

The kitchen was a full size kitchen that led to a dining room that seated ten people.

"We're totally having sex on that table," Thano said in a seductive voice.

Nodding in agreement, we made our way to the bedroom. My hands immediately came up to my mouth as I took in the sight before me.

The room was absolutely the most beautiful room I'd ever seen. "Look at the fabrics and colors they used in here," I gasped. The use of the cream and blue colors was beyond breathtaking.

Thano let out a chuckle. "Only you would notice the fabric and not the flowers."

In that moment, I was overcome with the smell of flowers. There were vases of daisies everywhere. Every color and every size.

"I can't believe your dad did this!"

Taking me in his arms, Thano captured my eyes with his. "My father had nothing to do with the flowers. I asked for that to be done."

My heart melted on the spot and my stomach fluttered.

"I love it. It's very romantic."

His lips moved gently along my jaw line as my body erupted in goose bumps and my breath stalled.

"You haven't even begun to see romantic yet, ladybug."

"Yes, please."

Pressing his lips to mine, I got lost in the kiss like I always did.

What was I even thinking earlier when I tried to leave? My life would never be the same without Thano. He was the very air I needed to breathe.

He whispered against my lips, causing a shiver to run down my back. "Love me, forever."

"Forever," I softly replied.

Thano slowly began to lift my shirt over my head while he continued to speak.

"Never doubt my love for you."

With a lazy shake of my head, I whispered back, "Never."

Reaching behind my back, he expertly unclasped my bra and removed it. His mouth was on my nipple as his hand played with the other, building my desire.

"Thano," I gasped as he moved his lips down my stomach while dropping to his knees.

Unbuttoning my jeans, he peered up and smiled at me. The same one that showed his dimples, and absolutely made my heart soar.

My jeans and panties were quickly pulled down while I stepped out of them and kicked them to the side. With a quickening heartbeat, I pulled Thano up and started to undress him, and not in the slow romantic way he undressed me. It was frantic and rushed. I needed to feel him up against my bare skin.

He engulfed me in an embrace, eliciting a moan from each of us.

"You feel so good," he said, lifting me up while I wrapped my legs around him.

Walking us over to the bed, he gently laid me down. Every nerve ending in my body was on fire.

"Slide up the bed, ladybug."

I quickly did as he asked. I wasn't sure how Thano seemed to make every time we made love feel like our first time, but he did.

His hands moved up my legs as my body trembled from his touch. No one could ever love me like Thano. He released my deepest desires.

My back arched as he took a nipple in his mouth and pushed his fingers inside of me, pulling a long deep moan from my mouth.

"You're mine, Kilyn."

Thrashing my head back and forth, I gripped the satin bedspread. My body ached from the need to release what was building. "Yours, forever yours."

His lips moved up and across my neck as I felt my orgasm beginning to grow.

Thano's lips pressed against mine while he pushed my legs open with his knee and slowly slid into my body. I was so worked up, I knew the moment he moved I'd come. I needed it. I longed for it more than I ever had.

Pulling his lips from mine, he began to move agonizingly slow in and out of me while placing his mouth against my ear. His hot breath caused my eyes to practically roll to the back of my head. I swear, when he made love to me it was my high. My rush. The drug I longed for with every single breath I took.

Sucking in a breath, Thano slowly released it. "I can't wait to make you my wife," he whispered in my ear.

My chest fluttered with his whispered words as my orgasm rushed across my entire body as we cried out each other's name.

My arms wrapped around his neck while his lips crashed to mine.

We came together. In one of the most beautiful rooms I'd ever been in. Our whispered names against each other's lips sounded as if they were echoing in the room.

It was the most intimate, beautiful, romantic, and unbelievable moment of my life.

I wasn't sure how long we had lain there as my fingers moved lazily over his back.

"Do we have to leave this hotel room?" Thano asked, breaking the silence.

With a giggle, I responded, "I wish we could stay here forever!"

Looking into my eyes, his expression turned serious. "Kilyn?"

With a smile, I replied, "Yeah?"

"How would you feel about eloping?"

I couldn't help myself from laughing. When he didn't laugh back, my smile dropped and my eyes widened in an astonished look.

"You're serious?"

"Dead serious."

My heart froze as I looked at him with a dumbfounded look on my face.

With a sigh, he pushed his hand through his already messy hair then dropped it. With a shake of his head, he focused back on me. His eyes looked troubled and the only thing I could think of was his family wouldn't bless our union.

Tears filled my eyes as I looked down.

Would our lives always be like this? Always fighting to prove we belonged together.

Squaring off my shoulders, I decided our life together was worth whatever fight we had to go through and I was not giving up on another dream of mine.

Sitting up, I pulled the sheet up and covered my body. I wasn't sure I would be ready for his answer, but I asked it anyway.

"Why do you want to elope?"

## thirty

### Thano

THE LOOK IN KILYN'S EYES was a mix of fear and strength. I knew she thought what I was going to say was something bad.

"The moment my family finds out I've asked you to marry me, two things will happen."

She sucked in a deep long breath and braced herself. "The first will be my mother getting on me and saying it's too soon, even though we've been together for almost six months."

Lifting her brows in a quizzical manner, she asked, "And the second thing?"

"They will insist we get married in our church. If you weren't baptized in a Catholic Church, it will become a huge affair."

I could see her body physically relax. "They won't disagree with the marriage?"

With a laugh, I shook my head. "Baby, look around at this hotel room my father got for us. Do you really think he doesn't want you to be a part of our family?"

Her eyes searched around the room as she let out a chuckle. "I guess I'm letting my thoughts get ahead of me."

Reaching for her hands, I pulled them up to my lips. "Kilyn, my family is crazy. They are big and loud and no matter how long we are married someone is going to say something about you not being Greek. That's something we both need to come to grips with and realize that it doesn't matter. What matters is I love you and you love me. I want to spend the rest of my life together with you. As much as I love my family . . . you're going to be my new family."

Her lips parted as a small smile spread over her beautiful face. "Your mother will not be happy with us eloping."

I shrugged. "So we don't tell them."

When she looked away and took in a deep breath, I knew something was wrong.

"Talk to me, ladybug."

She swallowed hard and turned back to me. Her eyes were bright and full of happiness, yet they held a sadness there too.

"When I was little, I used to tell my parents that when I got married I was going to have a wedding on the beach. My mother would sit with me for hours, it seemed like, as we went through wedding websites and I planned my wedding. I even had a book that I would print stuff out and put it in there. I was no different than any other little girl when it came to dreaming of my fairy tale wedding. I even had a checklist."

I smiled and took her hand in mine. Shit. I can't believe how selfish I was being. By trying to save her from a Greek overload, I was stripping her of something she wanted.

"When that night happened with Peter . . . he stripped away every dream I ever had. In my mind, I thought for sure no man would ever want to be with a girl who was tainted."

My chest squeezed as I thought about what that fucker did to her. "Kilyn," I whispered as she held up her finger.

"Wait, let me say all of this."

I closed my mouth and gave her a nod.

"Until I met you, Thano, I didn't have any of those dreams anymore. You reached deep inside of me and turned my life back on. Piece by piece I felt myself coming back. On the outside I pretended like everything was great . . . and in some ways it was. But I was missing something I longed for. Love."

Her hands came up and cupped my face as the most breathtaking smile appeared. "Your love. You, Thano. I don't want to run anymore. I love you and I know the road ahead of us is going to be hard at times, but I don't want to start our life together running away and getting married."

With a smile, I slowly nodded. "Then we won't. Tell me what you want, ladybug."

Her eyes seemed to have kicked up their intensity. They were filled with love but also with a confidence I'd never seen before.

"I want a beach wedding. I want Claire there and her parents. I want your parents there. I want to shop for an expensive as hell wedding dress and I want to see you standing next to a beautiful blue ocean looking handsome as hell in a black tux."

My heart felt as if it was going to pound out of my chest. It was in that very moment I knew I was going to give her everything she asked for.

"Do you know how turned on I am right now?"

She laughed and shook her head. "Why?"

"Because I love how strong you are. You know what you want and you're not afraid to say it. It's sexy as fuck."

She wiggled her eyebrows and purred, "Should I keep telling you all the things I want?"

"Yes."

"I want you buried deep inside of me telling me how much you love me."

Pulling the sheet away from her, she let out a small scream and giggled while I pulled her legs down and got her flat on the bed.

Crawling over her, I slowly began working my cock into her until I was buried balls deep inside of her. I hovered my lips above hers and softly said, "Done."

PEERING OVER TO KILYN IN the passenger seat, my heart skipped a beat. Neither one of us was able to wipe the smiles off our faces. The last few days had been incredible. We only left the hotel room once and that was to go get lunch. The rest of the time we ordered room service and made love in every single room and on I swear every surface we could find.

"Have you told Claire yet?" I asked.

Kilyn turned and grinned from ear to ear as she looked at me. "No. I want to see her reaction in person."

With a lighthearted chuckle, I nodded. "So, do you want to pick a date?"

She sucked in her lower lip and began chewing on it. "Thano . . . I need to tell you something that I probably should have told you a few months ago."

My heart dropped. Her eyes turned serious and I swear my hands started to sweat as I wiped each one on my pant legs.

"Do I need to pull over or something?"

She chuckled. "No. Sorry, I didn't mean to scare you. It's just, with us being engaged, I feel a bit guilty for not saying anything. I don't want you to worry about how we'll afford to pay for the wedding."

My head snapped over as I looked at her. I quickly looked around and pulled into a grocery store parking lot and put my truck into park.

Unbuckling, I turned to Kilyn. "There isn't anything I wouldn't do to make you happy. You know that right?"

She nodded.

"I'm not the least bit worried about paying for our wedding. If you wanted to have it in a French castle, I'd make it work."

Lifting her brow, she tried not to laugh. "Mmm, that might be kind of fun."

Taking her hand in mine, I squeezed it. "I'm serious."

Her face softened. "I know you are and I love you for that. But that's not what I'm trying to say. Um, well, I'm just going to tell you."

I nodded and held my breath.

"When my parents died, they, of course, left everything to me. My father was very successful and was also very business smart. I kind of have . . . well . . . let's just say I'm not hurting for money."

Narrowing my eyes, I said, "Okay. Well, that's good baby, but I'm not worried about that. I get paid pretty well, so the last thing I'm worried about it money."

She nodded and gave me a weak smile. "Thano, my parents' estate is valued at over 5 million dollars, or it was the last time I met with my father's lawyer. With his investments and real estate properties, my father wanted to make sure his family was always taken care of."

I closed my eyes and slightly shook my head before opening them again. "What?"

Chewing on her lip, she nodded. "I hope you're not mad I didn't say anything, but I've never touched the money except to pay for college, and I haven't been to my house in about six years."

"Your house?"

"Yeah, my parents' house here in town. They also own a place in the Bahamas. That's where I went a few months back when I left for a few days."

I was so confused. "Why were you in an apartment or living at Claire's if you had a house?"

With a shrug, she gave me a weak smile. "I haven't been able to go back there. In all honesty, I'm afraid to go, and I really need to probably sell it. I'll never live there."

"Why?" I asked.

Her eyes filled with tears. "It would feel like I've lost them all over again if I stepped foot in there. I can't do it."

My heart broke as I saw the sadness in her eyes.

"What if I went with you?"

She sniffled. "You're not upset I didn't tell you about the money?"

I turned and opened my door, getting out of the truck. Walking around the front, I opened her door and pulled her out. Cupping her face with my hands, I looked directly into her eyes. "Kilyn, I wouldn't care if you had a billion dollars. I love you for you. This doesn't change anything about how I feel about you. If you told me you never wanted to touch your parents' money I'd be perfectly fine with that. This right here—"

Pointing between our two bodies, I smiled. "This . . . this is all I care about. You and me. Us."

Tears fell from her eyes as she slammed her body against mine. "I love you, Athanasios. I love you so much."

"I love you too, ladybug. More than you'll ever realize."

She pulled back and looked into my eyes. "My parents set aside an account that was strictly for my wedding. I used that money for college but my father's investors are good at what they do and it's made some money."

With a smile, I pushed a loose strand of brown hair behind her ear. "Then you plan the wedding of your dreams, baby. And if we need more money I've got money set aside."

She scrunched her nose up and said, "There's a hundred and twenty thousand dollars in the account so I think we'll be fine."

All I could do was stare at her. "Jesus, Kilyn. What in the hell kind of wedding book did you make when you were little?"

Laughing, she playfully hit me on the chest. "My parents both came from poverty. When they met in college, they made a vow that they would never know what it felt like to be hungry again, and they made the same vow when I was born. That's why my father became a doctor and my mother a lawyer. They worked hard for their money and made smart choices."

An idea popped into my head and I made a mental note to talk to Kilyn about it later. Now wasn't the time.

"They sound like they were amazing people."

With a sad smile, she replied, "They were."

Pulling her in, I hugged her. "Let's head home."

"Sounds like a plan."

On the drive back to Manitou Springs, Kilyn and I came up with a date for the wedding. June 7. It was her mother's birthday. It only left us with a few months to plan the wedding, but I assured her we could do it.

When I pulled into my parking spot, we both let out a sigh of relief.

"As much as I loved Dallas, it was such a whirlwind. I'm so glad to be home!"

Grabbing our bags from the back seat, I nodded in agreement. "Me too."

Kilyn skipped up to me and flashed me a huge smile. "Can we ask

Claire and Blake out to dinner to tell them?"

Her happiness was practically dripping from her smile. "Of course!"

She let out a squeal of delight and pulled out her phone.

"Claire!" she shouted as we walked up to our apartment.

"Are you and Blake free for dinner tonight? Yes! The little surprise getaway was amazing and that's what I want to talk to you about."

Her smile faded. "What? How do you know?"

Turning to look at her, I pushed the key into the front door and unlocked it. I couldn't help but notice the look of confusion on Kilyn's face.

I pushed the door open and my heart fell.

Oh, holy fuck.

"Athanasios!"

My eyes scanned over my entire family standing in my apartment.

"Claire, I can't talk to you right now. I'll have to call you back."

Kilyn hit End as we both stood there in shock.

Rushing over to Kilyn was a group of women led by my mother. When they stopped right in front of her, my mother reached for Kilyn's hand. She gasped and then held it up as everyone yelled out, "Opa!"

Closing my eyes, I silently cursed myself for ever trusting my father to keep a secret.

## thirty-one

### Kilyn

*I* STOOD FROZEN AS ABOUT forty people from Thano's family stood around me yelling out, "Opa!"

Peeking over to Thano, he had his eyes closed before he opened them and began searching the room. I was sure he was looking for his father.

"Oh, we need to start planning the wedding!" Aunt Maria exclaimed.

"Dress shopping is first! I have the perfect dress shop," Sophia added.

Katerina held up her hands. "Now, stop this. We are jumping ahead of ourselves." Taking my hand in hers, she pulled me to the middle of the family. "We need to get our Kilyn baptized in the church first!"

*Oh. Shit.*

I hadn't mentally prepared myself for facing this right now.

Lifting up on my toes, I searched for Thano.

"We need to have an engagement party. Just for the family."

My heart was pounding.

Katerina started to point to people. "Maria, you are in charge of the invitations."

"For what?" I quickly asked.

Katerina looked at me like I had grown two heads. "The engagement party! Oh, we'll have to start planning the meals now."

Conversations started exploding all around me. From decorations, to a band, to who was going to make the baklava.

The word alone made me want to gag. My hand went to my stomach just thinking about the baklava.

Ugh.

I frantically searched for Thano as I tried to make my way through the crowd. When Thano's cousin Sophia picked up my hand, she gasped. "It's beautiful. Oh, and look at your cheeks. It's so cute! They're flushed."

*I wonder why?*

"You look so beautiful."

And then it happened. Women started coming up to me . . . and spitting on me. Or making the sound of spitting. Little did they know they sucked at pretend spitting.

Pft. Pft. Pft.

Each time they did it, my face jerked back as if I was being mortally wounded.

"Thano!" I called out.

Phoebe came up and pulled my ring up to examine it. "Oh, it's gorgeous!"

Pft. Pft. Pft.

I was going to need a bath.

Jumping up, I desperately tried to find him.

"Thano!"

"Kilyn, I'd love for you to try on my wedding dress."

Everything in the room stopped. Including my breathing. Slowly I turned to face Katerina and swallowed hard. "Wh-what?"

Her smile grew bigger. "My wedding dress! I bet all it needs is a few tweaks."

My eyes grew in horror.

"THANO!" I screamed.

My body relaxed the moment I felt his hand on my back. "Yep, I'm on it."

Glancing up at him, I noticed the distraught look on his face.

"They ambushed us!" hc said as he guided me to the bedroom.

"How did they know?"

With a scowl, Thano hissed. "My father!"

When we finally made it to the bedroom, Thano pushed me and locked the door behind him.

Placing his hands on his knees, he dragged in a few breaths. "I've never . . . never seen them this insane."

I stood there staring at him as I tried to get my heart rate under control. I couldn't help it. I started laughing as I covered my mouth.

Thano glanced up and gave me an incredulous look. "What in the world do you find funny about any of this?"

Dropping my hands, I laughed harder, causing Thano to start laughing. Soon we were both laughing so hard, we had tears rolling down our cheeks.

The knock at the door quickly snapped us both out of our moment of weakness.

Thano looked at me with a panicked expression. "We need an escape plan."

"No, you need to change your damn locks!" I said.

He nodded. "That too."

Pulling out my phone from my back pocket, I hit Claire's number. "We need you."

"Oh, this sounds like fun. I'm not sure Blake would be into that kind of thing, but I'll ask."

I jerked the phone away from my ear and looked at it. "What the hell?"

"Kilyn! I'm kidding!"

Rolling my eyes, I made arrangements for us to meet them for dinner.

"How are you going to get away from the family?"

"We'll figure it out," I said as I watched Thano go to the window. "It might not be a very good plan, but we'll figure it out. Got to go. See ya in a few."

Hitting End, I pushed my phone into my back pocket and gawked at him. "You cannot be serious."

With a frown, he shrugged.

The knock on the bedroom door had both of us stopping and glaring at it.

It was Katerina. "Athanasios? Kilyn? Now is not the time for celebrating!"

I spun around and pushed Thano toward the window. "Go! Go! Go!"

* * * ❤️ * * *

## JUNE—THE BAHAMAS

STANDING IN FRONT OF THE mirror, I fought to hold my tears back. If I ruined my makeup Aunt Maria would have a fit.

Claire and her mother, Kim, stood behind me with a huge grin across their faces. "Oh my. Kilyn, you look beautiful," Kim gushed.

Claire and I froze as we looked around the room.

No one heard her. Thank God.

"I can't believe this day is finally here," I said in trembling voice. "Did the flowers finally arrive for the tables?"

The wedding and reception were being held at my parents' house on the beach. Well, I guess it was actually my house. When Thano and I arrived four days ago, I thought it would be hard to walk into the house knowing my parents wouldn't be here for my wedding. It was the opposite. My heart was filled with so much joy. Especially walking around and showing Thano family pictures. We had yet to go to the house I grew up in back in Colorado. I wasn't ready yet. But being here . . . this was a step in the right direction.

"Everything looks amazing."

Glancing over my shoulder, I smiled at Claire. "I couldn't have done any of this without you. I hope you know that."

With a smile and a quick nod of her head, she took my hands. "There were a few moments I didn't think we would make it." She leaned in closer. "Like the day you told Katerina you were not wearing her dress."

We both trembled at the memory. I had to hand it to Thano's mother, though; she handled each letdown with grace and poise. Of course, that was after she spat something off to me in Greek.

Turning back, I looked at my wedding dress. It fit me like a glove, hugging my curves until it flared out at the bottom just enough to make walking easy. Thano was going to die when he saw me in this.

My hands ran down my body as thought about what I had under the dress.

"You're blushing," Claire whispered as she reached over my head and placed the diamond necklace that my mother wore on her wedding day around my neck.

My shaking hand came up to it and lightly touched it. My voice faltered as I said, "It's beautiful."

Kim opened up the wedding book I had made all those years ago with my mother and put a check in the box that read, Mom's diamond necklace.

With a chortle, Kim walked up and showed me the book. "The only thing left to check is, Marry the man of my dreams.

When she handed me my bouquet, I covered my mouth to keep from crying. I'd have given anything to have my parents here, but I knew deep down inside they were with me. God, how they would have loved Thano.

Taking the flowers in one hand, I dropped my other hand to my side. "I'll check that one myself after the wedding."

With a wink, she shut the book and set it on the table.

"Your mother and father would have loved Thano. You can see how much he loves you when he looks at you."

Blinking rapidly, I tried to keep my hands from shaking.

Kim reached up and placed her hand lovingly on the side of my face. "They would have been so proud of you. I hope you know that."

With a weak voice, I replied, "I do."

"You're so blessed to have a new family who loves and cares about you my darling."

Looking into Kim's eyes, I smiled. "I am. But I'm more blessed having you and Scott in my life. I'll never forget what you've both done for me and the hurt you've had to go through."

Her hand lifted as her fingers wrapped around a loose curl framing my face. "I'm so happy you found happiness."

Pressing my lips together, I barely was able to speak. "Me too."

She leaned over and softly kissed my cheek. "I'm going to go check on everything. The wedding will be starting soon."

With a nod, I took in a deep breath as I watched her walk away. It was then my eyes caught Katerina's. She slowly walked up to me, reaching her hand out for mine as she squeezed it.

"You make him so happy."

Swallowing hard, I replied, "He makes me so happy."

She nodded. "Do you know what I admire the most about you, Kilyn?"

I shook my head.

With a crooked smile, she answered. "Your strength. I know the family can be a bit overwhelming at times."

With a chuckle, I replied, "At times."

"But you never let it scare you off. And most of all, you followed your own dreams."

Looking down for a quick moment, I peered back into her eyes. "You're not upset with me that I didn't want to marry in the church?"

"At first, I was upset. I will not lie. But times are different, and I've been stubborn in letting go of some of the traditions in the family. But in the end, I only want my son's happiness."

Reaching up, I quickly wiped a tear away.

She shook her finger. "Dab! Don't wipe."

Laughing, I nodded. "Yes ma'am."

Next to walk up was Thano's Yiayia. Placing her hands on my stomach, she said something in Greek that caused every other Greek in the room to start cheering.

"Opa!"

I swallowed hard and looked at Claire. She leaned in and said, "Rather that than them spitting on you."

"What did she say?" I asked Katerina.

With a wink, she took my hand in her hand. "She wishes you to have a baby before she dies."

"Oh," was all I could manage to say as I looked at her and forced a smile.

The door opened and Sara the wedding planner stepped inside. There were so many conversations going on, I had given up long ago trying to listen to them all. Katerina's sister and a few of the cousins along with Yiayia had been in my dressing room all morning. One of the Marias did my hair while Sophia, did my makeup along with Claire's.

"All right. It's time to clear out the room and get seated ladies."

I breathed a sigh of relief. I'd already told Sara I was going to need a few moments by myself before the ceremony. I loved Thano's family, but I still needed to get used to them.

Claire walked up to me and smiled. She looked beautiful in her champagne colored dress. The strapless sweetheart bodice made her already tiny waist look smaller, while the tiered ruffle gown added the perfect amount of fun for a beach wedding.

"Are you okay?"

With a quick nod, I said, "Yep."

Narrowing her left eye at me, she tilted her head. "Are you okay?"

My chin trembled. "I've never been so happy in my life, Claire. I'm so afraid I'm about to wake up and it's all going to be a dream. Do I deserve to be this happy?"

"Oh, Kilyn, sweetie. I promise you this is not a dream, and yes, you more than anyone deserves it."

I closed my eyes and counted to twenty as I took in a deep breath. "God, I hope no one spits on me as I walk down the aisle."

Opening my eyes, we both busted out laughing.

The light knock on the door drew my attention to it. Scott, Claire's father, poked his head in. "Hey. I was instructed to get you out Claire."

She glanced back at me and pouted. "See ya soon, babe."

I nodded and let go of her hand.

Scott held the door open for Claire and then shut it behind them.

Setting the bouquet down, I slowly walked around the room.

"I'm getting married," I whispered out loud.

Walking up to the window, I peered out. I could see all the white chairs set up on the beach. The long red carpet led almost to the water's edge as I followed it with my eyes.

My breath caught when I saw him.

Thano.

I covered my mouth as a sob escaped from my lips. He was dressed in a black tux standing next to his best friend Gus. My eyes drifted down and I giggled when I saw he didn't have any shoes on.

He was standing there in his bare feet and it had to have been the sexiest thing I'd ever seen.

Then his eyes locked on mine as my stomach dipped and my chest fluttered. He smiled and I returned the gesture.

I wasn't sure if he knew I was in this room or he felt me looking. Either way, I was lost in those eyes. Lost in his love for me.

Lifting my hand, I placed it on the window. I'm marrying this man. My very own Greek god.

The light knock on the door had me dropping my hand and stepping away from the window.

"Hey, darling. Are you ready?"

Placing my hands over my stomach, I giggled. "I'm so nervous."

Scott walked up to me and placed his hands on my arms. "I remember the day I married Kim."

Smiling, I asked, "Were you nervous?"

He pulled his head back and chuckled. "Nervous? No. I was scared to death."

I instantly felt my body relaxing.

"Then I saw her walking down the aisle and it was like pouf! I was no longer scared. I didn't need to know if we were going to be okay. All I needed was that beautiful smile walking toward me. When she finally made it to me all my worries and fears were replaced with pure happiness. That's the only way I can describe it."

With a wide grin, I looked down as I thought of my parents. Looking back up at Scott, I cleared my throat. "Thank you, for everything you've ever done for me. Everything. And thank you for standing in for my father today. As much as I'd love to have him here, I love that you're the one walking me down the aisle."

A tear slipped from his eyes as he quickly wiped it away. "I love you like you're my own daughter. I hope you know that."

Nodding, I whispered, "I do, and I love you."

"Now, come on before you have us both crying and you get me in trouble with Sara."

With a giggle, I leaned in and kissed him on the cheek. Scott took my flowers and handed them to me.

"Ready?"

Dragging in a deep breath, I replied, "Ready!"

## thirty-two

### Thano

**W**HEN SHE STEPPED AWAY FROM the window my chest squeezed.

Taking in a deep breath, I turned out and looked out over the ocean. The last time I stood in this spot it ended in a way I'd probably never forget. Frowning, I thought about how I didn't feel the least bit guilty.

With Kilyn everything was so different. It felt different. I felt different. I wasn't nervous. I wasn't worried.

Smiling, I thought about last night when I had a drink with my Pappou.

*"Tomorrow is the planting season," he said with a smile.*

*"The planting season?" I had a feeling this was my grandfather's way of saying I needed to get Kilyn pregnant quickly.*

*Taking a drink, he nodded. "Athanasios, do you know how love works?"*

*With a laugh, I tilted my head and replied, "I would hope I know a little something."*

*He shook his head, "Nah, you know nothing."*

*Laughing, I motioned for him to speak. "Tell me, Pappou."*

*With a smile, he leaned closer to me. "I'll tell you what my Pappou told* me the night before I married your Yiayia. You build love from the ground up. It takes watering and care. The sun will shine on it most days." He nodded as if lost in a thought. Lifting his hand he pointed up. "But . . . those clouds, oh, those clouds will move in and storms will come. You have to be her shelter, Athanasios. She is a strong woman, but she needs you by her side always. You tend to her with love and passion. A woman likes a strong man in and out of her bed."

I looked away, smiled and nodded. "I will always tend to our love."

"Good," he responded. "Now, when can I expect a child from your Irish beauty?"

The music began as Gus tapped me on the back. "This is it, dude."

I spun around and took in a deep breath.

My little cousin, Nichole, came skipping down the aisle. She was singing something as she threw rose petals up in the air. With a chuckle, I watched as she came to stop right in front of me.

"Athanasios! Kilyn looks like a princess!"

Everyone laughed.

Leaning down, I asked, "Does she look as beautiful as you do?"

Nichole's face lit up. "Yes!" She moved in closer and whispered, "Don't tell anyone, but I think she looks the prettiest out of everyone. I don't want to hurt any feelings."

I crossed my heart and replied back. "I won't tell anyone."

Standing, I watched as Sara motioned for Nichole to stand to the side. As she turned to leave she stopped and quickly spun around. "Oh! I heard Kilyn telling Claire that you were going to love what she had on under her dress too! I think it's another dress because they were both really happy about it."

My mouth fell open as I stared at her and Gus busted out laughing next to me.

Nichole spun around in a twirl and skipped over to Sara.

I cleared my throat and tried not to look at my parents.

Gus leaned in and said, "Jesus, I hope like hell that was captured on the video. I want so badly to see your face."

Hitting him with my elbow, I said, "Shut up, Gus. Just stand there and be quiet." I smiled when I saw Claire walking down the aisle. She looked beautiful. It took everything out of me not to start laughing when a few of my mother's cousins began to act like they were spitting on her. Claire must have jumped ten feet in the air as she looked at them with a horrified expression. When she made it up to the front she flashed me a smile.

"Is she okay?" I asked.

With a nod, she replied, "I've never seen her so happy or look so beautiful."

Heat surged through my body and I swear everyone could hear my heart pounding.

The music changed and the music began to play. "Here we go," Gus mumbled as I tried to calm my racing heart. He placed his hand on my shoulder and gave it a squeeze. I was glad he was here with me and able to be my best man.

The moment she appeared in front of me I was left breathless. She smiled as soon as she saw me. It was like we were the only two people as our gaze locked on each other.

It felt like it took them forever to walk down the aisle. I was so lost in her beauty I wasn't even paying attention to my crazy family.

Stopping in front of me, Scott lifted her veil and kissed her on both cheeks. Taking my hand, he placed her hand in it. "Take care of her."

With a nod of my head, I replied, "Always, sir."

Placing my attention back on the most beautiful woman I'd ever seen, I couldn't help but grin from ear to ear. "You truly are stunning. No amount of words could describe how beautiful you look."

She pressed her lips together before finding her voice. "You look so very handsome."

"Is it how you pictured it?"

With a chuckle, she answered, "So much better."

We turned to face the pastor and took the two steps up to him.

I wasn't even sure what all he said. All I knew was the love of my life was standing next to me and was about to become my wife.

Life could never get better.

═══ 🖤 ═══

THE WEDDING CEREMONY FLEW BY in a blink of an eye. Then it was pictures. That was fun trying to get my family to stop talking long enough for the photographer to get everyone in one picture.

Kilyn and I had requested a few minutes alone together before joining everyone for the reception. We stood there on the edge of the water and watched as Sara ushered everyone up to the house.

Turning, I cupped her face in my hands. "Finally. I'm alone with my wife." Pressing my lips softly to hers, I whispered, "Hello, Mrs. Drivas."

Her eyes lit up. "Say that again."

"Which part, Mrs. Drivas?"

With a giggle, she wrapped her arms around my neck. She went to kiss me when we heard cheers from the house.

"Opa!"

Laughing, I rested my forehead against hers. "Are you ready for a party like none other?" I asked.

"I think so. I do have something I need to tell you though."

Pulling my head back, I smiled. "You made plans to have a boat come up and take us away?"

Her smile made my knees weak. "Nope."

"Um, let's see. You told my mother no baklava?"

She frowned. "Ugh, I wish I could tell her that. Although, I've gotten good at avoiding it without her catching on."

I threw my head back and laughed. "Oh, man. I don't know. I give up, tell me."

Reaching into her bouquet, she pulled out a folded up piece of paper.

Cheers came from the house again as I heard my brother Thad yelling at us.

"Thano! Kilyn! Come on, everyone is waiting for you two!"

Glancing back that way, I held up my finger, motioning for him to give us another minute.

I glimpsed back to the folded paper and took it in.

"What is it?"

Her teeth sunk into her lip before she said, "Open it."

Taking the paper from her, I unfolded it. What I saw I was not expecting.

Lifting my eyes, I smiled.

"Is this . . . are we?"

She nodded. "I guess it was the luck of the Irish and your Yiayia's damn fertile loving hands she kept placing on my stomach all the damn time."

Pulling her into my arms, I spun her around as she laughed and I called out, "Opa!"

When I put her down, I looked into her green eyes. I tried like hell to keep my tears back, but I lost the battle. "A baby? We're having a baby?"

"Yep. Are you truly happy? I know this wasn't planned and I honestly have no idea how it happened." She lifted her eyes in thought. "Well, I mean I do, but you know what I mean."

"I've never been so damn happy in my life."

She giggled. "Good, because I'm happy too!"

My eyes searched her face. "Man, I love this life."

Her grin grew bigger. "Me too."

Reaching down, I swept her off her feet and carried her up to the house.

When we walked through the gate, I called out, "Guess what!"

Kilyn looked at me with horror.

Winking, I said, "The bride and groom have arrived!"

It didn't take long before we were surrounded by family.

The rest of afternoon and evening was filled with lots of laughing, drinking, dancing, and eating.

When they announced it was time to have the bride and groom dance, I walked up and took the mic from Nicholaus.

"First I want to thank everyone for traveling here for our wedding. It meant a lot to Kilyn and myself to have you all here. When Kilyn left it up to me to pick the song we would dance to, I knew immediately which song it would be."

I glanced over to my beautiful bride. "When Kilyn entered my life, I was living in darkness. Afraid to let life in. But the more I got to know this beautiful woman, the more I realized I didn't want to be in the dark any longer. She had a love for life that was infectious. Just being around her made me happy. It still does."

Kilyn looked at me with such love in her eyes, I swear I fell in love with her even more. "When Kilyn told me she loved me, I thought it was the best moment of my life. When she said yes to my marriage proposal, I thought it was the best moment of my life. But today . . . today, I realized something. We have so many more best moments ahead of us and knowing that makes me the happiest son of a bitch on the planet."

Cheers erupted again as Thad handed me a glass of champagne. Lifting it, I looked directly at my beautiful bride. She lifted her glass and winked. "So, before I dance with my beautiful bride, a toast!"

Everyone lifted their glass as I shouted, "Gia Mas!"

The room once again erupted in cheers of *gia mas* and *opa*.

I turned to the DJ and motioned for him to start the song as I jumped down off the chair and quickly made my way over to Kilyn. When the first notes of "I Love This Life" started, Kilyn jumped up and down.

"Yes!" she shouted as I picked her up and spun her around.

Setting her back down, I placed my hand on the side of her face and smiled.

"Stay with me forever."

Her hand covered mine as she smiled and replied, "Forever."

Placing my lips up next to her ear, I said, "We're having a baby."

Her head fell back as she laughed and screamed out, "Opa!"

## thirty-three

SIX MONTHS LATER

## Kilyn

THANO AND I STOOD AT the end of the sidewalk that led to the house I grew up in.

"Are you ready?" he asked as I pulled in a shaky breath.

Nodding, I replied, "I think so."

As we slowly started toward the front door, I realized that the only reason I stayed away from this house was because it was easier for me to forget the memories rather than deal with my parents' death.

Falling in love with Thano and finding out I was going to be a mother, I knew I needed to finally face my last fear.

We stopped, and I looked up at the large wooden door. My body trembled as I lifted my hand and placed the key in the lock. When I turned it and heard the click, it felt as if it rattled my entire body.

I faced Thano, fear etched on my face.

"I'm right here, ladybug."

Taking his hand in mine, I pushed the door open and took a step inside. Ahead of me was the familiar staircase I ran up and down for so many years. Instead of being filled with sadness, I was overcome with a sense of peace and happiness.

As I walked in, a memory of my father standing at the bottom of the steps yelling for me to hurry up or I would miss piano flooded my mind.

Covering my mouth with my hand, I didn't try to hold back my tears. I let them fall freely as Thano squeezed my hand to let me know he was still there.

Turning, I made my way into the family room. Everything was exactly how I remembered it. Even my mother's favorite candle sat on the coffee table. Dropping Thano's hand, I walked up to the fireplace mantel and grabbed the box of matches. Striking it, I lit the candle and let the aroma fill the air.

I laughed when I saw the unfinished puzzle in the corner.

"My father loved puzzles," I said as I walked over to it.

Glancing over to Thano, I saw him walk up to the baby grand piano and pick up a picture of when I was five.

"You look so adorable in this picture. I like the pigtails."

I wiggled my eyebrows. "Oh, yeah? Pigtails, huh?"

His eyes darkened. "I think you should wear them tonight."

I shook my head. "You're terrible. We are in my parents' house and you're talking about sex."

"I didn't say anything about sex. You're the one who took it there."

With a shrug, I smiled. "I'm pregnant. I'm allowed to take it there."

When he walked up to me, his smile faded some. "How are you holding up?"

"Honestly, it's not as bad as I thought it would be. I'm glad I kept the housekeeper coming, though. Everything looks so neat and clean. Bless her soul, she didn't move a thing."

Thano looked around. "Show me the rest of the house."

I did just that. Each room we entered I was swept away almost immediately in a memory. We saved my parents' room for last. Slowly opening the doors, I walked in. It was then the sadness swept across my body. The knowledge that my mother would never hold my son or daughter in her arms hit me as I felt my legs give out.

Thano had his arms around me and walked me over to the love seat that was positioned in the reading nook of the room. "Sit down, baby. Take a deep breath and slowly blow it out."

His thumbs wiped my tears away as I whispered how sorry I was. He placed his hand on my eight-month pregnant belly and smiled.

"Kilyn, you never have to say you're sorry. I won't even pretend to understand how this makes you feel. All I can say is I'm here for you and I always will be. I'll never leave your side."

I gazed into his eyes and saw nothing but love. Placing my hand on his cheek, I closed my eyes. "Thank you for being so patient with me."

"Kilyn, there was nothing to be patient about. You needed to do this on your own time."

With a nod, I pulled in a deep breath and slowly let it out. "I think I know what I want to do with the house."

"You do? That's good."

Standing, I looked around my parents' room and in that moment I swear I felt their presence.

"I want to do like what you suggested a few months back. Turn it into a place where young women who have been sexually assaulted or physically abused can come and stay. They can get counseling and live here until they get on their feet."

Thano stood and walked up behind me, kissing me on my neck. "I think that is a wonderful idea, Kilyn, and one your parents would be very proud of you for."

Spinning around, I faced him. "Will you help me make it happen, Thano?"

"Oh, ladybug. Eísai i zoi mou. There isn't anything I wouldn't do for you."

Wrapping my arms around his neck, my eyes fell to his soft lips. "Fíla me, Athanasios."

With a huge smile, he replied, "And kiss you I will."

"NO! NO! NO! YOU DO not make the spanakopita with frozen spinach! Are you insane?" Katerina called out as Dimitris moaned.

Shaking his head, Dimitris walked by and said, "Here we go again.

I'm going to watch the football game over at Athanasios and Kilyn's house."

I giggled as my father-in-law stomped out of the kitchen. Phoebe stood next me mixing something up for a dessert she was making.

Bumping my arm, she asked, "Kilyn, how is everything going with your parents' house?"

Nodding, I replied, "Good. Thad has been so amazing with helping to clear stuff out of the house. I don't think Thano and I will ever be able to repay him."

She huffed. "Don't even mention his name."

"Why?" I asked.

She rolled her eyes. "We broke up."

All conversation stopped as seven other women turned and looked at her as they all gasped. I stopped stirring the salad I was making and looked around the kitchen. It still baffled me how they could all be talking to each other, yet know what other people were saying in a totally different conversation. Katerina told me it was a Greek thing.

"What is this?" Aunt Maria said as she pushed Cousin Maria out of the way. Walking up to Phoebe, she pointed to her.

"Did he do something stupid? I'll kick him in the—"

Katerina moved across the room, holding up her hands. "Okay! Okay! Step back, this is my son we are talking about."

I tried to ignore the sharp pain that radiated down my back, but I gasped. Everyone turned and looked at me.

"I um . . . I forgot to add the olives to the salad."

Yiayia made a tsking sound. "Again? When are you going to have that baby? I could die before I get to see my great-grandchild. Don't forget the oregano, like you did last time."

With a forced smile, I secretly grabbed the oregano. Gesh. Would I ever live it down that I forgot to add oregano and Greek olives to the Greek salad?

Katerina turned back to Phoebe. "What happened? I'll kill him if he did anything to hurt you."

"Oh, no, it wasn't anything like that. I asked him about marriage and he said he wasn't ready for it. I told him I was. I want to have a baby."

All the women nodded their heads while some even commented about how old Phoebe was getting. Even though she was almost twenty-four.

I was currently the only person still making my dish, while everyone else tried to figure out why Thad was afraid of commitment.

Dumping the olives that I bought at the market into the salad, I said a prayer I had the right ones this time. I bought the ones that were clearly marked Greek and even asked a woman who to me looked Greek, but was actually Italian. We both agreed they were Greek olives.

Finally, they all went back to their cooking and Phoebe stood next to me again. Peeking over to her, I asked in a hushed voice, "So, if you and Thad are not together, does it bother you being here at his house?"

She gave me a weak smile. "A little, but I'll sneak out before dinner. I really love being here with everyone, though. I'm going to miss this."

My heart broke for her and all I really wanted to do was hit Thad in the balls for being so stupid.

Looking down at my beautiful creation, I grabbed a handful of feta cheese and began sprinkling it over my salad. With a satisfied smile on my face, I picked up my wooden spoon and started to mix my cheese in when the pain hit me again.

"Oh, God," I whispered as I dropped the spoon and grabbed onto the counter.

"Kilyn?" Phoebe asked as she bent down and looked at me.

I was breathing slowly.

My eyes darted over to her as I mouthed, *contraction*. I knew she would most likely be the only one in the room to stay calm and go get Thano.

"What?" she screamed out. "It's time! It's time!"

Closing my eyes, I shook my head. "So, I was wrong on that one."

Lifting my head, I tried to smile as Katerina yelled out, "Dimitris! Athanasios!"

"No! It's okay, we don't have to—"

It was too late. Thano ran into the kitchen like something was on fire.

"What! What's wrong?"

"She's in labor!" someone shouted out.

Thano's expression turned to one of pure fear.

"Ohmygawd! What?"

I tried to laugh and make light of it. Of all the places to go into labor, why was it at the Drivas' house with seven other family members there?

I swear, Thano leapt over the table to get to me. When he swept me off my feet, Phoebe yelled out, "Opa!"

Glaring at her, I shook my head. "No!"

"Yes! You're having a baby! We need to celebrate!"

"I'll finish making the food! You go to the hospital," Aunt Maria said to Katerina.

I started hitting Thano on the shoulder. "Thano!"

He quickly made his way through the kitchen and living room. "Dad! Kilyn's in labor. Her bag is at our place, can you go get it?"

"No! No! Claire can get it!" I cried out.

"I don't mind getting it. I'll pick up Thaddeus and Nicholaus on the way."

Oh. Lord.

Hitting Thano again, I said louder, "Thano. Remember what we talked about . . . for when the baby was born?"

He gave me the goofiest smile. "Yes, the bag. I'm on the bag, baby."

Closing my eyes, I calmly said, "No. Not the bag."

"Dimitris, you drive separate and get the boys; Maria, Sophia, Phoebe, and I will take my car."

My head fell forward as I moaned.

"Are you okay, Kilyn?" Thano asked as he quickly walked to the front door. I had to admit, I was somewhat turned on he was carrying me like I weighed nothing. Of course, lately all he had to do was breathe on me and I was turned on.

Good Lord, look at the man. Handsome as sin. I'd love to feel his scruff on my thighs right now making me—

"Mama, can you call Gus for me?" Thano called out as he stopped at our new Honda Pilot. Gently setting me down, he opened the passenger door. "Shit, I hope your water doesn't break in the new car."

I was halfway in when I turned and shot him a dirty look.

Seeing I was not happy with him, Thano smiled. "Right, who cares if it does!"

He shut the door and ran around to the driver's side and jumped in. Reaching for his phone, he hit a number and handed the phone to me while he pulled out to the street.

"Who are you calling?" I asked.

"The doctor! We have to let him know you're in labor."

When the doctor's office answered I let them know my name and that I was having contractions. By the time I ended the call, Thano had about ten voice messages.

"How does news travel so fast in your family?"

He chuckled but kept his eyes focused on the road.

Clearing my throat, I squeezed my eyes shut and worked through what felt like another contraction. It wasn't as bad as the one before so it was easy to hide it from Mario Andretti.

"Thano, you need to slow down or you'll get a ticket, baby."

"Nah, I'm not speeding."

Rolling my eyes, I rubbed my hand over my stomach. "Hey, just curious if you happen to remember the conversation we had a few weeks back about when the baby was due? You know . . . the one where we both agreed it would just be us at the hospital?"

He took his foot off the gas and mumbled, "Oh, fuck."

"So, when I asked you to talk to your mom and dad about it, I'm going to safely assume by everyone's reactions, you never had that talk."

Thano put on his signal and pulled over into a gas station parking lot.

With a huge smile on his face, he looked at me and proclaimed, "I've got this!"

Shaking my head, I looked straight out the window. He didn't have it.

It was time to put plan B in motion.

# thirty-four

## Thano

MY HEART DROPPED WHEN KILYN looked away from me. The only thing she asked me to do was tell my parents we didn't want the family there for the birth. And I failed.

"I swear, baby, I'll fix this."

She shook her head and wiped a tear away. "Thano, I love your family, you know that. But I want this to be our time. Just you and me. There is no way you can stop them from coming to the hospital now."

Letting out a frustrated moan, I dropped my head. "I fucked up. I'll call them now and tell them not to come."

"No. That will just hurt their feelings. It's time for plan B."

I pulled my head back in shock. "Plan B? You had a plan B you didn't tell me about?"

Hitting Claire's number, she simply said, "Yep."

"Claire, hey . . . oh, dear God. Yes, I'm in labor—who told you?"

Kilyn slowly turned her head and glared at me. "Aunt Maria, huh?"

"Oh, man," I mumbled.

"Yeah, you guessed it. Plan B is in full swing. Right, you've got my bag? Perfect. Yep, I already called them. Right. Sounds good. See ya soon."

I shook my head in confusion. "Wait. Claire knew about plan B?"

She chuckled. "Please, Claire came up with plan B. We need to head to Memorial Hospital instead."

"What?"

She hit another number, "Yes, hello, this is Kilyn Drivas calling again. We need to invoke plan B of the birthing plan. Oh, good, he hasn't left yet. Perfect."

My mouth dropped open. "Wait. Who all was in on this plan B?"

Kilyn turned and looked at me. "Me, Claire, and Dr. Hopkins' office."

"Yet you didn't feel like you could tell me?"

She continued to stare at me and then a look of sheer pain swept over her face.

"Shit! Another one. Drive, Thano! Drive!"

I HAD PURPOSELY LEFT MY phone in the car. I knew my parents would be calling me and wondering where in the hell we were. It wouldn't take long before one of them tracked us down here at Memorial, especially with Kilyn still only five centimeters dilated.

Knowing what I needed to do, I told Kilyn I was running down to get coffee. She'd been given the epidural thirty minutes ago, and I could already see how much more relaxed she was.

With a deep breath, I reached in the car and looked at my phone.

One hundred twenty-six missed calls.

Shit.

My father was the safer bet. "Athanasios! It's Athanasios, be quiet! Where in the world are you?"

Clearing my throat, I replied, "We didn't go to General. There was a change of plans."

"They're not at—"

"Dad! Wait!"

He stopped talking. "Dad, I fucked up."

"What did you do? Is Kilyn okay? The baby?"

"Oh, yeah, yeah, they're both fine. A few weeks ago, Kilyn and I talked about when the baby was due, how we wanted to handle things. The only thing she wanted was for it to be the two of us, only. I was supposed to talk to you and Mama about it and I forgot."

"I see."

"Dad, it's not like Kilyn doesn't want the family to see the baby, it's just . . . the family can be a bit overwhelming. Ya know?"

He chuckled. "I know, son. Believe me, I know."

Running my hand through my hair, I sighed. "Dad, she had a plan B. She knew I was going to mess up and she made arrangements to go to another hospital if we needed to. I feel like a total asshole for her having to use it. Hell, for her having to have it in the first place."

"It's okay, Athanasios. The only thing that matters now is you're about to be a father."

I smiled as I walked back into the hospital. "Yeah, I am."

"I'll handle the family, don't you worry. You spend time with your wife and baby and call when you're ready for us to come visit."

Hearing my mother in the background, I couldn't help but laugh. "Handle the family? What do you mean you'll handle the family?"

"Thanks, Dad."

"Don't you worry. Kiss Kilyn and tell her we all love her."

Hitting the elevator button, I replied, "I will. Thanks again, Dad."

Getting off of the elevator, I started toward Kilyn's room. One of the nurses was walking up to me. My heart began to beat faster. If something happened I'd never forgive myself for leaving.

"There you are. It looks like your baby decided to make an appearance right now."

"What? Right now? As in now, now?"

She chuckled. "Yes, Dr. Hopkins is in the room now and Kilyn is ready to push."

I quickly picked up my pace to almost a run. When I walked into the room, the other nurse smiled. "There he is!"

Kilyn turned and looked at me. I could see the fear in her eyes as I made my way over to her side. Leaning over, I kissed her lips. "This is it."

She wearily nodded her head. "I'm scared."

Shaking my head, I took her hand in mine. "No. Don't be scared. You're the strongest woman I know. You've got this."

Her eyes filled with tears. "Right. I've got this," she whispered.

Kilyn spent almost an hour pushing. Sweat was covering her face and I could see how tired she was.

The doctor looked up and smiled. "One more good push and your baby will be here, Kilyn."

She thrashed her head back and forth. "I'm so tired. Tell him to wait another day."

I couldn't help but laugh. Slipping my arm around her, I said, "Come on, baby. One more time and that's it. You'll be holding our baby in your arms soon. One more push."

She looked at me with a serious look. "What will you do for me if I push once more?"

My mouth snapped shut as I looked around the room. Everyone now had their eyes on me.

"Um . . . I'll, um . . . well, what do you want me to do?"

Oh, shit. Please don't ask for anything sexual. Please.

"I want a hot fudge sundae, desperately. If I push this baby out, will you go get me one?"

I physically breathed a sigh of relief. "You dodged the bullet on that one," one of the nurses said.

"Yes! Baby, I'll get you ten if you want!"

She turned to Dr. Hopkins and said, "Let's do this!"

Less than two minutes later and our baby girl was crying.

Tears streamed down my face as I watched them wrap our daughter in a pink blanket and hand her to Kilyn, who wore the most beautiful smile I'd ever seen. Her face glowed with happiness as she took our daughter into her arms.

When her eyes met mine, I couldn't grin hard enough. "Our daughter. We have a baby girl, Thano."

Moving my eyes to the most precious, and beautiful, creature I'd ever seen, I stared at her. Her little eyes stared up at me as I slowly shook my head.

"Hey, baby girl."

Kilyn held up our daughter's hands and counted each finger and re-peated the process with her toes. Gazing down at her, Kilyn whispered, "She's perfect."

My finger moved lightly over her soft cheek. "She's beautiful, just like her mother."

Lifting her eyes to meet mine, Kilyn's chin trembled. "Thank you," she said as I pinched my eyes together in confusion.

"Why are you thanking me? You did all the work."

Pressing her lips together, she smiled and shook her head. "Thank you for coming into my life and giving me yet another amazing gift."

I leaned over and kissed her. Pulling back slightly, I whispered against her lips, "Thank you. And don't think I didn't notice you put your hair up in pigtails after I left."

Her face flushed as I kissed the tip of her nose.

One of the nurses walked up to me and smiled. "Okay, Dad. The baby's name was being left up to you if it was a girl. Do you have one picked out?"

Kilyn lifted the baby up for me to take. Scooping her up in my arms, I looked into my daughter's eyes. It was as if she was trying to tell me something. *Probably not to name her Maria.*

With a huge smile, I nodded my head. "I have."

"Well? What is it?" Kilyn asked with an inquisitive look.

Sitting next to her on the bed, I held our daughter so we were both looking at her. "She looks like you, Kilyn. Look at how light her blue eyes are."

Kilyn ran her finger through the small amount of dark hair. "My mother had the most beautiful blue eyes. She has my mother's eyes," Kilyn softly said.

"She also has your mother's name. And your father's."

Her eyes snapped up to mine as she pressed her lips together. Tears filled her beautiful green eyes. I knew what the name was going to be the moment Kilyn and I decided if it were a girl, I would pick the name. I couldn't imagine how she felt not having her parents here to share in this joy with us. This was my small gift to her.

I slowly spoke the name of our daughter while I watched my wife cry tears of happiness.

"Kira Kelly Drivas."

Kilyn buried her face in her hands as she cried. Quickly getting herself calmed down, she wiped her tears away and kissed our daughter on the cheek.

"It's beautiful. So amazingly perfect."

Placing Kira back into Kilyn's arms, I took a memory snapshot of this moment.

My garden was full. I would tend to it every single day for the rest of my life. Sheltering them from the storms and showering them with love.

My two beautiful girls.

My ladybugs.

## epilogue

FIVE YEARS LATER

### Kilyn

*I* WATCHED AS KIRA AND Robert ran around the backyard trying to catch a butterfly.

"Get it, Robert! Catch it for me!" Kira shouted.

"Good Lord. That child is so bossy, and I swear my son seems to drop and roll when she says to."

With a chuckle, I nodded my head. "It's the mix of Irish and Greek, I think. She's bossy."

Kira screamed in delight as Claire and I looked back out at them. They were four months apart with Kira being the older of the two.

"Stay still, Kira. It's going to be on the top of your head. That's good luck, you know," Robert said as he placed the butterfly on top of Kira's head.

Her smile was wide and bright. "Is it there?"

Robert frowned. "Of course it's there."

Turning to look at Claire, we both laughed.

"So, this is the calm before the storm, huh?" Claire asked.

With a nod, I glanced around at all the birthday party decorations. "Yep. I told Katerina only immediate family, but you know everyone will show up."

"With food."

I rolled my eyes as I looked at all the party trays I had ordered. I wasn't sure what I was thinking. I told myself it was for all the parents of Kira's classmates. Even though I knew they would all devour the Greek food the moment they saw it.

"You remember preschool when you tried to put out the cheese and fruit trays?"

With a nod, I frowned. "I remember."

"No one ate them. They went for the baklava and kourambiedes!"

"Don't remind me. Katerina ended up putting the trays in the bathrooms!"

Claire laughed.

The back door opened and my handsome husband came walking out carrying a cake. I jumped up and clapped my hands. "Kira! Your cake is here!"

Running over to Thano, she started jumping. "Daddy, let me see!"

He set it on the table and picked Kira up. Her dark curly hair was blowing in the wind. Reaching up, I pushed it behind her ears. Those baby-blue eyes lit up when she looked at her daddy.

Her mouth fell open as she gasped, "It's the most beautiful cake I've ever seen!"

I couldn't help but smile bigger. Kira was obsessed with butterflies and the cake was covered in them. It was a two-tier cake done in pink and purple with little handmade butterflies sticking out on sticks.

"Phoebe did a beautiful job!" I exclaimed.

Claire took a picture of the cake. "I still can't believe she opened up her own cake decorating business."

"I still can't believe Thad broke down and married her!" Thano said with a laugh.

Hitting him on the chest, I shook my head. "Now to get Nicholaus married off."

Thano rolled his eyes. "You sound like my mother."

My mouth snapped shut and I glared at him. "Bite your tongue."

Laughing, he pulled me into his arms. The black shirt he had on made his green eyes pop even more as he gazed at me with a seductive look.

Placing his hand on my face, he rubbed his finger over my lips. "Have I told you how beautiful you look today?"

My teeth sunk into my lip as I shook my head.

"Really? That's a mistake on my part. I'm going to have to make it up to you."

"How?" I asked in a whispered voice.

With a crooked smile, his eyes turned dark. "I'm thinking pigtails, and rope."

I fought to hold the moan in. "I'm thinking that sounds perfect."

"Pappou! Yiayia!" Kira screamed out as she ran past us.

Thano and I both looked to the back door as family member after family member walked through it.

"Opa!" was called out as I buried my face into Thano's chest. His laughter rolled through my body causing a warmth to spread quickly through it.

Placing his finger on my chin, he lifted my eyes to his. "Se agapó, Kilyn."

Smiling, I felt my heart grow so big I was sure it would burst from my chest. "I love you too, Thano."

The End

# acknowledgments

Darrin and Lauren—Thank you for your continued support. I love you both!

A huge thank you to everyone who helps me do what I do. You know who you are!

The Readers—Thank you for all of your love and support. I couldn't do this without y'all! Thank you for letting me share the stories in my head with you! Love you to the moon and back!

Last but not least. Thank you God for the blessings you have given me. The journey is bumpy at times, but I know you are always by my side.

## about the author

KELLY ELLIOTT IS A NEW York Times and USA Today best-selling contemporary romance author. Since finishing her bestselling Wanted series, Kelly continues to spread her wings while remaining true to her roots and giving readers stories rich with hot protective men, strong women and beautiful surroundings.

Kelly lives in central Texas with her husband, daughter, and two pups. When she's not writing, Kelly enjoys reading and spending time with her family.

To find out more about Kelly and her books, you can find her through her website.

www.kellyelliottauthor.com

# other books

STAND ALONES
The Journey Home
Predestined Hearts (Co-written with Kristin Mayer)
Who We Were (Available on audio book)
Stay With Me
Searching For Harmony (Releasing July 2016)
Made For You (Releasing fall 2016)

WANTED SERIES
Book 1–Wanted
Book 2—Saved
Book 3—Faithful
Book 3.5—Believe
Book 4—Cherished
Book 5 Prequel—A Forever Love
Entire series available on audio book
The Wanted Short Stories

LOVE WANTED IN TEXAS SERIES
Spin off series to the WANTED Series
Book 1—Without You
Book 2—Saving You
Book 3—Holding You
Book 4—Finding You
Book 5—Chasing You
Book 6—Loving You**
Entire series available on audio book
**Please note Loving You combines the last book of the Broken and
Love Wanted in Texas series.

BROKEN SERIES
Book 1—Broken
Book 2—Broken Dreams
Book 3—Broken Promises
Book 3—Broken Love
Book 1-3 available on audio book

THE JOURNEY OF LOVE SERIES
Book 1—Unconditional Love
Book 2—Undeniable Love
Book 3—Unforgettable Love
Entire series available on audio book

SPEED SERIES
Book 1 -Ignite
Book 2 -Adrenaline

YA NOVELS WRITTEN UNDER THE PEN NAME
ELLA BORDEAUX
Beautiful (Releasing June 7, 2016)
Forever Beautiful (Releasing fall 2016)

# play list

(CONTAINS SPOILERS)

Russell Dickerson—"Can't Quit You"
After Savannah dies

Cole Swindell—"You Should Be Here"
Thano walking around the cabin

Diamond Rio—"One More Day"
Thano after talking to his father about Savannah

Cole Swindell—"I Just Want You"
Thano and Kilyn dancing and she breaks down

Faith Hill—"Breathe"
Thano and Kilyn make love in the cabin for the first time

Selena Gomez—Camouflage"
Kilyn and Thano talking in her office

Jake Coco—"If I Were An Artist"
Thano and Kilyn outside of bathroom at restaurant

Dierks Bentley—"Say You Do"
Thano asking Kilyn to tell him she had missed him

Selena Gomez—"Survivors"
Thano and Kilyn leaving restaurant after they get back together

Chris Lane—"For Her"
Thano takes Kilyn to Dallas and asks her to marry him

LOCASH—"I Love This Life"
Kilyn's favorite song.
Thano finding out Kilyn is pregnant and the wedding song

CPSIA information can be obtained
at www.ICGtesting.com
Printed in the USA
BVOW06s0005020617
485799BV00010B/55/P